Nigel Williams is the author of sixteen novels, including the bestselling Wimbledon Trilogy. His stage plays include *Class Enemy* and a dramatization of William Golding's *Lord of the Flies*. He wrote the screenplay for the Emmy and Golden Globe award-winning *Elizabeth I*, starring Helen Mirren. His BBC Radio 4 comedy series *HR* (featuring Jonathan Pryce and Nicholas le Prevost) is now in its fourth series. He has lived in Putney for thirty years.

They Came From SW19

Nigel Williams

corsair

Constable & Robinson Ltd
55–56 Russell Square
London WC1B 4HP
www.constablerobinson.com

First published in the UK by Faber and Faber Limited
1992

This edition published in the UK by Corsair,
an imprint of Constable & Robinson Ltd, 2013

A copy of the British Library Cataloguing in
Publication data is available from the British Library

ISBN: 978-1-47210-678-0 (paperback)
ISBN: 978-1-47210-740-4 (ebook)

Typeset by TW Typesetting, Plymouth, Devon

Printed and bound by CPI Group (UK) Ltd, Croydon, CR0 4YY

1 3 5 7 9 10 8 6 4 2

For
Ned, Jack and Harry

PART ONE

I

The worst thing about my dad dying was my mum telling me about it.

When I get to forty-two, I hope they shoot me. I know quite a lot of forty-two-year-olds and they are all a real problem. It is a very difficult age. My biology teacher is forty-two, and when I found that out, it explained a lot of things about him.

Forty-two-year-olds – I've noticed this – rarely bother to finish their sentences. You find them hanging round the corners of the house, pouring each other drinks, lighting each other's cigarettes and saying things like, 'Bobbo, of course . . .' They don't need to say any more than that. Everyone knows what follows. Mere mention of the name 'Bobbo' is enough to activate hundreds of Bobbo stories which everyone has been telling twice a day ever since the 1960s. The Good Old Days! Get with it! The world is changing!

Mum is forty-two.

I know this because she says it, on average, about eight times a day. She always says it differently. Sometimes she sounds really surprised, as if she'd only just been handed her birth certificate. Sometimes she says it as if it is some horrible truth that must be faced. But mostly she says it as if it were my fault.

It isn't my fault! I know if I weren't fourteen she wouldn't be forty-two, but the two things are not, as my biology teacher would say, 'causally related'.

The day my dad died was a hot, dry day in early September. It didn't look like the sort of day on which people died. It was more like the sort of day you expect at the start of a holiday. Even the sky above the tiny roofs of Stranraer Gardens was, from what I could see of it, the deep blue of the sea on travel posters.

I didn't even know he was ill. They had called Mum while I was at school and she had left for the hospital before I got home. She got back from St Edmund's at around eight o'clock. I was sitting in the small room at the head of the stairs – the one he always used to call his office. The front door opened and slammed shut, and the wall next to me shook nervously. My dad was always very proud of the fact that we lived in a six-bedroomed house. It's meant to be a three-bedroomed house, but the Maltese plumber who had it before us put up an amazing number of walls and partitions and screens. From the outside it looks like another dull little terraced house, but when you're inside it you feel like a rat in a maze.

Immediately I heard the front door I switched off his computer. I knew it was her and knew the first thing she would do would be to listen at the bottom of the stairs to see if she could hear the hum of the machine. I've tried muffling it with scarves and old raincoats, but the house is so small that she always hears. She's frightened that it's going to rot my mind and turn me into a hunchback.

She's left it too late. My mind is rotted to compost and I am about as close to a hunchback as you can get.

She waited for a moment at the bottom of the stairs. Then she went through into the kitchen and I heard her moving around in an aimless sort of way. From the kitchen she went into the hall. I heard her making a small, mewing noise.

After a minute or so, I heard her come up the stairs and wait on the landing. Why was she waiting? Had I done something wrong? Of course my mum always moves around the house quietly and fearfully, like a woman listening hard for the nastier kind of burglar. But, as soon as her face came round the door, I knew we were looking at a problem. She worries about everything, but this time I could see it wasn't my inability to practise the saxophone.

She has long, *grey* hair, and she was brushing it back from her face. She looked like she did the day she told me about – to use her own words – 'the marvellous thing men and women do with their bodies'. For a moment I thought she was going to give me an update on this particular bulletin – the disgusting thing men and women do with their dachshunds, perhaps – but instead she said, 'A terrible thing has happened, Simon!'

She left it there. I was obviously supposed to say, 'What, Mother? Do tell me!' But I didn't. I just carried on looking at the floor. I have very bad eye contact, she tells me. Bad eye contact, bad posture and terrible skin.

'Norman has gone from us!'

Hey, Mum – where's he gone? Barbados, or what?

'He's gone, Simon! Gone! Gone! Gone!'

I was getting the message. He was gone. But where, Mum? You know? Be more specific.

She put her hand up to her forehead and started to rub it anxiously. She flinched a little as she did this. Then she lowered her face towards the floor and snaked up sharply so that she was looking into my eyes. 'He has gone,' she said, 'to Higher Ground!'

Something about the way she said this suggested to me that she was not referring to the Lake District.

She sat down heavily on the black sofa in Dad's office. The one he intended to use for clients. I used to fool about and pretend to be a client sometimes, which seemed to amuse my dad a great deal. Mum, looking slightly out of place in the room, brushed the hair back from her eyes. Then she looked off into the middle distance, as if she was trying to find her own personal spotlight.

'O dear Lord Jesus, who died on the cross for us!' she said – she really did – 'Oh God! He was forty-three!'

I did not like the use of the past tense, my friends.

'Oh my God!' she said again, and then, clenching her fists tightly and drumming them against her forehead in double-quick time, she squeaked, 'What does it all mean, Simon?'

This is typical of the way forty-two-year-olds talk. They cannot hold an idea in their heads for very long. A thought occurs to them and out it comes – like bread from a toaster. You have to go through their pronouncements very carefully and decode them. What did all *what* mean?

She got up from the sofa and came towards me. About three yards away, she stopped and shot out both arms. She looked as if she was about to sing. For a moment I thought she *was* going to sing (my mum is capable of such things when we are alone together). But she just stayed there, her arms at an angle of roughly 110 degrees to her body. I didn't give her any encouragement. After a while she put her arms down in the sort of resigned, hopeless way in which people take apart tents or deconstruct folding tables.

'You must,' she said, 'listen to the Lord Jesus!'

She didn't say this with much enthusiasm. Then she stepped back and looked at me sadly. She always looks cold, does my mum.

'I wish you'd tell me your emotions,' she said in a small voice. It was typical really. Something was my fault again. I was supposed to throw myself into her arms, or what? And what emotions? I'm fourteen. I don't have emotions.

Now that her arms were well and truly down, she seemed inclined to test out the old legs. She walked north–north-east, in the direction of the very large colour photograph of me that hangs on the wall next to my dad's desk. I put the points of my fingers together and looked over them at a spot about a foot above her head.

Then she gave it to me straight: 'Norman is dead!'

She paused dramatically. And then added, 'A heart attack.'

Why didn't she say this earlier? Why did it take three minutes of pacing round the room to lead up to it? But, now she was in specific mode, she kept on coming with the facts.

'He died', she went on, 'at five fifty-one. Our time.'

I want to know what time he died in New York, Mum! That'll make it easier. If I'm to get a fix on this event, I'd like to cross-reference it internationally. I want to know what effect this will have on the world money markets.

'His breathing', she went on, 'became "laboured and stertorous" at about three forty-five, and by teatime he was in . . .'

Here she paused, obviously confused about what he was in. Finally she came up with, '. . . serious difficulties.'

She was making him sound like he was entered for the Fastnet Race. Although – maybe dying is like ocean racing. I wouldn't know. I just wished she'd stop giving me all this blow-by-blow stuff. But she had started and she was going to finish.

'At four-o-three a man called de Lotbinniere came to give him cocoa and take his temperature. But that was a mistake.'

I should think so. From the sound of it, Dad was well past the hot drinks stage. I looked up. I could see her wondering how far she should go along the de Lotbinniere front.

I hunched my shoulders and sucked in my cheeks. For some reason I found myself wishing I could lay my hand on my glasses. It would have been nice to have something between my eyes and the rest of the world. To take my mind off what she was saying,

I started to think about this de Lotbinniere character. What was he doing wandering around hospitals waving thermometers in the faces of dying people? Shouldn't someone put a stop to his activities?

Mum had moved on from de Lotbinniere. She had that glazed expression you often see on her face when she is trying to tell you any story in which she is the main character.

'I went out for a cup of tea from the machine, which was at the end of the corridor by the glass doors and did soup as well. Hot, thick tomato soup, it said. Although I wanted tea . . .'

A haunted look came into her eyes. I could not have said whether this was to do with the soup-versus-tea controversy, or the death of the man to whom she had been married for twenty years.

'It gave me the soup which turned out to be oxtail. And while I was getting my change he had a second coronary thrombosis.'

This would in any normal person's hands have been the end of the story. But not for my mum.

'I was weeping profusely, of course. And hurling myself at Daddy and attempting to take him in my arms.'

This was not something she had done much of when he was alive. Or going through what passes for life at 24 Stranraer Gardens. But, clearly, Norman Britton was a lot more of an attractive proposition now he was no longer with us. Dead people can't answer back, can they? Dead people do just what they're told.

'And de Lotbinniere returned at this point and approached me from behind.'

I had known that she would have to return to de Lotbinniere. There is a weird logic to my mother's tales. The small parts always run away with the main narrative, although they themselves are often upstaged by the things that really obsess her – like brands of instant coffee or the design of furniture covers.

'Paul de Lotbinniere is a graduate chemist from Leeds and is only doing nursing as a temporary thing. He hopes to have his own gardening business, although it's proving immensely difficult at the moment. Apparently people have lost interest in gardening.'

Paul de Lotbinniere, eh? Come on, Mum, tell me more, do! Approached you from behind! De Lotbinniere! My man!

I had gone back to looking at the floor. It seemed the safest place to look. Just behind the desk, my dad had stencilled a large thing that looked a bit like a rhubarb leaf with bits chopped out of it. In the middle he had written my name and my date of birth.

SIMON BRITTON
MAY 1ST
1976

He had left spaces for all the brothers and sisters who were supposed to come pattering along after me. Who, mercifully, failed to appear. As I began to look at it, I began to think that this was how my dad's gravestone would look. A name and a date or two and a bit of the old fruit-salad carving.

I didn't cry or anything but decided to move my eyes away. There was a feeling in the room, although I couldn't have said precisely where. I couldn't have said what it was either, but I did know that that was the only good thing about it.

'. . . a cup of tea with de Lotbinniere while he wrote out the certificate and they took Norman away. Oh darling, darling, darling!'

I couldn't work out whether this referred to me or Dad or de Lotbinniere. So I said nothing.

She was on the move again for the next remark. She went over to the black bookshelf in the corner. She put one hand on it and

peered in my direction. She seemed to be having trouble getting
me in focus. I could see her quite clearly. She has a chapped
look, does my mum. She's been cured, like a herring, in the tiny
kitchen that my dad could never afford to replace, and round her
eyes is a web of small lines etched into her skin. They're marks
of worry and of ageing, I know, but sometimes I imagine they're
long-healed cuts from a razor and that it's my dad and I who
made them.

'He always wanted to be buried at sea.'

This was news to me. I somehow couldn't see Mum and Dad
ever having the kind of conversation in which they would get
round to talking about such things. But I still said *nothing*. I have
to live here. You know?

Mum continued: 'I said, "Why?" He said because he loved the
sea. I said, "I like John Lewis's, but that doesn't mean I want to
be buried there." He loved John Lewis's. We must remember to
be positive about this.'

With this remark she shuffled across the bare, polished floor-
boards, arms out. At first I thought she was going to try for
a clinch, but at the last moment she decided against it. She
stood about a yard away, looking suddenly bleak and small and
miserable. And then she remembered to be positive. It wasn't
that big a deal. Her husband had *died*, that was all! I could see
her worried little eyes looking for the pluses, and eventually she
found one of them.

'He will be in actual, direct contact with Derek and Stella
Meenhuis! And he will actually be able to see and touch and
experience fully the Lord Jesus Christ!'

Fond as I was of Derek and Stella Meenhuis, I couldn't see
that it was worth dying in order to get in touch with them again.
Neither am I one of those people who think it will necessarily be a
big deal to look God in the face. But my mum had got on course
now and she came closer to me, anxious to apologize in case she

had mistakenly given the impression of being disconcerted by watching someone die of a heart attack.

'We are going to *talk* to him!' she said, in the sort of eager way she used to recommend one of our cheap holiday breaks in a caravan park on the South Coast. 'We are going to talk as we have never, ever talked before, Simon. This isn't bad, darling! It's just . . .'

She struggled for the inappropriate word and, in the end, found it: '. . . just . . . *different!*'

2

I have a very bad attitude towards death. I'm terrified of it.

I know this is wrong. I know that there'll be bright lights and that Jesus will lift me up in his arms and that I will find myself in a large and harmonious choir – something that is never likely to happen to me while I am alive – but I don't *look forward* to stiffing.

I couldn't even work up much enthusiasm on my dad's behalf. While my mum started on one of her favourite topics – the precise geographical layout of heaven – I found myself looking round the room to remind myself of the few small things that had been his, before the loving hands of the Almighty cradled him in bliss eternal. It's pathetic, I know, but looking at furniture he'd sat on, or pictures he'd looked at, seemed to help.

As she droned on about the wonderful quality of the light Over There (she always makes it sound like one of my dad's brochures for his holiday cottages in Connemara) I looked down at the old man's desk. Below me, just to my right, was a pair of his glasses. He left them there, beside the Anglepoise lamp, because he only used them for reading. Next to the glasses was a letter that he must have been looking at before he got up to walk to wherever he had his first heart attack. At the bottom of the page the guy had written, rather optimistically, 'See you Thursday.'

You should never say things like that. You never know if you're going to see anyone on Thursday. When you kiss goodbye to your wife (or whoever) in the morning, don't say, 'See you tonight.' That's tempting providence. Say, '*Might* see you tonight.' And if she gives you a hard time about it, you just tell her. There is no guarantee.

I saw those glasses horribly clearly. As if they were correcting my sight, from where they lay, on the shabby wooden desk. I could hear everything very precisely too. In the street outside, someone was playing a radio. The song on the radio was the Pet Shop Boys singing 'What Have I Done to Deserve This?' I could hear the Maltese plumber's water pipes singing along with them and, above my mum's head, see the shelf that my dad had put up in the spring of 1986. It took him the whole spring to do it, but it still slopes, dangerously, towards the floor.

My mum shook her lank, grey hair and blinked like something from the small-mammal house. She'd moved on from the nature of Heavenly Light and had got on to how we would all float around like *spacemen* when we reached the Halls of Jesus and how we would not need to eat *as such* but would always be sort of *three-quarters of the way through a most delicious meal.* Something about my expression must have told her that even this was not going to get me to look on the bright side of this issue. She looked at me rather plaintively and said, 'Auntie Diana will be so pleased to see him!'

I didn't agree or disagree with this.

'They always had so much in common,' she went on. Then she folded her hands together, lowered her head and, without asking anyone's permission, went straight into public prayer.

My mum is a leading member of the First Church of Christ the Spiritualist, South Wimbledon. Why didn't I mention that?

What do you take me for? It isn't something I advertise. Only a few people at school know. It is, for reasons that will become clear, impossible to keep it from the neighbours, but whenever I am out with First Spiritualists I try to make it clear from my posture and expression that I am absolutely nothing to do with them.

I don't know whether there was ever a Second Spiritualist Church of South Wimbledon, but, if there was, I guess the First Church soon ran it out of town. The First Church has some very heavy characters in it *indeed*. In spite of a Youth Drive and the Suffer Little Children campaign, not many of them are under forty-five. But even the wrinkliest members can still act funky.

Four years ago, for example, my mum and I were on the Used Handbag Stand at the twice-yearly Bring and Buy Sale, when Rita Selfridge offered to buy my mum's trousers. The ones she was wearing. She offered her five pounds for them and asked her if they qualified as Used or Nearly New. My mum didn't do anything – she never does if people are rude to her – but my mum's friend, Mabel, who is seventy-five, threw herself at Rita Selfridge and bit her, quite badly, on the neck.

The First Spiritualist Church of South Wimbledon was founded early this century, by a woman named Ella Walsh. They don't actually use the word 'founded'. What she did was to 'renew' a body known as the Sisters of Harmony and Obedience, a church which had been in her family for over a hundred years. Ella Walsh was the great-granddaughter of Old Mother Walsh of Ealing, of whom you may have heard. Old Mother Walsh was a prophetess who lived in a hut very close to what is now the North Circular Road. She had a dream in which she saw a huge snake wind itself around the planet. Fire came out of its mouth, and it bore the inscription TWO THOUSAND YEARS GO BY. It talked as well. It said that a woman was coming who would save the world and make it whole. She would be announced by a boy prophet 'of pure heart and mind' and, when she came into her ministry, 'all mannere of thynge would be welle'. If she didn't, it was going to gobble up the world. Some snake!

After Old Mother Walsh died, her memory was kept alive by her daughters and granddaughters. The Walshes bred like rabbits. Eliza Walsh, for example, had no fewer than six phantom pregnancies as well as the twelve that produced babies. Finally, around 1890, just after the Walsh family moved to Wimbledon, Ella Walsh, the Mother and Renewer of the Sisters of Harmony, was born.

Ella took the Sisters in a new and exciting direction. She kept some of the rules and regulations and printed a limited edition of *The Sayings of Old Mother Walsh*, and added her own angle. She brought in spiritualism, and soon there just wasn't room for much of Old Mother Walsh's doctrine, even though scraps of it survived and were still about when I was young. 'Evacuate the noise of the bowel in your own place!' for example. Members of the First Church still rush out of the room if they suspect they are about to fart.

Like all churches, the first thing it did was to set about getting some money in the bank. Ella Walsh met a guy called Fox, and, more importantly, got in touch with his brother, who had died four years earlier in a boating accident near Chichester.

Fox was *loaded*.

Ella Walsh and Fox spent many a happy hour talking to Fox's brother. He was, it turned out, feeling pretty good about being dead. Apparently being dead was a lot more fun than being alive. They had snooker and whisky and quite good boating facilities over on the Other Side. And, after they'd contacted Fox's brother, they called up all sorts of other people – including Robespierre and William Thackeray. It was all such fun that Ella married Fox and Fox gave her thousands of pounds to build the First Spiritualist Church.

She must have creamed off most of the money, because the First Spiritualist Church makes your average scout hut look like the Taj Mahal. It is a kind of tin and concrete shack, somewhere at the back of South Wimbledon station, and I'm always hoping some enterprising businessman will see that it has restaurant potential and offer us money for it.

It has no restaurant potential.

On the back wall there is a letter from Sir Arthur Conan Doyle, thanking the First Spiritualist Church for all their help and saying how great it was to talk to them. The letter is signed, in his absence, by one Rebecca Furlong, and it's only when you look at the date that you realize it was written fifteen years after Sir Arthur snuffed it. He sounds pretty chirpy, and gives no indication, in the text, that he has croaked. He doesn't really mention much about himself at all. But maybe after you've been on the Other Side for a certain length of time it all gets pretty samey. Certainly, dead people seem pretty keen to get on down to the First Spiritualist Church of South Wimbledon, so there can't be a lot happening over there.

If I ever die they won't see me for dust.

Pike and Hannah Dooley won't have the chance to ask me how am I doing, and do they have skateboards in the afterlife. Marjorie can use every single one of her internationally renowned psychic tricks on me and I will guarantee not to respond. And Quigley, oh Mr Quigley – he can rap the table for as long as he likes but I will not be answering!

They did great business, apparently, after the First World War. In the early 1920s you couldn't get in. Just before the war, Ella and Fox had had a daughter called Rose and – guess what! – she turned out to be a Psychical Prodigy. Rose, as far as I can gather, was a real all-rounder. She wasn't as hot on Jesus as her mum had been, but when it came to automatic writing, Ouija board, ectoplasm and something rather dodgy-sounding called cabinet work, there was no one to touch her in South London. About the only thing Rose Fox didn't do was levitate, but, as she was nearly sixteen stone, that is hardly surprising.

I saw her when she was in her mid-seventies. She rolled into Sunday service supported by Mr and Mrs Quigley and gave us this big speech about how the spirits never talked to her any more. The last time anyone from the Great Beyond had given her their valuable time was, apparently, during something called the Suez Crisis, when she had had a short conversation with the late Admiral Nelson. 'They want me to join them,' she said. 'Their silence beckons me!' And then, as people frequently do down at the First Spiritualist Church of South Wimbledon, she burst into tears.

I quite often burst into tears on my way there. On one occasion, when I was about seven, my mum had to untwist my hands from about every gatepost in Stranraer Gardens. 'It's not as if it's the Spanish Inquisition,' she used to snap.

No, it was the First Spiritualist Church of South Wimbledon! That was what was worrying me. If it had been the Spanish Inquisition it would have been fine. I thought I knew where I stood with the Spanish Inquisition.

Some people blamed Rose Fox for the decline of the First Spiritualist Church. She went too far, people said. There were all these poor bastards who had lost relatives in the First World War, trying to get in touch with them. But with Rose it was hard to hear anything through the table-rapping or the squelch of ectoplasm being flung about the room by men in black jerseys. She started to take photographs of the spirits too, and that is how she came to be accused of trickery.

'Did I ever tell you', my dad said to me once, when we were walking, as we often did, in the direction of the off-licence, 'about how Rose Fox was photographed beneath the spirit reality of Franz Josef of Austria?'

'I don't believe you did,' I replied.

Whereupon, from his pocket he produced a black-and-white photograph of a plump woman in a loose white dress. It was hard to make out what was behind her – a chair, a table and what looked like a wardrobe of some kind. But what was directly above her head was easier to see. Hanging in the gloom, at a height of about five feet, was the gigantic face of an elderly man with mutton-chop whiskers and a helmet with a steel point on it. I happened to know, because we were doing it at school, that the face balancing on Rose's bonce was that of the last ruler of the Austro-Hungarian Empire.

'My God,' I said, 'it looks just like him!'

'It does, doesn't it?' said Dad.

He wrinkled his lips appreciatively, as if he was already tasting the first drink of the day. 'It also', he went on, 'looks amazingly like a photograph of the old boy that appeared in the *Illustrated London News* in June 1924!'

That was typical of my dad. He always took great delight in any reports of trickery. And anything that reflected badly on Rose Fox, who was a great heroine of my mum's, always went down particularly well.

The worst thing Rose Fox did was not to organize spirit photographs of internationally famous dead people – it was to get married. She got hitched to a man called Stuart Quigley, in the year the Second World War broke out. Quigley died in 1950 and was so boring that no one could bear to speak to him much, even after he'd croaked. But, before he opened that last little door into the unknown, he managed to make Rose pregnant. And so it was that in 1948 Rose Fox gave birth to the man born to make my life a misery – Albert Roger Quigley, MA – part scout leader, part amateur opera singer, part Christian, part Spiritualist and one hundred per cent complete and utter arsehole.

Quigley is an assistant bank manager. My mum once took me

into his branch to show me his name, which is written up on a board. He is billed just below someone called Mervyn Snyde, who looks after International Securities. I think they are making a grave error of judgement in letting anyone know he's there. Quigley, like quite a few other members of the First Church, is downright sinister. It was quite horrible to think that someone like him should be left alive when my dad was dead.

I didn't start crying until after my mum had left the room. But the thing that started me off wasn't the fact that Quigley was still above ground. Or the thought of my dad lying on a slab with all his dental-work showing. It wasn't the thought that I would never see him again, because he still seemed too real for me to imagine that as a possibility. I mean, that guy in the letter, right? He'd planned his Thursday round Norman, you know? And I had so many things that I could have been doing with him, now, tomorrow, the day after tomorrow, that it was literally impossible to believe that he wouldn't be doing *any* of them.

The thing that started me off was the last thing my mum said before she headed off down the stairs. She tried a tentative embrace, patted my head vaguely and went across to the door. She looked, I thought, almost pleased with herself as she turned back to me. I didn't crack. I just kept right on looking at her, with my head slightly to one side. I think I was trying to look intelligent. My dad always used to say that intelligence was the only thing that made humans bearable. Which makes his ever being involved with the First Spiritualist Church even more puzzling.

'Over There,' she said, 'they are probably organizing some form of official welcome for him!'

I goggled at her. All I could think was that my dad hated parties. Especially official ones. In order to avoid replying, I looked out of the window. Over Here, the late afternoon sun was slanting down on to the impassive red brick of Stranraer

Gardens. I could see our cat slink into the opposite garden, her
shoulders pressed towards the ground.

'We are going to be talking to him in the very near future,' she
said. Then she walked back towards me and nodded significantly.
'I am sure that he has a great deal to discuss with you. And I have
a very great deal to tell *him* now that he has Passed Across!'

There was something almost menacing in the way she said this.
She straightened her narrow shoulders and gave me a blink from
those worried little eyes of hers. 'Conversations with Norman,'
she said, 'are only just beginning!'

With a kind of smirk, she bounced out of the room. I could
hear her steps on the stairs, sounding, as usual, a note of warning,
of some kind of trouble on the way.

That would be the last thing the poor old bastard wanted.
He finally gets through with the mortgage and the weekly
shopping and putting the rubbish in a grey plastic bag and
trying to fit it into the dustbin, when what? She's calling him
up and telling him the news about the latest jumble sale and
my failure to pay attention in French. I would have thought
the only plus about being dead was not having to listen to her
any more.

She'll have him back before he knows it, I thought. She'll
send his ghost out to Sainsbury's.

It was Sainsbury's that did it. I suddenly saw my dad wheeling
the trolley round the delicatessen section. The way his face lit up
at the sight of the salamis and the smoked fish was beautiful to
behold. I saw him purse his lips as he sorted through the bottles
of rosé wine, trying to find that special one that was going to
make an evening with my mother bearable. I saw him finger his
paunch at the check-out counter and grin when he caught sight
of the chocolate biscuits, Swiss rolls, soft drinks and all the other
things I had managed to smuggle aboard the wagon: I saw his
big, round face and neatly combed, balding hair, and I saw the

heavy gold ring on his left hand. I saw him. You know? I saw him.

It was only then that I thought: He's not coming back any more. I'll never see him again as long as I live. And I may not see him when I die, either.

I put my face down on his desk then, and cried like a baby.

3

A friend of my mum's once said that my dad looked a little seedy, and at the time I was very offended. But there was some truth in the remark. When I saw his clothes, without him, in the weeks after his death, I could see that that was what they were. The suits were neither flash nor respectable. The jerseys were all torn and ragged, and the pairs of shoes (my dad loved buying shoes) were never quite expensive enough to achieve whatever effect he had intended.

But he was more than his clothes. None of his possessions made sense without him. And what made it even harder to understand that he really had died was the fact that, as is usual in the First Spiritualist Church, he was not buried. Not by us anyway. A day or so after he was transferred from the hospital to the funeral parlour, the undertaker rang my mum and said, in an unctuous tone, 'Will you be wanting to arrange a viewing, Mrs Britton?'

'No,' said my mum.

'What I mean is,' said the undertaker, sounding a touch peevish, 'he is here at the moment. If you want to see him . . .'

He hasn't run off or anything! You know?

I was listening to all of this on the extension – which is the only way you ever find out anything in our house – and this last remark was followed by the longest pause in British telephone history. I seriously thought my mum had gone off to make a cup of tea.

Eventually the undertaker said, in a wheedling tone, 'He looks very nice now.'

Come on down! We've laid on tea and biscuits and a video!

'He really does look at peace. It's amazing what we can do!'

I thought this was a bit much, frankly. I wouldn't have said my dad was a good-looking guy, but I didn't think he needed the services of an embalmer to make him palatable.

'No one,' said my mum, eventually, 'will be coming to see Norman.'

'Oh . . .' said the undertaker, going back into peevish mode. 'If that's how you feel . . .'

In that case we'll take him out of the window. He's taking up space! We'll screw the old lid down and get on with it.

'Anyway,' the guy said finally, 'he will be here till about a quarter to five . . .'

So boogie on down while you have the chance! I mean, what do you require here? A funeral, or what?

'No, thank you very much,' said Mum. 'Thank you for the opportunity of a viewing, but in this instance the family must decline.'

The guy on the other end of the line was obviously dismayed at this unwillingness to test-drive his mortician's skills.

'My church', said my mum, with a certain amount of prim pride, 'does not believe in burial as such. We give you carte blanche as far as Norman's corpse is concerned. Do with it as you will!'

'I see,' said the undertaker.

You could sense him trying to work out what this signified. Did it mean absolutely anything went? Were they to be allowed to stick him in a trolley and wheel him round the local supermarket? Or give every last bit of him away for medical research?

'You do . . . er . . . want him buried?' he said finally.

'Buried? Not buried? What's the difference?' said my mum.

'Well,' said the undertaker, 'to us, quite considerable.'

'Is it?'

'Well, we don't usually find ourselves dealing with non-burying situations. Cremation and burial are, so to speak, our raisons d'être.'

'Quite,' said my mum, rather meanly.

It was possible, of course, that the guy was wondering whether to give my dad the full five-star treatment. *Burmese mahogany*, you could hear him thinking, *silver-plated handles, top-quality professional mourners.* Indeed, when the bill came in, it looked as if we had been charged for exactly that.

'Are you a Hindu?' he asked eventually, with some caution.

'Certainly not,' snapped my mum.

He was well and truly stumped now.

'Well, Mrs Britton,' he said in the end, 'we shall try and dispose of your husband's body in a way that we hope will be suitable as far as you are concerned.'

'What you do with his body is irrelevant. I will be talking to Norman in the next few days, and I assure you that one of the things we will not be discussing is his funeral.'

'Indeed,' said the undertaker. Then, clearly desperate to regain some professional self-respect, he said, rather brightly, as if none of this conversation had taken place at all, 'Would you like any photographs of the event?'

My mum started laughing at this point. I was rather with her actually. 'Photographs?' she said. 'Photographs?'

I think the guy was simply wondering whether he would be required to furnish proof that he hadn't sold the cadaver to some fly-by-night surgeon.

'Norman', she said pityingly, 'has gone to a place more beautiful and more peaceful than anything you could imagine.

You can't take photographs of it and stick it on the mantelpiece. You can't get package holidays to it. But those of us who have talked to people who have had first-hand experience of it know it is utterly, utterly beautiful!'

'I'm sure,' said the undertaker feelingly.

And, leaving the poor sod trying to work out for himself exactly what place she was talking about, Mum put the phone down.

This must have happened about a week after Dad died. But I don't remember much about the days that followed that first, awful conversation with my mum. Perhaps because the night that followed it was so eventful.

It was hot that autumn. The evening they took him to the hospital went out like a Viking funeral. I didn't cry for long. I was frightened she might hear me. I cleaned up my face and sat looking out of the window. The plane-tree opposite looked how I felt. It hadn't even got the energy to turn brown. But the sun was going gently, winking back at me from the windows of the neighbours' houses in the way it can do, even when someone you care about dies. A few streets away, on the main road, a police car or an ambulance made the noise I most connect with cities – the pushy, important wail of a siren.

Down the street I caught sight of a few stalwarts from the congregation, trying to park a car. You can never keep them away from a death. But they were on the job with unusual speed. Maybe someone Over There had tipped them off.

Like many other things in the First Spiritualist Church, the parking was a team effort. Hannah Dooley, in a tweed skirt and a double-breasted jacket, was waving madly at the bonnet, while Leo Pike was sneering at the boot through his gold-rimmed glasses. I couldn't work out what his expression meant. Maybe it just meant that Pike drove a large, uncontrollable Ford that was at least ten years old. This was a brand-new Audi. The guy in it was important business.

The door opened and Quigley got out. Yo, Quigley! New wheels! You tapped into the bank's computer, or what? Pike held the door for him. No one cringes quite like Pike. Humbling himself in the sight of God is not enough for him. He would crawl to me if I let him. As I watched his wintry little face, his shoulders hunched in his tweed jacket, his constant, half-bowing motions as Quigley emerged, I found myself wondering, once again, how it was that someone so humble could be, on occasions, so fantastically menacing.

Hannah Dooley loves Pike, but the reverse is not the case. Maybe Hannah loves him because she loves all the things people throw away, and Pike has the look of something left out for the binmen. Left out but not taken. If I was a refuse-disposal operative, I would have nothing to do with him, but Hannah Dooley gives him the kind of tenderness she bestows on old chairs and smelly bits of carpet. She pulls them out of people's gardens and waves them at the householders who are guilty of casting them aside. With her wrinkled face bright with eagerness, she calls, 'Are you *really* throwing this away?' To which my dad always used to reply, with scarcely controlled fury, 'We are trying to, Miss Dooley. We are trying to!'

Quigley was followed out on to the pavement by his wife and daughter. The wife is called Marjorie, and says things like, 'Is there a plentiful sufficiency of baps?' The daughter is called Emily. She is good at the cello. Need I say more?

Some years ago, Marjorie, Emily, Hannah and Pike (who is a kind of unofficial chairman of these three) all decided that I was going to learn to play the saxophone properly. They bought me the examination syllabus. They bought me a year's supply of reeds. They used to leave my instrument outside my bedroom door after evening prayers at our house. But they had reckoned without me. They couldn't actually wrap my lips around the horn and inflate my lungs until I made a noise. Only my dad was allowed to hear me practise.

Hannah Dooley shambled up to Quigley and started to whisper something in the great man's ear. Quigley likes Hannah Dooley, but you never know which way he is going to go. I could see his big, bushy, black beard waggle up and down as he nodded at something she said, then he shot a quick glance at her when he thought she wasn't looking. Sometimes he stroked the ends of his beard and lifted his nose rather sensually as he did so. Quigley is proud of his beard. I think it's the kind of beard that conceals a great deal more than the owner's face. When he had finished the listening/stroking routine, he turned smartly and walked towards our house. Even from the first-floor window you could see that his hand was in his right trouser pocket and was grasping his balls firmly. Just in case anyone tried to give them ideas.

The *whole* Quigley family was wearing flared trousers, including Emily. Flares and bright colours. When someone croaks in the First Spiritualist Church, you let the relatives know you don't feel negative. Pike was last across the road, waiting, as he usually does, for a car to come into sight before scampering in front of it like a spider. Pike is really keen to rip through the gauze that separates us from Sir Arthur Conan Doyle. Maybe he thinks he'll get his hair back on the other side.

Quigley rang the bell. You could tell it was Quigley. He hit it hard, as he always does. He kept the volume very steady and – the giveaway this – he left it that extra five seconds, as if to say: *It's no use hiding behind the sofas, guys! I know you're in there!* Downstairs I heard my mum scurry out of the kitchen and scrabble at the door.

There was a pause as she opened it, then Quigley said, 'Great day for Norman!'

'Yes,' said mum, rather feebly.

'He's crossed!' said Hannah Dooley.

'We're so pleased for him,' mumbled Pike.

'Yes,' said mum, again sounding as if she was past feeling pleased for anyone.

I heard Quigley's big feet come into the hall. 'Have you experienced him yet?' I heard him say.

I assumed he was talking about my dad. He certainly sounded very up about the whole dying business. And I knew to my certain knowledge, that, after me, my dad was Quigley's least favourite person in the Wimbledon area.

'I . . . I'm not sure,' said Mum.

Mum is never fantastically sure about her spiritual powers. And the Quigleys do nothing to bolster her confidence in this area. 'I sort of . . . had a whiff of him on the stairs.'

'Yes!' This from Mrs Quigley.

'But then,' said Mum, 'he was always on the stairs.'

He was actually. He was always on the stairs or in the hall. He hung around his own house like he was a lodger did my dad. As I sat listening to the Quigleys, I could almost see the poor old sod. I could see his ragged little moustache, his beaky nose, and I could hear his voice, rolling the words round his mouth like he was a voice-over for a cheese commercial: 'I never wanted to be a travel agent!'

That was a frightening one. There were guys out there who could just *make* you be a travel agent. And presumably the same people were lying *in* wait for me. They could saunter up and offer me even worse fates than the ones they had forced on my old man. 'Ever fancied being a *greengrocer*, Simon? If you want to keep the use of your legs, I advise you to get your head round the old *fruit and veg*.'

The Quigleys clumped through to the kitchen.

'Ohhh,' I heard Marjorie say. 'You've got a new bin unit!'

She sounded really excited about this. Hearing her reminded

me of my dad's reaction the first time he had seen it. He had said it was the most elegant wooden sculpture to surround a plastic bucket he had ever seen. He also said it was something called 'post-modern'. Which, I think, is a term of approval. He was at Oxford, my dad, but he never did anything with it, apparently.

'It's actually a bin-*housing* unit,' my mum was saying.

I sat on the stairs and pulled at my T-shirt. If you can fluff it out, it makes you look as if you have quite a respectable chest. When I had finished fluffing out my T-shirt, I held out my right arm and tried to coax out my bicep. It did not seem to be its night.

Downstairs they started laughing about something. Emily was joining in, the way she always does. I sat there, thinking about my dad. I couldn't face going downstairs and telling everyone how terrific it was that he had stiffed. The window alongside me, which looks out over what Dad always called 'the most disgusting back passage in London', was coated with fine, grey dust. Why did we always live in places that other people had tried, and failed, to care for? And why was it we could never make them right? Once upon a time, years, years ago, I could have sworn we had lived in a big, clean house where the lights always worked and there was a garden you could go into without stepping in something nasty.

I suppose Dad had made money once, a long time ago. Well, he certainly wouldn't be making any now. If they have cash on the Other Side, it's probably a bit like those currencies they have in eastern Europe. Not even worth earning.

After a while I heard a snuffling sound on the landing. When I investigated, I found Pike rifling through the airing cupboard. He was holding up a green jacket.

'Was this your father's?'

'Yes,' I said.

'Nice jacket,' said Pike.

I went up to him and took it from his hands. I'm only fourteen but I'm as big as Pike. I put my face very close to his and said, 'I'd better hang on to it, don't you think? In case he drops back for it.'

Pike snorted. 'Oh,' he said, 'you don't come back in the body. You don't come back as yourself.'

'What are you coming back as, Pike?' I said. 'A natterjack toad? That might be a big improvement come to that . . .'

Pike snickered. 'Toads are nice.'

'Compared to you, Pike, the toad is Man's Best Friend!'

I heard a cough in the hall below. There, looking up at us, was Quigley. I could see more than I wanted of his teeth and nostrils. He spread his arms wide, as if he was about to conduct an imaginary choir – something he quite often does at bus-stops or (alarming, this one) when driving the car.

'Simon,' he said. 'We have come a-visiting!'

The last time my dad had seen Quigley was in the First Spiritualist Church Five-a-Side Football Team. Quigley had somehow got them a game with a nearby public school, and an enormous boy called Hoxton had put no fewer than eight goals past my dad.

'Jump high high high, Norman!' Quigley had called in a light voice as they ran back after goal number nine had slipped past my dad.

'And stuff the ball up your arse!' my dad had called in a loud, fruity voice.

'New car,' I said.

Quigley smirked. 'The Lord rewards His own.'

Pike was slobbering over the banisters. It was time to go.

'Well, Mr Quigley,' I said. 'I have to be going out now.'

'Simon,' said Quigley, 'don't you want to get in touch with Norman? He's very, very, *very* strong at the moment. This is a very crucial time in his spiritual development.'

I heard my mum call: 'Will you have some root beer, Mr Quigley?'

The First Spiritualist Church disapproves of all alcoholic drinks unless they are made 'at home and cleanly in the sight of the Lord'. Which leaves the more adventurous a lot of scope for 300-per-cent-proof spirits of the kind that are best taken in through the scalp. The last time my dad had finished off a bottle of his home-made gin he had tried to put a pair of his underpants on Quigley's head. Quigley had beseeched him in the sight of the Lord to abjure 'strong wine and wickedness'. After that I was sent to bed.

I started down the stairs.

'I'm sorry, Mr Quigley,' I said. 'I have to go out.'

Quigley put his head to one side. 'And where is young Simon going to, I wonder? Is he going to tell us where he's going, do you think? Or what time he's going to be back? What do you think, Mother?'

This was to Mrs Quigley, who, with my mum beside her, had appeared at the kitchen door.

'I'm going,' I said in a quiet, patient voice, 'to see if any Unidentified Flying Objects have landed on the Common. I'll be back for supper. OK?'

4

It is a perfectly reasonable assumption that there are intelligent beings somewhere else in the universe. They may be more than intelligent. They may be very, very intelligent. So there is a *possibility that they are on their way to the earth.* And if they do get to land, I don't see why it shouldn't be in sw19. That's my position.

If you look at the literature, you will discover that the aliens have landed in quite a number of suburbs all over the world. A group of squat but distinctly humanoid creatures dropped in on a residential district just outside Munich in the winter of 1979. A bunch of 'leathery-faced people in cloaks' was seen coming out of a large silver object in a commuters' sector of Barcelona as recently as 1989.

I am not saying I have seen them. But a hell of a lot of perfectly sane people *have.* I am not denying that irresponsible individuals invent sightings. Or that the ufological movement has as many crazies associated with it as, say, the Conservative Party. I do not believe, for example, that Hans Kluigtermeier was, and I quote, 'anally raped by a group of nine entities in red cloaks just outside the town of Poissy-le-Vaugin in northern France, *last September*'. But the volume of evidence is so considerable that it is irresponsible to ignore it. Why, I ask you, should we be the only intelligent life anywhere in the galaxy? They are out there. And they may well be on their way here.

My friend Mr Marr is actually an electrical engineer. I mean, he really does go out and mend things for the Council. No one has tapped him on the shoulder and tried to take him away in a van just because he chooses to clip on the old infra-red binoculars and get out there on the Common every night, clutching a tape-recorded message saying WELCOME in thirteen languages.

There are those who say he *should* have been taken away in a van years ago. I know this. He knows this. But he is pretty calm about it. 'I know I may never see them, Simon,' he says to me sometimes. 'But if they *do* come, and if they decide to come to Wimbledon, I want to be there to see it!' Which seems reasonable.

He's a bit like those people at the January sales. You know? Who camp out for weeks in advance because they're terrified of missing a bargain. Or the guys who doss down outside the Royal Albert Hall because they want to be first in with a chance to hear some brilliant cellist.

He was waiting for me on the corner with his Thermos.

'Who knows', he said, as we walked up the hill towards the War Memorial, 'what will come out of the sky tonight?'

I didn't answer this.

'It's a nice, clear night for them, anyway,' he went on.

'Indeed, Mr Marr,' I said. 'I hate to think of them getting wet.'

He laughed. He does have a sense of humour does Mr Marr. You can take the piss out of him and he doesn't mind.

'Weather is no problem for the aliens. They laugh at weather.'

I didn't ask how he knew this. Partly because, on the corner of the street, I could see Purkiss and Walbeck waiting for us. Walbeck was jumping up and down on the pavement and grinning. As we got closer, he pointed a finger at the sky and shook his head violently. Purkiss laughed.

Purkiss is small with a shock of black hair and the beginnings of a hump. Walbeck is huge but lost. They both wear anoraks. Walbeck is deaf and dumb. But he is fantastically talkative. I've worn out many an envelope in conversation with Walbeck.

As usual, Mr Marr just nodded to them as we passed and they fell in behind us. He lets them come along, but they're not top-quality ufologists. They're apparently very unscientific in their attitude to the beings who are hurtling through space-time towards Wimbledon Common. I often worry whether the four of us are *enough*. You know? What will it be like when they spin down out of the upper atmosphere and cop a load of me, Mr Marr, Purkiss and Walbeck? Will they be impressed?

'You're a dark horse, Simon,' Mr Marr said as we climbed the hill towards the Common. It was dark now, but still warm. We were moving past bigger houses than ours. Houses that seemed to put out their secrets for all to see, but were, nonetheless, more mysterious than the cramped terraces of Stranraer Gardens. 'You never say what's on your mind.'

'Do you reckon?' I said.

He looked at me sideways.

'But you're on the right side, anyway!'

Mr Marr reckons that we as a society are not doing enough about the extraterrestrials. When you think of all the money that is put into medical research and the English National Opera – why can't we put aside a few quid to welcome the boys in the saucers. You know? I mean, what are they going to think?

He's particularly keen on what he calls 'instrumentation'. I think this comes from being an engineer. He has instruments for listening to them, instruments for picking up their lights, instruments for talking to them and an amazing variety of gadgets for making the long night watches easier. Things to rest your head against, things to put your feet on, little chairs to make sure you are pointing towards the night sky at the right angle and little trays that enable you to have your dinner and keep your eyes on the Crab Nebula at the same time. We all miss a lot of stuff, Mr Marr says. We wander around looking at the ground − and up there, there's a party going on!

His wife died ten years ago. She was apparently the most beautiful woman you could ever wish to look at. Her name was Mabel. I've seen her photograph, and it obviously doesn't do her justice. She has just the one head, but she definitely has an alien look about her. She was a terrific cook though, Mr Marr says.

'Well . . .' he said. 'Anything happen today?'

'My dad died!'

He was the first person I had had to tell. For some reason it made me feel tremendously important. It didn't seem a difficult thing to say. It was the sort of thing real men said to each other. I was so concerned with actually saying it, rather than thinking what it meant, that it came out wrong. I wanted to sound serious but unweepy. Instead, I sounded positively chirpy about the whole business.

Mr Marr stopped. 'Oh, Simon!' he said. 'Oh *Simon!*'

He's from the North, is Mr Marr. He has this funny voice and this great big tuft of ginger hair that sticks up in surprise from his head. He's really nice.

'Should you be out tonight?'

'It's OK, Mr Marr. Honestly.'

Purkiss looked at Walbeck. He pointed at me. Then he raised his hands above his head. Then he pointed at the ground and made what looked like shovelling movements. They could have been something different, of course. It's always hard to tell with Purkiss.

Walbeck was looking at him, as usual, in total puzzlement. I don't think he and Purkiss really communicate. They resent being so much together, I think – which, from both their points of view, is an entirely understandable reaction.

Mr Marr took over. He set himself in front of Walbeck and said in a slow, clear voice, 'Simon's father is dead.'

Walbeck nodded seriously. Then he turned round and started to wander off down the street. Maybe he thought Mr Marr had said, 'Go home to bed.' It's that bad with Walbeck.

Mr Marr turned to Purkiss. 'Bring him back,' he said, 'and don't try to tell him things. Write them down, OK?'

'Yes, Mr Marr,' said Purkiss, in a high, squeaky voice.

Somehow all this was helpful. When I'm around Purkiss and Walbeck, it almost seems a plus that I am me. Mr Marr was making off up the street with big, confident strides, clearly anxious not to miss any aliens.

I must say that it felt like a good night for them. Although it was late summer, it was still warm. That wind seemed to promise something. There was no one now on the quiet, wide streets that surround the Common. The thought that out there, somewhere between the stars and the moon, was my dad's soul (I believe in the soul) gave the night a special feeling. As we came up to Carew Road and headed towards the War Memorial, I kept my eyes on the planets.

Over to the left was something that I thought might be Venus. It turned out to be the masthead of the Sun Life Assurance Building. I looked to see if I could make out

the Great Bear or Orion's Belt, but all I came up with was
a group of stars that seemed to be laid out in the shape
of a condom. Was there, I wondered, a star called Durex
Major? When you looked closer, however, you could see
that it looked more like an aubergine. Or, indeed, a Renault
Espace.

I see condoms everywhere. I am obsessed with them. It's
pathetic. The chances that I'll ever get to use one for anything
remotely like the purpose for which it was intended are very,
very low. The best thing I could do with one, really, would be to
pull it over my head and breathe in deeply.

I gave up and looked at the moon. You know where you are
with the moon. It was in the usual place – just to the right of
Wimbledon Public Library – and it was the usual colour – De
Luxe Oatmeal, the colour we've painted our bathroom. It has
lost its glamour, has the moon. Too many people have been
there. These days, they say, the Sea of Tranquillity is littered
with probes and undercarriages and the remains of astronaut
picnics.

It's the far galaxies that get to me. All I want to hear about is
Sirius Four and Betelgeuse and Star BXY5634256 in the Milky
Way. Stars that are light years away, and moving away from us at
speeds you couldn't begin to imagine.

Khan says it's all to do with something called String
Theory. Khan is in my class, and, although he is only about
three feet high and his father is an Islamic sex maniac, he
does know about physics. Apparently the world was all string
before it was what it is now. Or something like string. It's
full of things that are so dense that matter sort of pours into
them – white dwarves and black holes. And it makes a noise,
too. There's a sort of background hum out there, like static
on a radio. There's Solar Wind and Solar Dust and Bargons
and Protons and, according to Khan, something called Axion

Radio, which is not a local broadcasting station but some vibration that happened *minutes* after that key moment 150 billion years ago when everything was in excess of one billion Kelvin. Don't ask me who Kelvin is – some friend of Sharon's or Tracy's, I suppose.

I don't *know*. That's what makes looking at the sky so absolutely amazing.

'I liked your dad,' Mr Marr was saying, while I thought about the universe. The War Memorial was in sight now. Beyond it was a dark patch of grass and the shallow pond next to which Mr Marr always takes up his observation post. 'He was a nice bloke.'

'Yes,' I said, 'he was a nice bloke.'

My dad always used to say that you should be very suspicious of people who said you were a nice bloke. It means they really despise you, apparently.

My dad said a lot of things that were quite hard to fathom. I didn't think it was true that Mr Marr despised him. Dad despised himself, I suppose. At least, he said he did. When he wasn't claiming to be the greatest unpublished novelist in western Europe.

He hadn't always been a travel agent. He had been a lot of other things while he was trying to be a novelist, but he had ended up as a travel agent. Which, it seems, was the worst possible thing that could have happened. Some jobs, he used to say, go quite well with writing. A guy called Trollope worked at the Post Office. Melvyn Bragg is a television personality. But, according to my dad, there has never been a really successful writer who was also a travel agent. The two just do not go together.

'He was a disappointed man in many ways,' said Mr Marr, who had moved into the past tense a touch too easily for my liking, 'but he was a man of real calibre.'

I nodded. I just do not *get* remarks like that. *Calibre!* Get serious, why don't you? Mr Marr would never have said that about Dad when he was alive. He used to drink with him sometimes, but I don't think he knew him well enough to decide whether or not he was of *real calibre*. Whatever that may mean. And what, while we were at it, did he mean by 'disappointed'? It wasn't his fault they made Dad become a travel agent and forced him to marry my mum.

Mr Marr was practically running now. He always gets like that when he's close to the action. It's as if he expects the aliens to sneak in a landing before he's in place. And that somehow, if he *wasn't* on his canvas chair on the edge of the Common, it wouldn't really count. You know? Like when you tell yourself that if you don't get to the red light before it changes you'll die at school today.

He put up the canvas chair. Walbeck and Purkiss, as usual, hung back in the darkness. Walbeck, his head tilted so far that the point on the end of it practically brushed the back of his jacket, was staring at the stars like they were the faces of old friends. What's so great about Walbeck is that he *really* expects them. Any moment now. He just can't wait to start nodding and waving at the little green guys, and trying to get them to write him messages on the back of that envelope he carries with him.

'Walbeck's frisky,' I said.

Sometimes he seems to pick up what you say. As I made this remark, he started to frolic on the patch of grass, waggling his head to and fro and grinning as he did so. Mr Marr looked at me. He had a deadly serious expression on his face. 'Tonight', he said, '*is* the night!'

It was funny. He says that every night. The fact that, so far, in ten years of watching there has not been a sign of them only makes him more convinced that he is getting closer to the moment when, from a saucer hovering over the birch trees, a steel ladder is let down on to the Common and entities start shinning down it and asking the way to the nearest fast-food restaurant.

My dad was like that about his book. Every time he got a letter back from a publisher, he was convinced that, this time, it wasn't going to start:

Dear Norman Britton,
    I am afraid we are having to return the MS of *Jubal's Lyre* to you. Much of it has a Dickensian breadth but ultimately it fails to convince. The drawings, however, impressed us all!
Yours,
A. Bastard

Things were always just about to get better for my dad. Which is perhaps why he got on so well with Mr Marr. 'The thing about old Marr,' Dad would say, 'is that he's committed. You know?' Sometimes he would add, with a little wink, 'There are those, of course, Simon, who maintain he should *be* committed. If you take my meaning . . .'

I sat next to Mr Marr on the grass, and I could see that he was sort of quivering, like a retriever. As I looked up at the sky, I could have sworn I heard a distant humming sound.

Watching for the aliens is always a nerve-racking business. You never know when they are going to come. Every time a car backfires or a plane flies in low over Raynes Park, Purkiss and Marr are up and gibbering like loonies. Quite often Mr Marr has started the tape and we're halfway through 'We hope you had a pleasant journey and that our atmosphere is proving satisfactory' before we all realize that we have been straightening our ties for a 150 cc Kawasaki.

Tonight was different. Tonight was the night. There is some mysterious force at work in the world, because I swear I had foreknowledge. Even before all this happened, I *knew* that something was on its way and that, by the end of the night, my life would be utterly changed.

5

We were about twenty minutes into the session. Purkiss had already frothed at the mouth at a Boeing 747. Walbeck suddenly started rubbing the top of his head with the palm of his hand.

'What does that mean?' I asked Purkiss.

'It means', said Purkiss, 'that he's hungry.'

I didn't get this.

Purkiss looked rather superior. 'It's his impression of a cheeseburger,' he said.

From the High Street I saw an elderly man in a dark grey suit walking towards us. Jacob Toombs. Toombs is an elder of the First Spiritualist Church, which means he can do anything he likes apart from shag the choir in full view of the rest of the congregation. He was walking in a very peculiar way. Each time he lifted his foot he waggled it around in the air before placing it, very carefully, on the ground in front of him. He looked as if he was trying to avoid dog turds.

Toombs was elected an elder a few years back, after a pretty dirty campaign in which a lot of famous dead people endorsed his candidature heavily. He's pretty extreme, even by First Spiritualist standards, but I couldn't work out why he was carrying on like a man trying to walk along two separate tightropes at the same time. Then I remembered.

'Place the foot carefully upon the ground,' Old Mother Walsh is reported to have said, 'and hurt not any living thing with the soles of thy feet.' Toombs was trying to make sure he was doing right by the local insects. Every so often he stopped and peered closely at the pavement to check they were all all right. Then he looked over his shoulder.

About twenty yards behind him I could see my mum, Pike, Hannah Dooley and the Quigleys, all waggling their feet like astronauts. They were on their best behaviour because Toombs was there. Why had they brought him to see me? If they'd brought Toombs with them, it must be serious.

Toombs looks great, which is more than can be said for most members of the First Spiritualist Church. He has a hawklike nose, fierce blue eyes and a great mane of white hair. It's when he opens his mouth that the problems start. You think he's going to make with some deep remark about the meaning of the universe. In fact, what you usually get is, 'There's nothing worse than a bad-mannered dog!' Or, 'The English abroad often wear shorts.' That, for Toombs, would be a *pretty bold* statement. He is usually a lot less controversial than that.

He was staring at me now as he got closer. Was he looking deep into my soul? Or was he trying to remember whether he or his wife was taking the kids to school in the morning?

When they got close enough, they sort of formed up in a line – something the members of the First Spiritualist Church are incredibly good at doing. Then Quigley coughed and stepped forward a pace. 'Well, Simon,' he said. 'Mr Toombs has got something to say to you.'

A look of panic ruffled the calm of Mr Toombs's handsome face. *What was it?* his expression seemed to say. Quigley looked sideways at him and muttered something. I couldn't hear what it was. Then Toombs took two paces forward from the line and cleared his throat. 'Simon,' he said, eventually, 'your father is dead!'

A lot of people seemed keen to emphasize this fact. As if I hadn't heard them right the first time. As if I might have thought they'd said, 'He's in bed,' or, 'He has a bad head.' *I am getting the message: he is dead!*

'But', Mr Toombs went on, 'there have already been very strong messages coming through from him.'

'What kind of messages?' I asked.

I didn't care for this. They seemed almost pleased about whatever it was my dad had had to say. All I could think was that this sort of behaviour was not typical of Norman. He was not a talkative man.

'Messages about his deepest feelings.'

This was even weirder. The one thing my dad never liked to talk about was his deepest feelings. And he hated other people, especially my mother, talking about *their* deepest feelings.

Mr Toombs was nodding solemnly. Quigley stepped up to the elder, whispered in his ear and then retreated to the line, combing his beard for nits as he did so.

'There have never been quite so many messages coming through so soon after a coronary thrombosis,' said Toombs.

'Really?' I said.

Purkiss and Walbeck were busy clocking all this. Mr Marr had the bins trained on the front gates of Cranborne School. He was absolutely motionless. From the look of him you would have thought a green man with horns and a ray gun was drifting out past the Porter's Lodge at that very moment. But maybe he was just trying to ignore Quigley and company.

'And we are of the opinion', went on Toombs, 'that Norman has something very important to tell *you.*'

He prodded me in the chest with his forefinger. I looked straight at him.

'That is why we have come,' he went on rather menacingly. 'We want you to join with us now in trying to make contact with him. We must find out exactly what his problem is.'

'His problem', I said, 'is that he's dead.'

Quigley gave a superior laugh. 'We have a very simple view of the world, don't we, Simon?' Then he turned to Mr Marr, who, like Nelson, was keeping his eye to the lens. 'How are the "little green men"?' he asked.

Mr Marr did not respond to this. He twitched slightly though. He hates aliens being called 'little green men'. As he says, we don't know what shape or size or colour they'll be. And why be so sexist? They may be hermaphrodites.

Mrs Quigley weighed in next. The First Spiritualists often talk like this. As if they all had one sentence in mind and had agreed to share it out between them. As if they were all controlled by some central brain.

'The feelings are very, very bad,' she said, in a low voice – 'very, very negative. We feel he has something very, very important to tell us. And he can't quite get through.'

'Maybe we need a bigger aerial,' I suggested.

Mrs Quigley looked intently at me. She gave me the impression I had just uttered a great and important truth. 'Yes – maybe we do!'

I just stood there looking at them. Then my mum said, 'Please, Simon. For me. Will you? For me.'

This is it with mums. There you are, trying to have a rational conversation, and then, suddenly, they're looking deep into your eyes and reminding you that, just over fourteen years ago, you were in their womb. So – you were in their womb! Just because you were inside them they think they have some kind of hold over you! Actually, Mum usually says something even more embarrassing than that. So embarrassing that I can hardly bring myself to write it down: 'I carried your maleness inside me for nine months and a day.'

I was frightened she was going to say something along those lines now. Right here, in front of Emily and everything. So I did the quite tactful thing I do at such moments. I sucked at my teeth and looked at the ground. But I could still feel her looking at me. Eventually, I looked back at her. She had come out as she was, in her flour-covered apron. She seemed smaller and more frightened. The way she always does when the Quigleys are around.

I smiled and said, 'OK.'

Walbeck pointed at the sky and shook his head vigorously.

'I'm sorry, Walbeck,' I said, making sure he had a good, clear view of my mouth, 'but they probably won't come if I stay. You know?'

I'm sure it's true, actually. I'm sure none of this would have happened if I'd been there. Nothing ever happens when I'm around. I have to be surgically removed to create an event. If you see what I mean.

They were still looking up into the night sky as I was led away by the delegation from the First Spiritualist Church. Mr Marr was drinking deep, straight from his Thermos. Purkiss was sitting cross-legged on the grass, trying to read *Flying Saucer Review*. And Walbeck, his big, round face anxious and pale, was looking after me. Every so often he would point up at the stars and give me a rather woebegone thumbs-up sign. He puts a lot into his gestures, and when I gave him one back I tried to make it worthy of his very high standards. I got my thumb to sit up straight and then I made it quiver like a dog that has sighted a rabbit. Walbeck is a connoisseur of sign language, and even he looked impressed.

'I got this terrible feeling,' said my mum as we turned down towards Stranraer Gardens, 'that something was wrong. Just after you went out.'

Mrs Quigley came in here, before Mum said anything embarrassing. 'Emily', she said, 'had a very strong feeling in the toilet.'

'Well,' I said, 'Dad spent a lot of time in there.'

Everyone nodded seriously at this remark.

Mum clutched my arm. 'I went into the spare bedroom,' she said in a low voice, 'and he was *there*! He was ever so tangible, Simon. And he isn't happy about something.'

Quigley nodded seriously. 'He has a lot to tell us – a great deal to say. We all feel it.'

Dad had absolutely nothing to say to Quigley when he was alive. I couldn't see why being dead should have made him any more communicative. But, in the First Spiritualist Church, people tend to get a lot livelier after they've croaked. Guys who, when they were alive, would not give you the time of day can't wait to tell you how terrific it is on the Other Side, and where they went wrong in the brief period of time allotted to them to hang around South Wimbledon.

Dying is a big event for the First Spiritualist. I sometimes think that what would really suit them would be a gas explosion right outside the church – and then the whole lot of them could get blasted over to where the action is.

I noticed that they had formed up into a kind of protective shell around me. Pike was a little way ahead, over to my right. Hannah Dooley, Mr Toombs and Mrs Quigley were behind to my left. The north-west exits were covered by my mum and Quigley. Emily hung in close to my offside rear in case I should try to bolt west-south-west as we came in to Durham Gardens.

'Well,' said Quigley, in a conversational tone, over his left shoulder, 'has Jesus Christ entered your heart yet, Simon?'

'Not yet, Mr Quigley,' I said. 'But you never know!'

'You never know,' he repeated, with somewhat forced cheerfulness.

The big thing in the First Church of Christ the Spiritualist is honesty. Everyone is very honest with everyone else. If you have body odour, people will tell you about it. You know? And they are razor-sharp about Faith. It's not like the golf club. You don't just join. It's not really enough to be born into it, which is perhaps why so many people leave – especially around my age. They are always asking you whether you *really* believe, and whether Jesus has *really* entered your heart.

I think the only reason I haven't left is that I have nowhere else to go. While my dad was alive, none of it seemed to matter too much.

'Norman,' Quigley had once said to him, 'are you happy with the Lord Jesus? Are you comfortable with Him?'

My dad had given him a cautious look. 'I think we get along pretty well. You know?' And he turned to me and gave me one of his broad winks. Then he raised his right buttock and mimed a farting movement.

He never really liked conversations about JC. And he never talked to me about those things. Maybe now he was dead he would have a bit more to say about it all. I found myself quite looking forward to his views. What he said, of course, depended on which of us got to him first.

We were marching, in good order, down Stranraer Gardens. We were coming up to the shabby front door of number 24. We were waiting patiently while my mum groped in her apron for the key. We were stepping over the threshold.

Mrs Quigley stepped in first, her long red nose twitching with excitement. As she moved down the hall she was practically pawing the carpet in her excitement. When she got to the bottom of the stairs she turned round and flung her arms wide. 'Yes,' she said, 'oh *yes*! He is very strong. Very, very strong. Still!'

If anyone was going to get on the line to the late Norman Britton, her face seemed to say, it was going to be Marjorie Gwendolen Quigley.

6

Mrs Quigley is a sensitive. I don't mean she *is* sensitive. She's about as sensitive as tungsten steel. She is *a* sensitive, the way some people are bus conductors or interior designers. She is in touch with things that dumbos like you and I did not even know existed until people like Mrs Quigley clued us in on them.

She knew, for example, that Emily was going to fail Grade Four Cello. Not because Emily Quigley is tone-deaf and has fingers about as supple as frozen sausages, but because she *knew.* The way she *knew* that that ferry at Zeebrugge was going to roll over and kill all those poor people. Why, you may ask, did she not get on to the ferry company and tell them not to bother with this particular service? Or, indeed, get at the Associated Board of Examiners? She *knew*, that was all. It was fate — right?

She usually keeps quiet about her prophecies until they have been proved correct, but occasionally she will go public a little earlier than that. Remember the nuclear war in Spain at the end of 1987? That was hers. Or the tidal waves off Boulogne in the August of the following year? Seven thousand people were going to die, according to Marjorie Quigley. A lot of us thought that house prices would be seriously affected.

She was extra-sensitive tonight. After she had pawed the carpet, she lifted that long, spongy nose of hers and sniffed the air keenly. Her nose is the most prominent thing about her face. The rest of it is mainly wrinkles, that dwindle away into her neck. On either side of the nose are two very bright eyes. They are never still. They come on like cheap jewellery.

'Norman!' she said, as if she expected my dad to leap out at her from behind the wardrobe in the hall. 'Norman! Norman! Norman!'

'He wath in the toilet,' said Emily. 'I had a thtwong feeling of him in the toilet!'

You could tell that nobody much fancied the idea of trying to make contact with Norman in the lavatory. Marjorie's nose and mouse-bright eyes were leading us to the back parlour, scene of some of her greatest triumphs.

They always have the seances in the back parlour – a small, drab room looking out over the back garden. It was here, a couple of years ago, that Mrs Quigley talked to my gran. Never has there been such an amazingly low-level conversation across the Great Divide.

'Are you all right, Maureen?'

'Oh yes. I'm fine.'

'Keeping well?'

'Oh, yes. On the whole. Mustn't grumble. You?'

'We're fine. How are Stephen and Sarah?'

'Oh, they're fine. They're all here, and they're fine.'

It really was difficult to work out who was dead and who was alive. My favourite moment came when La Quigley, running out of more serious topics, asked my dear departed gran, 'What are you all doing Over There?'

'Oh,' said Gran – 'the usual things.'

The *usual things*, my friends! They are dead, and they are still running their kids to piano lessons and worrying about whether to have the spare room decorated. What was the point in dying if that was all you got at the end of it?

I had the feeling, however, as Mrs Quigley settled herself at the table, that tonight's rap was going to be a little more heavy-duty. The team got into their chairs and pulled themselves up to the table like they were the board of some company discussing a million-pound tax-avoidance scheme. Only I remained outside the circle.

'Come,' said Mrs Quigley. 'Come, Simon!'

I came.

Have you ever been to a seance? Do you imagine something vaguely exciting? With the curtains drawn and the doors closed and the night wind banging at the window? A weird, black-magic affair, where people push glasses around on heavy tables, or levitate, to the sound of heavy breathing? With the First Spiritualist Church of South Wimbledon, it isn't like that at all.

For a start, there is no build-up. You draw the curtains, yes. But after you have taken the hand of the person next to you, off you go. There are no preliminaries apart from a short prayer, which Quigley was giving out as I sat down.

'O Jesus,' he was saying, 'all of us here at 24 Stranraer Gardens are very keen to get in touch with Mr Norman Britton, of this address, who died earlier today at a hospital in the Wimbledon area.'

That's Quigley. He gives it to Jesus straight. Like he was talking to Directory Enquiries, or something.

'You' – I could tell from the way he tackled the first letter of the word that he meant Jesus – 'see everything. You see wars, famines, victories, defeats and also, of course, You see . . . us!'

I breathed out. Once Quigley gets on to the Lord it's time to go out and get the popcorn. Those two can talk for hours. Or, rather, JC can *listen* for as long as Quiggers can dish it out.

'Tell us, Lord,' he went on, 'about Thy new arrival. How is he? And can He . . .'

Here he stopped, aware that he had vocalized the first letter as a capital and that he wasn't supposed to be talking about Jesus but about my dad. He gulped and struggled on, careful to demote the late Mr Britton to the status of mere mortal.

'. . . can *he* – Norman Britton, that is – talk to Thy children here at 24 Stranraer Gardens on today, Wednesday the fifth of September?'

That's Quigley. The date. The time. The map reference.

Jesus said nothing. He never does. People do not expect him to.

'And,' went on Quigley, 'Lord, if Norman has a message for any one of us here – any word of advice from Thy Kingdom on the Other Side – please may he come forward and speak, as we trust in Thy mercy to reveal him!'

There was absolutely no response to this.

Quigley, rather like a guy on the radio filling in time between records, prayed a bit more. 'Thy crop has been a good one, Lord, and the economy, as far as we can tell, is moving out of recession and into Steady Growth.'

Here he stopped, clearly aware that he was losing all grip on his capital letters. To mask any confusion he might be feeling, he squeezed his eyes tightly shut and drove forward into the next sentence. 'But Britain still lacks a spiritual dimension, Jesus, and many people live their lives in complete ignorance of Thee.'

He lifted his head at this point, opened the Quigley peepers and looked round at the assembled company. His gaze ended on yours truly. I could have sworn he was trying to pick me up! It was only one step away from 'Hi, let's go back for a cup of coffee!' You know? There was that much sincerity in the old Quigley glance.

There was still absolutely no sign of Norman.

Quigley ploughed on bravely. 'Television is about to be deregulated and, as a result, there is a danger that pornography will be pumped into our homes. Old values are under threat. Motorways . . .'

He stopped. He now had his head bowed over the table. His fingers masked his forehead. He peered over them at the assembled company. He obviously hadn't quite got the heart for motorways. Once again he looked in my direction. I had adopted the sort of half-and-half attitude to prayer I had perfected for the rather less intense religious services on offer at Cranborne School, Wimbledon. I sat at a slight angle to the vertical, with my eyes hooded like a hawk's. This was the only concession I made to the spiritual. You could see this freaked Quigley. Was I on the team or wasn't I? Was I working for the opposition?

'Motorwayth', said Emily Quigley, picking up the ball and moving well with it, 'are an evil, Lord! They blight the beautiful countwythide. Thupport and thuccour uth in our thtwuggle to thtop thith ditheathe that thweatenth the thtandardth of the Thouth-Eatht!'

She has no shame, Emily. She looks for the nineteenth letter of the alphabet and she works it in whenever she can. Content-wise, however, she had clearly scored a hit. People were nodding as if they all felt this was something that needed saying.

My mum's eyes were blinking very fast. She pulled at her straggly grey hair and, in the reedy, worried tones she always used to talk to him, she said, 'Norman . . .'

This was clearly something that had to be stopped. The guy had not yet had clearance from air-traffic control and here she was weighing in with a direct address, using his first name. You could tell from the way both Quigleys looked at her that the death of her husband had not improved her standing in the very competitive field of psychic phenomena.

Mrs Quigley made her move. I felt her hand flutter in mine

slightly. And then, one or two firm tugs at my wrist. On the other side of her, Emily started to brace her right shoulder. She knew her mum. When Mrs Quigley goes for it, you get out the protective clothing and nail the furniture to the floor. She is serious business.

'Oh!' said Mrs Quigley. 'OH! Oh! Ohhhh!' We all knew the main show had started. There is a fantastic amount of upstaging in the First Church of Christ the Spiritualist, but nobody was going to give Marjorie Quigley anything to worry about. They knew a class act when they saw it.

'Oh!' she said, as if someone was pushing a large cucumber up her bum. 'Oh! Oh! Oh! Ohhhhhhhh!'

Then she started to tug hard at my hand. I held on as hard as I could, but she was moving into top gear. On her other side, Emily had whipped away her hand as if someone had just passed a few thousand volts through it. Her mum was sort of snaking forward and then bouncing back in her chair, then giving us a few good pelvic thrusts, before starting the whole movement over again. She looked as if she was in the middle of some complex, experimental swimming stroke.

'Oh!' said Mrs Quigley, as if she was getting used to the cucumber – even, perhaps, to like it a little. 'Oh! Oh! Oh! Oh! *Ohhhhhhhh!*'

She was bucking like a rodeo rider now. At any seance the rule was always to give Mrs Quigley a good strong chair, because there was no chance it was going to keep its four legs on the floor for any longer than was absolutely necessary.

On the other side of the table, Quigley was waving his hands. 'O *Jesus!*' he was saying. 'Oh *Jesus Christ!*'

It was hard to tell whether Quiggers was talking to the Son of God or was merely in a panic at the unexpected violence of his old lady's seizure. She always gives good value, but this one was a real corker. Everyone else was, quite literally, keeping a low profile. Pike's profile was so low his nose was hitting the table. Toombs, one hand in my mum's, the other grasping Hannah Dooley, was getting his head well down between his knees. He looked as if he was about to chunder all over the carpet. Only Marjorie's old man, who had broken away from his two tablemates and who had bared his lips above his yellow teeth like a nervous horse, was giving it anything at all. But he never fails her.

'O Jesus,' he said, 'are you come amongst us?'

As if in answer to this, Mrs Quigley gave a loud howl and headed for the floor like a rugby forward crossing the line. My hand snapped out of hers. She must have gone about five yards. Then she started to writhe.

Mrs Quigley writhes brilliantly. She does an aerobics class with my mum, who says she can hardly get her knees in the air. But get her in a darkened room and mention Jesus a couple of times and she is doing things a world-class athlete could not manage. She goes in about eight different directions at the same time.

Quigley got to his feet, his eyes shining. *This*, his expression seemed to say, *beats anything at the National Westminster Bank.* 'What is it, my sweet one?' he said. 'What is it, my sweet precious?'

Mrs Quigley started to grunt. The grunt was new. I thought it was pretty good. I don't think Quigley was too sure about it. He kept looking at her as if she was about to drop her drawers and flash her gash at us.

'Darling,' he said, reaching for her hand. 'Darling . . . Darling . . . What is it, sweet darling?'

It's a normal day, Quigley. I always do this. Remember?

Quigley looked up at the light fittings. 'Jesus,' he said, fixing his eyes on them, 'what is the spirit that is in her? Jesus? O Jesus? Jesus? Jesus?'

Jesus was still saying *nothing.* Mrs Quigley started to bang her head on the floor. Over on the other side of the table I saw Pike sneak a look at his watch.

She made us wait for it. She always makes us wait for it. But when the voice comes out it is always good. This time it had a weird, distorted effect on it. It was hard to see how she could have possibly produced this timbre on her own, but what La Quigley doesn't know about voice production could be written on a very small postcard. A guy from the Society for Psychical Research once frisked Marjorie just before she got in touch with the late Elvis Presley. Although she was clean, she made, I am told, a noise like a container ship's fog-horn and broke three windows.

But this voice was really creepy. It had a sharp little edge to it. It sounded lonely. There was an ugly ring to it, too, as if it belonged to someone who had mean, nasty things to say about the world.

Whoever it belonged to, it was calling my name.

'Simon!' it said. 'Simon Britton! Simon! Simon! Simon Britton!'

Everyone looked at me.

'Yes?' I said, in as calm a voice as I could manage. 'That's me. What exactly can I do for you?'

7

You don't talk directly to the dead.

Over There, just like over here, you always have to go through someone if you want to do things properly. It's a bit like when I used to phone my dad's office and his secretary would say, 'I'll see if he's in.' I knew this meant that he was in but that she wasn't sure if he wanted to talk to me.

The dead are like that. They are guarded by a whole load of spirits, with names like Peony and Goldenrod, and by the time these have kept you hanging round for hours, telling you their life stories, you sometimes wish the dead would hire competent secretaries.

Sometimes you get crossed lines. You're looking for Aunt Elsie or little Camilla, but Lloyd George or Philip Larkin or somebody like that barges in and tells you what a great time they had on earth.

This voice of Mrs Quigley's was a *spirit*, right? The next thing on the agenda was for us all to start asking it who it was and where it came from. Spirits don't volunteer any information. They don't walk around with ID cards pinned to their robes. And they have to be wooed. Sometimes there are things they don't want to tell you. Sometimes they are too busy to talk to you.

I was buggered if I was going to woo this spirit. I didn't, to tell the truth, like the sound of it. It rather freaked me out, in fact. And so, as so often happened at our seances, it was a member of the Quigley family who led us further down the passage to that Other World that lies in wait for us all.

'What ith your name?' Emily said.

There was a pause while Mrs Quigley thought of a name. 'Gossamer,' she said eventually, in a thick voice. Was this another celebrated spirit? A founder member of the Durex empire?

My mum is always good with the lower spirits. She'll spend hours asking them how they float and what they eat and are their clothes comfortable. She often asks them really personal questions about their habits. I've heard them get quite offended.

'Are you at peace, Gossamer?'

The voice took on a slightly babyish quality. 'I . . . at peace . . .'

'Oh good,' said Mum. 'Oh *good*!'

'I at peace, but . . .'

Quigley moved in, fast. 'But what?'

He tends to threaten the more junior spirits as if they are hostile witnesses in a cross-examination.

'Gossamer?'

Mrs Quigley was writhing again.

It sometimes occurs to me that it was only during seances that the Quigleys could say what they really felt about each other. Normally Mrs Quigley was subject to the usual restrictions that apply to married people. She had to sit there and grit her teeth while her husband went on about the mortgage rate, the need for competitive small business and the very real power of Jesus' love. In the middle of a seance she was at liberty to grunt and throw herself around the room and ignore everything the assistant bank manager said to her.

'Gossamer?'

'Go away!'

'Gossamer?'

'Fuck off!'

The spirits often use bad language. Especially when Quigley is asking them personal questions. I have often thought of going into a trance myself simply to have the pleasure of telling Quigley to go and fuck himself with an iron bar. As yet, I fear, I have not had the nerve to do so.

'Gossamer?'

Mrs Quigley's voice became plaintive and girlish.

'What-a matter?'

Quigley looked as if he was trying to resist the temptation to honk into his inside jacket pocket.

'Gossamer . . . have you a message for Simon?'

'Methage for Thimon?'

Gossamer had gone babyish in a big way. Quigley responded by trying to out-yuck him/her/it.

'Yes. What message for li'l Simey? What message 'oo got?'

Mrs Quigley came back with the sort of scream Dracula comes out with when faced by garlic or wooden stakes. She drew her knees up to her chin and started to bang her right arm on the floor in pretty strict rhythm. At the same time she pushed her crotch up at Quigley as hard as she could. He looked impressed. When her voice came through, it was a tiny croak, distant and faraway. 'Simon?' it said. 'Are you there, Simon?'

'Is this Gossamer I'm talking to?' said Quigley in a no-nonsense voice.

It didn't sound like Gossamer. It sounded like someone on a car phone going into a tunnel.

'Gossamer gone . . .' said the voice. 'I am not Gossamer.'

'Who are you?' said Pike, clearly feeling the need to be included in all this.

'An old spirit,' said the voice – 'one from the dawn of time. A tired spirit. A tired spirit that wants to sleep.'

'What was your name?' said my mum – 'when you were on the earth?'

Mrs Quigley thrashed a little. There was dead silence in the room.

'On earth,' said the spirit, 'I bore the name of Norman Britton.'

'And what', asked Quigley keenly, 'was your address?'

'Address?' said the spirit, feebly. 'How do you mean – "address"?'

It obviously didn't know about addresses. They don't have addresses over there, guys. There is a marked absence of the Filofax.

'Which house . . .' said Quigley, sounding a bit like my mum talking to a Swedish lodger we had once, 'which *house* did you *live* in?'

'I . . .'

There was a tense silence. Then Mrs Quigley frothed lightly, twitched a little and said, 'I Gossamer. I come back!'

Everyone looked pretty cheesed-off at this. I think we all felt we had had Gossamer. He was fine as far as he went, but it was time to make contact with new and more exciting shades.

'We want to talk to Norman,' said Quigley, keenly, 'not to Gossamer. Can you put us in touch with Norman? Norman Britton.'

'He was a travel agent,' said Mum. 'He had a shop in Balham High Street.'

Quigley glared at her.

'Norman,' he said, in an insistent tone. 'Norman Britton.'

'I Gossamer,' said Mrs Quigley, brightly.

This whole thing was beginning to resemble a bad transatlantic phone-call. Should we, you could see Quigley wondering, just leave a message and ask the guy to ring back? If we did get through, were we going to get any sense out of him?

'Why can Norman not sleep?' Pike asked.

Maybe because of all you guys getting on the line and asking the old spirit pointless questions! You know?

'Is there something that troubles you?'

Mrs Quigley groaned. Long and low and quiet. 'Ohhh! Ohhh!'

'Thay if you have thinned!' said Emily Quigley. Typical Emily. She'd never have dared talk to my dad like that when he was alive, even during the period when he was into the High Anglican church, Putney. I was quite prepared for my dad to get on the line and start talking about his period of Error – which is how the First Spiritualists referred to his going over to another church. But he didn't.

'What is your message for Simon?' asked my mum. 'What do you want to say to him?'

He didn't answer. This was, I have to say, absolutely typical of my dad. You could ask him a question and he would take literally days to reply.

'Want to say . . .'

'Want to say what?' Quigley sounded like a man trying to encourage his pet snake to dance.

There was no reply.

My mother, in a rare moment of independence, said, 'You frightened him off!'

'Don't be *stupid*!' said Quigley. 'Don't be *utterly stupid*!'

He was crouched over his wife, massaging her hands. Eventually that voice came out of her again. It was the one I didn't want to hear. The voice of a child alone in a large house at night. It had fear in it, but it also had the things that make you afraid – darkness, and the things that comes out of darkness and makes you afraid to go to sleep. It was like a sinister baby

– something very young that has already had another life and is only pretending to look at the world for the first time.

'I lived my life . . . I drank my wine . . . I broke my bread . . .'

'Yes?' said Quigley. 'Yes?'

Suddenly the voice changed again. It dropped an octave. It really was a bass voice, a voice thick with cigarettes and whisky, rich with the things that had helped to end its owner's life. It was my dad, I swear it. Although it was Mrs Quigley's lips moving, it was his voice I heard.

'Simon, old son . . .' he said.

It was so *like* him, you know? Right down to the way he couldn't finish sentences. I couldn't help myself. I just couldn't help myself. I wanted to talk to him so much. I wanted him to say the things he always used to say to me. Not big, important things, but just those ordinary remarks that let you know you're still here and ticking over. I was so desperate to hear his voice I didn't care if it came from the mouth of Marjorie Gwendolen Quigley.

'What, Dad?' I said. 'What's the matter? What do you want? What's the matter?'

Very slowly, Mrs Quigley started to lift her head off the floor. It wobbled loosely during the ascent, very much as Mum's does when she is doing her aerobics on the bathroom floor. Madame Quiggers did not look well. She always says that intense mediumship can damage you permanently and that very intense spirit possession can take thirty years off your life. If these calculations are correct, she could well be joining Norman for a face-to-face confrontation rather sooner than she had anticipated.

What was weird was that she was looking straight at me, but she obviously couldn't see me.

'Oh Simon,' said my dad's voice, seeming to come from the pit of her stomach. 'I am . . . I am . . . condemned!'

'Condemned to what, Dad?'

'To walk the earth.'

I could see Pike give a nervous glance out of the window. He takes these things very seriously, does Pike.

Suddenly Mrs Q started to writhe again.

'Walk the earth where?' said my mum, in a rather worried voice. 'In any particular place? Or sort of roaming about across the sea, and so on?'

Although this was clearly exactly the next question on Quigley's mind, he gave her a pitying look.

Mrs Quigley was working up her writhing and thrashing nicely. When she was at domestic-blender speed, the cucumber-up-the-bum effect was reintroduced. It now sounded as if a team of construction workers was hammering it into place. 'Oh!' she said. 'Oh! Oh! Ohhhhhhh!'

'Where, Norman?' said Mum, who really did sound genuinely concerned about the quality of the old man's afterlife. 'Where are you?'

The voice came again, and it was still my dad's. He could have been in the room. You know?

'Repent, Simon!' he said, in a deep, hollow voice. 'Repent! You hear me? You must repent!'

Repent of what? Was it my fault he had kicked off? What had I done that was so wrong?

'Free me, Simon! I beg you, free me! Free me!'

By now Mum was practically screaming. 'Where, Norman? Where are you?'

Rio de Janeiro? The Algarve? Have you come back as a lighthouse keeper in South Uist, or what?

With a snap, Mrs Quigley rose to a sitting position. It was not what any of us expected her to do, but, like a great actor, Mrs Quigley often throws in something very low-key, bang in the middle of a high dramatic passage. It surely does keep you watching. Quigley, her ever-faithful support act, ran to her side. He raised his hand to her face and kept it there for a full thirty seconds. Pike's eyes were starting out of his head on stalks. Hannah Dooley was openly weeping.

This time Mrs Q gave us a new voice. It was my dad still, but he sounded as if he had been put through a mixer and someone had added echo, reverb and a few hundred dBs of extra bass on the way. It had a threatening ring to it, too – some traces of that earlier spirit voice. The voice that reminded me of a frightening and frightened child.

Mrs Quigley's tongue lolled out of her mouth. She started to laugh. Or, rather, something inside her started to laugh. It wasn't a very pleasant sound.

'In what part of the world,' said my mum, in pleading tones, 'are you condemned to walk?'

'Wim – bel – don!' said my dad.

8

Great!

Not only does he die, he is condemned to walk the earth and find no rest. Worse than that, he is condemned to roam around Wimbledon for the next few thousand years. Have a heart, O Spirit of the Universe! Wimbledon is bad enough for an afternoon. With house prices the way they are, quite a few people are stuck there for rather longer than that. But at least they can look forward to stiffing.

My dad was one of the undead. He was not being allowed to pass to the Other Side. He was going to miss the tea parties and the organized games. Although he wasn't an enthusiastic Spiritualist, he often said he looked forward to seeing Auntie Norah again after she fell under the train at Norwood Junction. But even that was to be denied him. *What had he done to deserve this?*

He used to get ratty about the neighbours. He could be quite vicious when asked to hoover the front room. But he was not what you would call a bad man.

He said what he thought, did my dad. Maybe that was his crime. I remember the two of us came across a large poodle having a crap on the pavement outside our house. Dad picked it up by the collar and hurled it and its half-ejected turd into the middle of the road. Whereupon a woman in a fur coat threw herself upon him and demanded to know what he was doing with her dog. 'Give me your address,' said my dad, 'and I'll come round and shit on your doorstep!'

He was basic. He was noisy and loud, and he was earthy to the point of being gross. Whether he was singing an Irish song called the 'The Galway Shawl' or clapping me on the back or trying, unsuccessfully, to kiss my mum, he was very much of this world rather than the next one.

But he wasn't a bad man.

I could think of no good reason why he should have been doomed to roam up and down the local streets, or float in and out of the Wimbledon bookshops, trying to pick up the latest paperbacks with his see-through fingers. I did not understand why it was that Mr Lustig, the deputy headmaster, was going to be allowed to walk through him on his way to church, or why the Thompson family from three doors down, whom he had always hated, should be allowed to shoulder their way through his thick chest and big, balding head on their way to the pizza parlour.

It was to do with something I had done. It sounded to me as if he was being punished for something I had done. What *had* I done? For a moment I thought he might have been trapped on the earth he had enjoyed so much because I hadn't appreciated him properly. And then it occurred to me that I had probably done quite enough bad things on my own account to allow something like this to happen.

I have done plenty. I am an averagely bad person. Fourteen earth years give you plenty of time to plumb the depths of human depravity. We cannot all be Emily Quigley. I have done things that would make your glasses steam up just to *mention*. You know? I am a sinner.

I do, for example, from time to time, indulge in a spot of self-abuse. I say 'from time to time'. That isn't quite accurate. I wank like a man demented whenever I get the opportunity. And I do seem to get an awful lot of opportunities. Nobody gets me to go on mountaineering trips or enter swimming galas or any of the other things that are supposed to be good for masturbation. They let me get on with it. As a result, although there are times when my hand does come off my chopper, I have to admit that they are fairly well spaced. I don't think it's going to make me go blind, but it must be having some effect. Maybe I'm going deaf. People are always saying I don't seem to hear what they're trying to tell me.

Could my wanging off until the sheets crackle be the reason why my dad had been condemned to waft through Wimbledon for the foreseeable future? I seriously thought about this possibility as I went to bed that night. But, then, you are not rational when someone you love kicks the bucket.

I lay awake, I remember, staring out at the moon above the street and trying, unsuccessfully, to keep my hand off my dick. There's a poster on my wall. It's of Bruce Lee, the Master of the Martial Arts. Looking at Bruce no longer gives me the thrill it once did. I keep it there because it reminds me of how simple and decent things used to be when it was enough to watch Chinamen kicking each other. As I gazed up at Bruce's iron-hard stomach and the three red sword wounds on his chest, it reminded me of the good old days before pubic hair. I missed them.

The Quigley family had stayed over, something they did quite a lot if they thought one of us was in spiritual danger. They were always trying to insinuate themselves into our house when my dad was alive. But he used to do things like open the front door and call 'Homes to go to!' if they stayed past ten. Any later than eleven and he would appear in his pyjamas and begin winding the alarm clock.

'We need to be with Sarah,' Quigley had announced after the seance was over. We had asked Jesus, and Jesus had thought it was a fantastically good idea that they stayed. Toombs and Dooley had gone for their bus, and Pike had shambled off to his second-hand Ford, dubbed by me Lethal Weapon III.

I could hear Quigley snoring. He didn't just snore, he made a sort of satisfied grunting sound in between snores. At one point I could have sworn his old lady was giving him a blow job. I kid you not – the noise he made was remarkable. But, when I got up to check, it turned out Mrs Q was sleeping with Emily in a room at the back of the house. Quigley was capable of sucking himself off, mind you. There are no limits where Quigley is concerned.

At about four I got up and went for a walk. I walked along the landing and looked in on my mum. She was lying with her nose in the air, giving out a light snuffling sound. Mrs Quigley and Emily were locked together in a rather awkward-looking clinch. Between them was Emily's teddy bear, whose name, in case any of you are interested, is Mr Porkerchee.

I went back to my room and looked down at Stranraer Gardens. Surely, I thought to myself, they wouldn't make him roam Stranraer Gardens? Death brought you some privileges, surely? He might not deserve the Elysian Fields, but he hardly deserved *that*.

And then I saw him. He was standing outside number 20. Everything about him said *ghost* in very large letters indeed. And, if he wasn't actually roaming, he looked like a man on the verge of roaming. He looked pretty condemned to wander to me.

He was wearing white, as ghosts tend to do. A kind of long smock, almost down to his ankles. He was barefoot, of course, and there was, you had to admit, a kind of ghostly yellowish glow about him – although that could have had something to do with the fact that he was standing under a sodium lamp.

The only other serious effect death seemed to have had on him was to deprive him of his glasses. But, I guess, Over There, you have no need of glasses. It certainly hadn't made him any more decisive. He was just hanging round looking vague – the way he used to when he was alive. Maybe, I thought to myself, he hadn't been assertive enough to get through to the Other Side. He looked a bit like one of those guys you see at airports, waiting for their luggage to come round on the carousel.

I just assumed it was an optical illusion – in a couple of minutes, I'd look back and it would be gone. Either that, or we'd get a few special effects – a shooting star or a voice booming out round Stranraer Gardens telling us our days were numbered. But my dad proved to be as low-key posthumously as he had been when above the sod.

I lay down on my bed, closed my eyes and counted to a hundred. Then, very slowly, I pulled myself up to the window and looked out. He was still there.

That was when I got really frightened. At first I lay, not moving, listening for some other effect that would tell me that what I was seeing was supernatural. They do that in films. They play the music and you *know*. When it really happens, you do not know. It's like death itself. One minute you are worrying about where the next cheeseburger is coming from, the next you have stepped into another world.

I didn't dare look again. I lay there, sweating, in the darkness. Then I decided to wake up Quigley.

I mean – this was his field, right? And, appalling as his old lady was in most departments, she had been proved one hundred per cent right about this one. She had said he would roam Wimbledon, and there he was – roaming. I also felt, and I'm almost ashamed to say this, that it would be useful to have an adult male around. Quigley the Squash Player is quite famous in the Mitcham area. When he starts to call you Sonny Jim, you run for the door if you are wise. When he carried the cross in the pageant organized by the First Church (yes, he *was* playing his hero), he almost threw it across the room when he got to Golgotha.

Without daring to look out of my bedroom window, I tiptoed along the landing. Quigley was in the spare room, lying under the grubby duvet, his right foot protruding from one end. It looked more like a vulture's claw than a foot. His beard was bolt upright. It looked, as usual, as if it had nothing to do with Quigley. As if it had just perched on his chin for a couple of hours and was soon going to flap off to join its pals. His mouth was wide open and his arms were folded across his chest. I looked at them for some time, wondering how he managed to keep them there while remaining asleep. Maybe there was some religious significance to it.

I shook him hard by the shoulder.

'Mr Quigley!'

'Uh?'

'Mr Quigley!'

His eyes clicked open. His head jolted back into the pillow. Then he sat up, ready for action.

'Simon? Yes?'

He is a leader of men, is Quigley.

'Mr Quigley . . . I . . .'

I stopped. I just didn't know how to describe what I had seen. Then I said, 'I've seen my dad!'

Quigley's chin went into pleats. His nostrils flared. He described a very small 180-degree turn with his head, while keeping his eyes fixed on mine. 'Simon, where have you seen him?'

'In the road outside.'

Quigley nodded. *I was wondering when this might happen*, his expression seemed to say. But he didn't seem in a hurry to get over to my bedroom to check out the phenomenon. I was surprised by this. I would have thought a guy with Quigley's background would have been reaching for the specimen jar and getting on the line to the Society of Psychical Research before you could say astral plane.

'Yes!' he said. 'Yes!'

I suppose he might have been frightened he might not see the apparition. As it was, his old lady's talents had been confirmed by an unprejudiced observer. It was also possible that the prospect of actually seeing my dad roam Wimbledon, rather than talking about it, made Quigley a touch nervous. My dad could have come back for any number of reasons. One of them might even be Quigley.

'Let us pray, Simon,' he said. 'Let us kneel in prayer.'

'All right.'

He grabbed my hand and sprang out from under the duvet, keen as ever to get on the line to Jesus Christ, God the Father or whoever else was on the switchboard at four in the morning. He was stark naked.

I kid you not, he had the biggest chopper I have ever seen in my life. It was gigantic. It bounced around furiously for a moment or two, and then Quigley, as if he had only just remembered it was there, jammed both hands over it. I thought at first he was going to start twanging it backwards and forwards, like a piece of elastic, but instead he said, 'O Lord, Thou seest my nakedness!' I didn't say anything. I left this between him and Jesus Christ of Nazareth.

Quigley did not quite have the neck for the full-frontal nude approach to the Almighty. Or maybe he was just cold. He wrapped his balls in the duvet and knelt by the bed. For a moment I thought he might still, in fact, be sound asleep. Maybe I was asleep. Maybe we were all of us dead to the world and it was only my dad, out there in the lonely street, who was really alive.

I knelt. I don't mind saying that. I knelt.

Look, I was impressed. It isn't every day you see a ghost, is it?

'O Lord Jesus Christ,' said Quigley, 'help this boy! Help him through the difficult phase he is experiencing and return him as soon as possible to Thy bosom where so many others of us . . . er . . . nestle.'

There was a pause. Then I said, in my own time, in a low voice, 'Yes, help me!'

I needed help. It was either Jesus or an optician. I mean, either I was cracking up or else I had got the world badly wrong. Maybe it was a mistake to go around being proud of being so cynical. I was cynical.

'I am cynical, Lord,' I heard myself saying *out loud*.

Quigley was nodding furiously. 'Yes, Lord, he is! Alarmingly so, for one of his age.'

I wasn't sure I went all the way with this. But then, to my surprise, I found myself saying, 'I do awful things!'

Quigley shot a glance in my direction. He seemed keen to know more about this aspect of my life.

'Fleshly thoughts?' he said, in a rather wheedling tone.

'I . . .'

I stopped. I realized I didn't want to discuss my need to pull the wire with Quigley. Not, at any rate, as we were both placed at the moment. There was only a duvet between me and his enormous whangdoodle. Once I had got on to the subject of my dick, maybe Quigley would bring up the subject of his own equipment, and from there we would go on to discuss our private parts generally, after which it would probably be time for a bit of the old *gay sex*.

'I'm mean . . .'

Quigley's eyes were shut tight and he was chewing his moustache furiously. This was what he really enjoyed. Impromptu prayers at 04.00. Brilliant.

'. . . I'm selfish . . .'

Prayer is a very insidious thing. My advice is: don't start! Once you start, it is really hard to stop. Because it was true. You know? I really am mean and selfish. I give my mum a fantastically hard time. All she is trying to do is keep the house clean and give me a good education, and I sit at the table, pick my nose and think about nothing except the next television programme, the next video and the next chocolate biscuit. I sit like a mule and I undermine her. I know I do this because this is what she tells me about fifteen times a day. Which is why it is getting worse. I am getting really *good* at sitting like a mule. No one undermines like me, apparently!

So, as I started to list my faults – well, the clean ones anyway – it came as a fantastic relief. I felt I was talking to a real person, and that there was nobody else in the world I could talk to like that. I mean, not even Greenslade! You can say things to Greenslade, but not *those* things. I was praying. I was talking to Jesus!

'I am conceited as well. I think I know all the answers.'

'You don't know all the answers, boy!' my dad used to say to me. Especially if we were talking about current affairs. Along with, 'You're a long time dead,' and 'The mind is its own place,' it was one of his favourite sayings. As I said it I started to blub. *Again!*

Look – it had been a hard day. And as I said it I saw him as he had been in life, sitting at the wheel of our car while my mum went into the shops, reading a travel book and biting his lower lip. I saw him laughing like a hyena down the phone or coming out with one of those brief, completely inexplicable things he used to come out with at the dinner table: 'There are passages in Tennyson that force one to conclude he had experienced air travel. How can this be?' I saw him in life and I saw him in death. I saw him out there under the street lamp, *roaming.* And I sobbed my heart out.

Quigley put a manly hand on my shoulder. He kept the other one (thank *Christ!*) on the duvet. 'Cry, little one,' he said. 'Cry out your pain and your sorrow and your sin!'

That is normally the kind of line that would send me reaching for the sick bag. Not then.

That's what I mean about praying. I was enjoying it. I could see the man on the other end of the line. He looked a bit like Peter Falk in *Columbo*, except he was in pyjamas and he smiled more than Peter Falk. He was as real, as solid and as lifelike as that hologram I had seen out in Stranraer Gardens.

'I'm sorry . . .' I was saying. 'I want to believe in you. I am sorry. I am sorry . . .'

I was talking Quigley's language. He let go of the duvet and put both his lean, muscular, Christian arms round me. There was nothing between me and the Quigley organ but my brushed-nylon pyjamas.

'Go to the window,' he said. 'He will be gone. He is at peace.'

9

Quigley was spot on.

There was absolutely no sign of my old man anywhere in the street. I checked out the upper atmosphere, but he wasn't whizzing around the chimney-pots either. Quigley stood beside me. He had given up the duvet. He seemed to enjoy the opportunity of flaunting his tackle at old Mr Walker opposite.

'He has gone, Simon,' he said, 'and Jesus is a bit like that.'

'He doesn't hang around either, you mean?'

Quigley laughed amiably. Now we had prayed together I was obviously going to be given a lot more latitude.

'Jesus can do anything for you. He can bring your daddy back and He can take him away. He can bring joy or sorrow, pain or pleasure.'

They had said he would be roaming and he had roamed. I had prayed and he had disappeared. The First Church of Christ the Spiritualist was scoring very high marks indeed.

'I'm sorry,' I said. 'I'm sorry I was cynical.'

'That's all right, Simo,' said Quigley, putting his left arm round my shoulder. I saw his willy bounce up and down and his balls go jingle-jangle in the direction of old Mr Walker. 'All I want to do, young shaver, is to love you and cherish you!'

'How do you mean?' I said, a touch nervously.

Quigley squeezed me, rather hard. 'Your daddy is with Jesus, and he's got a lot of personal things to go through before he is really at peace. But we're going to be talking to him about that, and getting him to come to terms with what his problems are. And you're going to help!'

I wiped a tear from my cheek. I must have looked a right dickhead. 'Yes, Mr Quigley.' I sniffed.

'Because' – here he stabbed me with his forefinger in quite an aggressive manner – 'what *you* do and think and feel affects *him*. How you behave affects *his* spirit.'

I was past debating this remark. You know the bloke who fell off his camel on the road to Damascus and started to hallucinate? St Paul – that's the guy. I think that what I had experienced was probably very like what happened to him. And, just as St Paul resolved to keep off the hand-jobs and stop frenching the local Syrian girls, so I started to think how I could change my life so as to make things easier for the late Norman Britton.

'You have come to Christ!' said Quigley, raising his eyes to heaven. 'O Jesus!'

I looked sideways at him. Now I was almost a Christian, you would have thought I might find him a little less repulsive. Weren't Christians supposed to love their neighbours – all of them – even Quigley? I looked into my heart but found there was still no space for Albert Roger Quigley. If anything, I realized, I found him even more repulsive than usual.

'I am going to wake the others,' he said, his chopper waggling excitedly.

I must say, I would not have relished being hauled out of bed at four in the morning to be told that some idiot had just come to Christ, but this is the kind of thing Christians *adore*. They like anything a bit showbiz. You know?

'Marjorie!' he boomed, as he headed out on to the landing. 'Sarah! Emily! O Jesus!'

Was he going to put any clothes on? Was all this proving too much for him? Was he *ever* going to get any clothes on?

'Oh, Simon!' I heard him shout. 'Little Simon has come to Jesus!'

I heard Mrs Quigley squawk from the landing below – 'He's what?'

She didn't sound at all wild at the news.

'Simon has come to Jesus! Oh Marjorie! Oh Sarah! Oh Emily! We are getting such messages! We have seen visions, my children!' I went to the window and looked down at the street, at the very spot where I had seen my dad. I could see the actual section of pavement where he had been standing. I wanted to go down and mark the place. You know? Like pilgrims do. A placard: NORMAN BRITTON APPEARED HERE. And I felt fantastically sad too, as if I had just learned something, but didn't yet know what it might be.

It's funny. Everyone has been young but none of them really remembers. None of them remembers how complicated it is. How sometimes time goes too fast and sometimes it goes so slowly you want to get up and push the hands of the clock round. How you never get the things you want when you want them because all you know how to do is to want. You want so much, so many things. And none of them seem to be for you.

When I turned round, my mum, Emily, Marjorie and Albert Quigley were filling up the door to my bedroom, beaming at me like I was the school photographer.

'Oh Thimon,' said Emily, 'thomething thtupendouth hath happened! You have theen Jethuth'th light!'

I was beginning to have doubts about the wisdom of having prayed with her dad. If I went back now there was going to be a major incident. It occurred to me that there was something pre-planned about all of this. As if they knew, or had somehow

contrived all this to happen, not *just* because it was good to get a
guy to come to Jesus but because . . .

Because what? I didn't know. And it certainly wasn't an issue
I could raise out loud. My mum was peering at me. She looked,
I thought, vaguely disappointed.

'Let's get on our knees,' said Quigley, who seemed to feel
uncomfortable when he was off them for more than ten minutes
at a time, 'and thank Jesus!' To my relief, he was wearing pyjama
trousers.

The others had no difficulty in coping with this. They
swarmed into the room, found themselves a nice quiet space
and got the old knees in contact with the carpet. I was the last
to get down, after one more nervous glance in the direction of
the street. Quigley was in touch with Jesus before I even hit
the deck.

'Thank you, Jesus,' he said, 'for showing little Simo his
daddy.'

Here he flashed a quick look at Marjorie. Once again I had
the uneasy feeling that there were things on the agenda that little
Simo was not going to be told. There was a desperation about
the guy. As if he wanted me to go further. To get a full confession
down in writing so that he could use it for . . .

For what?

'And now,' Quigley went on, 'Simo is going to talk to you
about his new-found faith!'

He is? I looked up at the rest of the family, who were all waiting
for me to begin. More praying. In those days I was naive enough
to think that prayer is conversation without the hypocrisy. And
when I started to pray, I made the fatal mistake of saying exactly
what was on my mind.

'Jesus,' I said, trying to keep my tone matey without being
offensive, 'you know how much I . . . er . . . liked my dad and
how much I . . . er . . . want to see him.'

You could tell this wasn't enough for Quigley. He shot me one short, fierce glance. I tried again.

'If he really is walking the earth,' then tell me . . . tell me why . . .'

A strong right arm gripped mine. A fierce, bearded face was thrust into my line of vision. 'Simon,' hissed Quigley, 'you don't make deals with Jesus!'

Why not? He's supposed to be a nice guy. He's a Jew, for Christ's sake – why not make deals with Him?

'Faith,' said Quigley urgently, 'is a leap. Faith is a jump. You must believe, Simo. You must have faith. And then blessings will flow!'

Mrs Quigley nodded furiously at this. My mum was looking at me, red-eyed. She looked as if she was beginning to have doubts about the session.

'There is no time left,' said Quigley. 'You must believe *now*! *Now! Now! Now!*'

You can't take Jesus back to the shop, guys. He doesn't come on approval. He is even harder to dispose of than a subscription to the *Reader's Digest*.

'I . . .'

'Do you want your father to be at peace? Do you want his soul to find rest? Do you want to be able to talk to him? To hear his voice sweetly like the . . .' Quigley groped for a simile '. . . lark?' he asked eventually.

I looked around at the circle of faces. 'Well,' I said cautiously, 'I . . .'

Quigley started to tremble violently. 'Don't play games with Jesus Christ!' he said, in the tones of a man addressing a baby crawling towards a live electricity cable. 'Don't mess around with the Living God, Simo! This is an *urgent* matter!'

But why? Why was it suddenly so urgent? He was upping the stakes the whole time. I knew for my own sake that I had to say

I believed in something. I didn't particularly want it to be Jesus. But there didn't seem to be any alternative.

'I . . .'

'Say it, Simo, please say it! I beg you!'

Did he get commission, or what? I felt I was on top of a cliff. I was going to step off and fall through the air. I was going to fall the way a seed falls, blown by the wind. And there, on the shore below me, was my dad. He would be waiting for me when I got there. And, if I said the words, he would be alive again.

'I believe . . .'

There was a hiss like air escaping from a cushion. Quigley was breathing out slowly. Why should just saying these words seem so important? I could change my mind about them later, couldn't I? I quite often said things I didn't believe. Would repeating the magic formula make it true? And what would it lead to?

From the expression on Quigley's face I suspected it might lead to plenty. Did he see me as some kind of potential Messiah? The First Spiritualists are always looking for the 'boy prophet of pure heart and mind'. Fox reckoned she had found him in a thirteen-year-old Bengali youth from Manchester, and Mr Toombs had made some pretty big claims for a Scottish farmer's son.

'I believe in . . .'

'In what, Simon?'

'In Jesus Christ.'

There was a nasty moment when I thought I was going to be expected to go on and say exactly what it was I believed about Him. And maybe to tell everyone why I believed whatever it was I did. But, before I was forced to get down to specifics, Quigley picked me up. His strong hands held me under the armpits and he sort of shook me at the window, as if I was a new baby of which he was especially proud.

'Alleluia!' he said.

They actually say that sometimes down at the First Spiritualist Church.

My mum, Emily and Marjorie came in right behind him: 'Alleluia!'

And then Marjorie stepped forward. The two of them folded me in their arms. I looked across at my mum, still on her knees in the far corner of the room. There was no way I could move. It was as if I suddenly belonged to this rather unappetizing couple. I looked up at Quigley's face, flushed with triumph. Once again I had the impression that this had not been done entirely for my, their or even Jesus Christ's benefit.

'Mrs Danby,' said Quigley, 'will be very pleased.'

His old lady smirked at him. 'Mrs Danby will be *delighted*!'

I had heard that name before. I couldn't have said where. It brought with it all sorts of memories – a smell of something sweet and heavy, like perfume. A noise like distant music, with light falling in long lines from a high window. And a feeling of longing for something that I knew I could never have.

But it also brought with it a voice that said, 'Don't ask too many questions about that name, Simon. Watch, wait and listen.'

I looked out of the window once more before I finally went back to bed. There was no sign of him. It was like he had never been there.

10

When I woke next morning I could have sworn I heard my dad's voice on the stairs. The sky at the window was the same pale blue as the day before. A breeze ruffled my face gently.

'What do you fancy for breakfast?' That was always his first remark of the day, as he stood outside my bedroom in his grey towelling dressing-gown.

'What is there?' I would reply.

There would be a panic-stricken pause, and then he'd say, 'Beans . . . I think.' Or maybe, '*Pain au chocolat* . . . possibly.' He never knew what there was.

So I'd get up and the two of us would stagger down to the fridge. We'd stand there, side by side, staring in at the pork pies and the tomatoes and the milk bottles, and then he'd groan. 'Me and drink are *through*!'

It was only when I opened my eyes fully that I realized I hadn't heard him at all. No one had said anything to me. Perhaps they were hoping that Jesus would wake me. I did, however, seem to have acquired a truly staggering hard-on. Maybe this had frightened Quigley off.

As I swung my feet out on to the carpet, I looked down at my erection resentfully. What use was it? What was it supposed to be *for*? As things stood, there seemed to be no chance of anyone taking it seriously for about another ten years. By which time my balls would probably have started to drop off.

My chest did not seem to have got any bigger during the night. My left arm was still slightly shorter than my right. I went to the middle of the room, closed my eyes, flexed my knees and allowed my head to loll to one side, thereby bringing myself into the first Tai-Ping position. 'You are focused, Simon,' I said to myself. 'You are in harmony with the Law!'

I allowed my trunk to roll forward and lowered my head between my knees. It is quite easy to fall flat on your face while perfecting the second position of Tai-Ping. Maybe Europeans are the wrong size, or maybe it's just me. I stopped short of full *bei-shin* and began the duck-jumps backwards and forwards across the room. But I hadn't the heart for *ten-shang-lai*. I groped for my school trousers under the bed, while listening hard for the Quigleys.

At the back of the house, from the kitchen, I heard what sounded like voices raised in song. As far as I could tell, whoever was doing it – and one of them was certainly Quigley – was also adding a sort of primitive drum beat by banging a wooden surface, hard. I looked at the clock. It was seven forty-five.

'I'm H-A-P-P-Y. I'm H-A-P-P-Y. I know I am, I'm sure I am because . . .' Drum roll. '. . . Jesus loves me!'

Bully for him. I was beginning to have second thoughts about Jesus Christ. I know he can heal the sick and raise the dead, but does he also have to make people carry on like the Treorchy Male Voice Choir at a quarter to eight in the morning?

When I had safely covered every bit of naked flesh, I made my way down the stairs towards the noise of the singing.

The kitchen door was closed. I put my ear to it. Things seemed to have gone quiet. For a moment I had this fantasy that the Quigleys were lying in wait inside – hanging from the

curtain rail upside down, perhaps, or concealed under brooms
and buckets in the scullery cupboard – and, as soon as I opened
the door, they would spring out at me like a shower of surprised
bats. I bit my lower lip and pushed open the kitchen door.

The first thing I saw was Mum. She was standing over by
the stove waving a spatula. She wasn't wearing the faded floral
apron, the one that Dad always said made her look like an Irish
chambermaid, but a bright new plastic affair. She looked as if she
had spent the night rearranging her hair.

I was about to say something, but before I could there was a
drum roll from the table and Mum started singing *on her own*.

MUM: I put my fingers in his garments.
    His flesh seemed cold and pale.
    On his hands and feet there were some marks so neat . . .

At which point the Quigleys came in, in four-part harmony:

QUIGLEYS: I think they had been made by a nail!
MUM and QUIGLEYS: *Oh Jesus!*
MUM: I rolled away the stone into the garden!
    I felt more than just a little queer!
    In his chest and side there were some wounds you could
not hide. . .

Here the Quigleys leaped to their feet and, with a sort of loosely
choreographed thrust forward with the right arm, sang:

QUIGLEYS: I think they had been made by a spear!
MUM and QUIGLEYS: *Oh Jesus!*

While they went through the next bit – which was about how
Jesus then pitched up waving a spear and a bunch of nails and

saying how they were no problem for Him – I made my way to
a vacant place at the table. I could see that on every plate was
something I had only ever seen before in a hotel – a full English
breakfast. There were sausages and tomatoes and eggs and bacon
and fried bread and mushrooms, and, in the centre of the spread,
a gigantic pot of steaming coffee.

All of the Quigleys looked amazingly clean. Their flares
looked as if they had all just come back from the dry-cleaners.
I wouldn't put it past Quigley to take a trouser press with him
wherever he goes.

When they'd finished, they all started chuckling, and Quigley,
switching all his attention to me, said, 'People call us the Mad
Quigleys!'

I'm not surprised, I almost said, as I grabbed what looked like my
plate and, after checking whether I had got as much as Quigley,
started chomping into the fried bread.

I somehow could not connect myself with the person who
had prayed to Jesus. How had I managed to do such a thing? As
I pounded bits of sausage into the egg yolk, I wondered whether
praying could be related to wanking. It was often hard to believe,
in the morning, that you were the person who had been pulling
his wire so energetically the night before.

Quigley was buttering his toast as if in time to invisible music.
'Well, young shaver,' he said, 'Jesus lives!'

There seemed no tactful answer to this. I just hoped no one
was going to mention last night.

On the other side of the table, Emily was trying out what
could have been a wink. 'Hallo, fwend,' she said.

'Hi,' I said, reaching for the toast.

Quigley's right arm shot out and grabbed my wrist. 'Haven't
we forgotten something?'

I paused. 'Sorry,' I said, and put my hands back under the
table.

After a decent interval, I said, 'Could you pass the toast, please, Mr Quigley?'

This, I thought, was about as good as you could get at 07.58 in the morning. But it wasn't good enough for Quigley. He grinned like a loony and waggled his head from side to side. 'Nope,' he said.

Christ, what did he want? 'I beseech toast, O great Quigley!' 'I fall on my knees, O Quigley, and crave the boon of toast!'

'Er . . .'

Quigley waggled his forefinger saucily. 'Jesus!' he said.

Could you pass the toast, please, Jesus? Was that it? And would it then rev up on the plate and fly in low over the salt and pepper?

Quigley pushed his face close to mine. I could see egg, sausage and tomato being ground to pulp by the Quigley teeth. 'Thank Jesus.'

He seemed quite chirpy about this. We were, after all, on the same side. For a moment I felt genuine remorse about not having thanked Him.

'Thanks, Jesus,' I said in a firm, manly voice. And then, in case there should be any doubt about this, I added, 'For the toast.'

Quigley beamed at me. 'Yes,' he said, 'thanks for the toast.'

'And,' I said, 'for the hot chocolate.'

'We haven't got any hot chocolate,' said my mum, swiftly.

I like hot chocolate. My displeasure must have showed on my face, because Quigley came in with, 'It's a boy child, Sarah.'

I knew this. I gave him a friendly smile and reached out, once again, for the toast. Once more Quigley's arm reached out and grabbed mine. Was I ever going to get any toast?

'Could I,' I said patiently, 'have some toast? . . . in the name of Jesus,' I added, thinking that the mention of His name might prod Quiggers into action.

He just sat there beaming. 'Not till you say the password,' he said.

A guy could starve to death here, surrounded by all this bacon and sausage and egg and fried bread. In many ways, Quigley was like a computer game. You know? You paid a lot of money to be frustrated. I just could not figure my way through his latest move.

'Pleath, Mithter Quigley, could I have thome toatht?' said Emily.

For a moment I thought this was merely a rather formal way of her addressing her old man. Then I caught on. 'Please, Mr Quigley,' I said, 'could I have some toast?'

'Good,' said Quigley, beaming. 'Good!' And he passed me the toast.

It was that simple. I was able to eat bread in my own home. I was in with the in-crowd.

The rest of the meal was uneventful. They didn't have grace after the meal. Nobody asked the Lord to make sure I had a good day at school. I was not handed a boxful of bibles to give out in break. I tell you, I was grateful when I pulled my blazer off the banisters and headed for the front door. Whatever it was they had in mind for me, it was clear that I was a high-priority project for the people at the top of the First Spiritualist Church. If they kept this up for long enough, I was going to start telling the folks up at school that they should welcome the Lord Jesus into their hearts. I tried to imagine myself saying this to Greenslade. It was neither easy nor pleasant.

For some reason, that morning, I decided to walk up the hill, instead of taking the bus up the main road. I started thinking about those extraterrestrials. There *had* been something odd in the atmosphere last night. I had never seen Mr Marr so certain that he was going to get a result. I went up through Elam Gardens and Holtfield Park, trying to figure out this Christian thing and whether it might have anything to do with the visitors from outer space. Could you be a Christian ufologist? I didn't see why not. There were people, according to Mr Marr, who reckoned Jesus came from outer space.

The first thing I saw when I came off Parkside and across the Common was Mr Marr's little canvas chair, his telescope, his night binoculars and the ten or twelve back numbers of *Flying Saucer Review* that are always to hand when he is waiting for the subjects of the periodical to show up. Everything was arranged just as it had been last night. It was like the lunch table on the *Marie Céleste*.

I was standing there trying to understand what all this might mean when a hand clapped me on the shoulder and a noise like an old goods train being shunted started up in my ear. Walbeck only makes one greeting noise and it is very distinctive.

He held up a small, grubby piece of paper, on which were written the words THEY TOOK HIM AWAY IN A SPACESHIP.

I looked at Walbeck. He pointed to the chair and the bins and the magazines. Then he nodded. He looked, I have to say, very serious indeed. I tried some direct speech.

'Where to?'

Walbeck gave me an odd look. *Where do they take people in spaceships? Margate?* He was writing. When things get bad, Walbeck writes.

another galaxy, of course!

Of course! He started to cover the paper again. I could see that it was covered with fragments of Walbeck's previous conversations. Discussions about joints and timber sizes (Walbeck is a carpenter by trade) lay next to words of comfort addressed to his elderly mum, and sometimes ran into them, so you got sentences that looked like ARE YOU ALL RIGHT THERE MUM FOR TEN INCH NAILS? Or I GOT YOU SOME OF THAT FISH YOU LIKE FROM THE BUILDER'S MERCHANTS YOU IDIOT!

The message intended for me read: purkiss and me went for a hamberger then we went for a kip at purkiss's place and when we come back around six in the morning we found . . .

I turned the page. On the other side was written SIX SQUARE FEET OF CHIPBOARD.

Walbeck always runs out of paper at the crucial moment. We went back to lip-reading.

'What did you find?'

Walbeck pointed at the chair, the magazines and the binoculars. Then he shrugged.

'Maybe he went home.'

Walbeck shook his head furiously. Then he made the conventional sign for Purkiss, which is a kind of crouch plus leer, and did a fluttering movement with the fingers of both hands. They had been to Mr Marr's and he was not there. I just *knew*, the way I had known about my dad. I knew when we left him peering up at the sky that something awful was going to happen. It was all laid out so neatly on the grass. Mr Marr would never leave his binoculars, and the canvas chair cost £15.99!

I wanted to stay and find out more. But we had run out of paper. There is a limit to the amount you can glean from pointing at things and grinning like an idiot. As I turned to go, Walbeck pointed at the arrangement on the grass. He looked really sad, suddenly. Then he pointed at the sky and raised his shoulders in a questioning sort of way.

'I know, Walbeck,' I said. 'Why should they take a nice guy like Mr Marr? He was on their side, man. Why should they take him?'

I walked on towards school trying to work this out.

The same reason they had come for my old man, of course. Because life isn't any fairer on the other side of the solar system than it is here. They come for the nice guys and leave the bastards behind. It's always people like Mr Marr and my old man who get tapped on the shoulder by the small men with green leathery skin and fifteen fingers on each hand.

There *had* to be a connection. I didn't yet know what it was, but there had quite clearly been an unusually high level of psychic activity in the Wimbledon area last night. The energy that was capable of lifting an electrical engineer off the Common might well have something to do with the fact that a forty-three-year-old travel agent had been dragged back from the grave to haunt 24 Stranraer Gardens.

11

Just before I got to the school gates, I got out *Tricolore 4* and started to read it. It lets people know you're a serious person, doing something like that. And, besides, I am in correspondence with a girl called Natalie, who lives in Clermont-Ferrand. As far as I can make out, Clermont-Ferrand is even worse than Wimbledon. I was deep into the bit where Olivier and Marie-Claude are trying to buy some cheese in La Rochelle. *Tricolore* never gives you the stuff you really need to say to French people, like, 'Can I hold your hot body to me?' It is all about how to ask for a full tank of *'super'* from the friendly *'garagiste'* and what to say when they have run out of cardigans in Nogent-le-Rotrou.

I was late. We were almost into First Period.

As I came up to the gates, I looked cautiously over the book and saw Khan and Greenslade. Khan was sitting on his games bag. Greenslade was going through his pink nylon rucksack with an expression of desperation on his face.

'Est-ce que tu as oublié tes condoms?' I said.

He gave me a superior smile. 'This is no time for you to be a dickhead, Britton. I have *lost* my geography project!'

I never mind people saying I'm a dickhead. It's the key to my popularity. I'm pretty controlled, if you know what I mean.

I wait before I speak, and if I'm not sure what to say – which is quite a lot of the time – I just give this mysterious smile. Greenslade says it makes me look like the village idiot.

This morning, for some reason, I really felt like blurting out what was on my mind. Not about my dad. About the aliens spacenapping Mr Marr. It was only when I thought about saying it out loud that I realized how crazy it would sound. Thinking how crazy it would sound made me wonder whether it was true.

'Tell Baines you'll bring it tomorrow,' said Khan in a deep voice. Khan is always calm about things. I think it's because he is so good at physics.

The three of us moved through the gates towards 4c, or Cell Block H as it is known. Behind us, Limebeare was getting out of his dad's BMW in that special way people get out of expensive cars.

What possible *reason* would they have for spacenapping Mr Marr?

He was an engineer. Maybe that was why they needed him. Maybe something had broken down out there on Alpha Centauri and he was the only guy able to fix it. Maybe the know-how of the London Electricity Board was the only thing that could save the atmosphere of some lump of rock light-years from SW19. They would set Mr Marr down, hand him a nine-headed spanner and, after he had done the job, he would be on his way back to Wimbledon.

Maybe they needed my dad *and* Mr Marr. You know? Maybe that was why he had appeared to me last night. Maybe they had ways of breathing life back into people so as they could do their evil will – although I could not, for the life of me, think why entities from a distant planet should want a travel agent.

'Why are we always late?' asked Khan, as we trudged along the corridor towards the classroom. He sounded as if he was going to get philosophical about this.

Maybe they had heard about him. Dad always said he was the best man in South London if you wanted two weeks in Provence with swimming-pool and maid provided. Maybe the fame of Sunnyspeed Tours had spread. And if there are galaxies where life-forms exist, on the other side of the long dark spaces that lie outside our solar system, why shouldn't the life-forms need travel agents?

'Flasher will kill us,' said Greenslade, looking morosely down at his feet. Greenslade is tall and thin. There is always a gap between his shoes and the bottoms of his trousers.

What, while we were at it, did Jesus Christ have to do with all this? Was JC somehow mixed up in the mysterious events of last night? What did I mean by 'Jesus Christ' anyway? I had certainly been pretty glad to talk to him, or indeed Him, last night, hadn't I? Suppose He really did exist – not in the way Quigley thought, but as a kind of mysterious energy source? We didn't necessarily mean the same thing when we said 'Jesus Christ'. Any more than Sarrassett Major and I mean the same thing when we say 'football'. Sarrassett Major means huge guys throwing each other at a ball, neck-deep in mud. I mean hanging round the goal and talking to Greenslade.

We got into class just before 'Flasher' Slingsby. I moved into my desk, carefully chosen because it is in the darkest corner of the room. If you sit very still, people think you are part of the furniture. Flasher came in, threw his briefcase on the desk and started to pace around, draw pretty shapes in white chalk and talk the incomprehensible rubbish for which teachers get paid.

I just sat there, my head in my hands, thinking about all this stuff and trying to make sense of it.

'Britton! What have I just been saying?'

I looked Mr Slingsby straight in the eye. 'You were talking about triangles, sir.'

This was safe ground. There was one on the board, for Christ's sake!

'What about triangles, Britton?'

'Well . . . about how they are . . . amazing, sir.'

There was muffled laughter. Britton was at it again.

'In what way are they "amazing", Britton?'

'Well, sir, they are equilateral. Sometimes.'

Mr Slingsby was enjoying this. He positively twinkled as he said, 'And is that what I was saying? That they are "equilateral . . ."?'

Here he gave the class a conspiratorial wink. They responded well. ' ". . . Sometimes." '

I looked round at the faces of the class.

'I'm afraid,' I said, 'I wasn't paying much attention.'

'Oh!'

Mr Slingsby sounded almost delighted at this news. He tapped his desk with his finger and gave me about twenty seconds to sweat.

'Indeed. And why were you "not paying much attention", Britton?'

I paused. I let him hang there for a good half-minute. Then I said, 'Because my father died of a heart attack yesterday afternoon, sir.'

I have seen guys dropped across, but none like 'Flasher' Slingsby was dropped across that day. 4c were giving his performance very close attention. He looked, I thought, like a man who has opened his desk and found his wife's head in it. I didn't say anything. I just looked at the floor.

'Britton, you . . .'

'I what, sir?'

He had dug the hole. He had jumped in. It was now up

to him to play himself out. The lads were definitely with me. Greenslade had folded his arms and, his head on one side, was studying Flasher's body language as if he was going to write an article about it for the school magazine.

'You . . . you shouldn't be here!'

I wasn't going to let him get away with that. I raised my head and looked straight at him. 'I thought it might take my mind off it, sir.'

I have never really let anyone at Cranborne School know too much about the First Church of Christ the Spiritualist. People can use information like that. People think I'm kinky enough as it is. Sometimes people ask why I have to leave early on Friday afternoons, but I do not – repeat *not* – tell them I am off to Gather in the Lord's Fruit in a High and Seemly Way (which is why Mother Walsh deemed the hours between three and six thirty on Fridays to be sacred). I say I am going to the dentist. They must be really worried about my teeth.

Flasher had turned a light pink. 'You . . .' He was opening and closing his mouth like a fish.

'It was very quick, sir.'

Flasher did not wish to know this. But I kept right on telling him.

'He was having a pint in the pub at lunch-time, sir, and by early evening he was . . . You know?'

My God, you could see Flasher thinking, *this could be me!*

'Simon, I'm . . .'

First-name terms! I kept my eyes on his face, waiting for his next move.

'How old was he?' he said eventually.

'He was forty-three, sir.'

You could tell he was dying to get the conversation back to sines and cosines and all the other wonderful things left to the world by Leibniz and Descartes. But there was no way he could do it.

I looked over in Greenslade's direction. Greenslade was carving a primitive figurine out of his rubber. Next to him, Khan was hunched forward across his desk. He looked as if he was about to put Flasher right on some tricky point of mathematical theory. The windows in our classroom are really high. I could only just make out the pale blue of the sky outside.

Flasher coughed. 'Don't you want to . . . be with your family at this time, Britton?'

'Not really, sir.' It's actually quite a relief to be here! Have you seen my family? 'I just feel . . .'

I started to play with my pencil.

Feelings are weird. Here, where I was surrounded by people who were actually *sympathetic* to a person when they heard that a close relative of his had failed to make it, I didn't really feel sad at all.

'I thought it would be better if I just carried on, sir.'

Flasher squared his shoulders. He is a captain in the Territorial Army. A year ago I was with him on Army Cadet Force manoeuvres in the Welsh Mountains. Limebeare, who was, for some unknown reason, a corporal, stole a bazooka from the armoury and shelled the village of Aberfach for three hours before being arrested by the local police. They handed him over to Flasher, and Limebeare said afterwards that he would rather have served three years in Carnarvon jail than pass the afternoon he did with Slingsby.

'Yes, Britton. Yes. I quite understand.' He looked at me in a somewhat worried way. 'I never know what goes on in your mind, old son,' he said. 'You're a secretive chap, Simon . . .'

You could see that he now thought he was in the clear. We had had this out, man to man. Although how he could say I was a secretive chap was, to me, a complete mystery. I'm an open book.

He came towards me between the grim wooden desks, and for a moment I thought he was going to put his arm round me. I wasn't finished yet.

'I *thought* it would . . . but . . . I don't think I can quite . . . manage it, sir.'

Flasher looked at me narrowly. For a second you could see him wondering whether this might not be a wind-up. You could tell he still thought this was a strong possibility, but it wasn't a chance he could afford to take.

'Would you like to go home, Britton?' he said.

'I think I'd just like to walk on the Common and think about things.'

No pupil of 4c had ever requested such a thing before. If this went on, it wouldn't be long before we started ordering hot chocolate and croissants to be brought to the desk.

'Is that all right, sir?'

'Absolutely, Britton. Absolutely!' said Flasher. 'But . . .'

'Yes, sir?'

'Don't do anything foolish, will you?'

'No, sir,' I said, in a voice that was meant to suggest that I was about to pen a short note describing Flasher's insensitive attitude to the bereaved and then swallow a few dozen Nembutal.

I got to my feet. Everyone was looking at me. I wondered whether to tell them the whole story. But I wasn't sure that Flasher was ready for my dad's coming back to life. He had not really had time to adjust to Norman's death.

I stopped at the door and gave him my best and bravest smile. 'Thank you, sir, for being so understanding about my problem. There are times when geometry just doesn't seem at all relevant.'

'I realize that, Britton,' said Flasher with some humility.

Very slowly and quietly I closed the door behind me. I could feel the lads' appreciation as I headed off down the corridor. A round of applause would not, I felt, have been out of place. All I needed now was to bump into Mr Grimond, the games master, and for him to ask me what the *bloody hell* I thought I was doing.

Mr Grimond would fit quite well into the First Spiritualist Church. He is stark staring bonkers. He has been known to hold boys upside down on the rugby pitch and swat the ball with their heads. He regards brain damage as character-forming, which, for someone of his level of intelligence, is an entirely consistent position.

I walked out through the main entrance, past the picture of Sir Roger de Fulton, a rather dodgy-looking customer in a blue dressing gown, and the huge pokerwork version of the Cranborne School motto QUID AGIS? Or 'Wha' Happenin'?' as we translate it. There was more sunshine outside than Wimbledon could really accommodate. The streets seemed rich with possibilities – the way they do when you know you're supposed to be at school.

I thought I had better go down the hill and take a look at Mr Marr's house. In my right-hand jacket pocket I could feel the weight of his front-door key, the one he gave me three years ago.

As I passed south of the War Memorial, I could see Mr Marr's chair, standing out on the Common. Next to it, all his stuff was still laid out. It looked lost, like someone's drawing-room suite abandoned in a junk yard.

Mr Marr had given his key to no one else. I was the only person he trusted. He had told me to use it only in emergencies. But this, to me, looked like an emergency.

'There may come a time, Simon,' he had said to me, as he handed it over, 'when people from another galaxy who are not

kindly disposed to us – and such people are probably out there –
may . . . you know . . .'

' "You know" what, Mr Marr?'

'Well . . . MIBs for example. You know?'

I knew. 'MIBs' stands for 'Men In Black'. In Deepdene, Ohio,
in 1958 Mr and Mrs John Wearing saw a large flying saucer three
miles out on the highway to Sawmills Bridge. It was hovering
over a petrol station. There was, according to Mr Wearing, 'a
sort of perspex shield where the driver's cab might have been
situated', and he claimed to have seen a large 'blob-like creature'
with its nose pressed to the windscreen. It let him know, without
using earth language, that the whole of the Midwest of America
was in grave danger.

Fine. These sorts of things are always happening.

Two days later, after the Wearings had contacted the local
newspaper and given an extensive interview, two men in black
suits turned up. They wore dark glasses and black trilbies but
were by no means the Blues Brothers. In 'cracked, automatic
voices' they warned Mr and Mrs Wearing that they had better
not speak of these experiences to *anyone.* I'm not, actually, quite
sure why or how the Wearings allowed the story to get out. I
mean, I hope they're all right. You know?

'If I should disappear without trace, you know what to do,' Mr
Marr had said to me.

'I know what to do!'

'Here's the number. Memorize it and destroy it.'

He gave me the top-secret telephone digits of a very senior
guy in the Wimbledon Interplanetary Society. I was to ring him
only in an emergency because, apparently, British Rail took a
very dim view of his receiving calls about non-terrestrial business
during office hours.

There was still no breeze at all. It was dead still that September.
On the house-fronts in Columba Road, the roses nodding on the

brickwork, as big as soup plates, looked as if they were waiting for something. And, as I turned into the cul-de-sac where Mr Marr lived, it seemed to me that the whole suburb was holding its breath.

I had forgotten the number of the chairman-for-life of the Wimbledon Interplanetary Society. I could not even remember the name of this rather crucial person. It would have been good to talk to someone about all of this, I thought to myself, although, from the little Mr Marr had told me about him, he sounded pretty flaked. Anyway, by making the call I would be admitting what had really happened. There was still a chance that Mr Marr had been taken ill or something, or had decided to go and see a relative.

Except he didn't have any relatives. And, if he had been taken ill, there was a card in his jacket pocket saying who he was. We take no chances in the Wimbledon Interplanetary Society. 'Be always on your guard,' Robert du Carnet, the secretary, had said at the last Annual General Meeting. 'Don't let *them* choose the time!'

We know that the things from hyperspace may want to blast us to bits. And that people who don't even believe they exist will be at even more risk than we are. We have a duty to survive, Mr Marr says.

He chose this particular cul-de-sac, for example, for very good reasons. He liked to feel his back was secure. Although, as I often pointed out to him, the aliens could easily come at him over the tennis courts. His house is a funny little semi-detached affair, with bulging windows and wooden beams stuck to the bricks that are supposed to give it an Olde Worlde appearance. There are three uncared-for rose bushes in the front garden. There's a white one for him, a red one in memory of her and a yellow one he planted just for me. He always said I was the son he never had. The white and red ones were supposed to grow into each other, but they never managed to do it. They just sort of droop grimly at each other across the ragged lawn. I don't know what this says about the old Marr marriage. My bush has gone crazy. It grows out in all directions and showers petals all round it.

The front curtains were drawn, which was odd. I was a touch scared. I peered through the frosted glass in the front door. All I could see was the shape of Mr Marr's bicycle. Through the letterbox I could see the usual pile of letters, plastered with stamps from all over the world. They write to Mr Marr from everywhere about sightings, landings, close encounters of the fourth kind and all the other things that those boring radio telescopes down at the Mount Palomar observatory fail to pick up.

I fitted the key in the lock. I pushed open the door and looked down the hall. The first thing I thought was: the blobs or the androids or the giant green lizards from Venus or whatever they were had paid Mr Marr a call.

12

Every drawer in the house had been pulled out. But it wasn't like burglars. Things had been piled neatly on the floor, as if someone was packing for a long journey. Underpants were in one pile, socks another, and by the door there was a neat line of shoes. Over by the window the aliens had made a start on the reading matter, which, as it was mainly about them, was unsurprising. They were halfway through a book called *The UFO Report 1991*. It was open at a chapter entitled 'Disturbing Encounters in Northeast Brazil' by Bob Pratt.

A sentence on the first page caught my eye. *If a UFO were to land in my backyard I would certainly not run out to embrace it. I would be very wary – and with good reason.* Somebody had underlined this remark. It wasn't Mr Marr, because he never writes in books. He's fussier about how they look than he is about what's in them. I say somebody. Something. Something which had used a Biro. I looked round carefully. There was a kind of chill about the place. I got up and went through to the kitchen.

Whoever had paid Mr Marr a visit had tried to make a piece of toast. Not very successfully. It was possible, of course, that these guys could handle speeds faster than light but a British toaster had them baffled. Mr Marr's toaster is, as it happens, a particularly dodgy piece of equipment. But why should they take the things out of the drawers? I sat on the bed and tried to think.

Could it be a burglar? But if it was a burglar, where was the broken window or the forced lock? I checked all over the house and there was no sign of any such thing. The next thing I did was to ring Mr Marr's office and ask if he had shown up for work. A woman at the other end said he hadn't. She sounded very surprised. 'He never misses,' she said. And then, 'Are you his son?'

That made me feel peculiar. I said I was his nephew. I don't know why. She didn't have any idea of where he might be if he wasn't at work. Which figured. There just wasn't anything else in his life. I was really getting worried. First my dad, and now Mr Marr. What was happening?

Why were all his things out on the floor, as if someone had been packing? Was it possible that he had run away? Had he done something awful and decided to leave without telling anyone? Surely he would tell me if he was in trouble. Wouldn't he?

Or was he playing them along? I thought about this as I loosened my school tie and paced about the empty front room, feeling like a detective. I quite liked this line of approach. Maybe he had expressed keenness to visit their galaxy, but asked if he could pack a few things first. The blobs or the lizards, or whatever they were, follow him back from the Common and stand over him while he makes preparations.

'Come on, Marr,' they say, 'Threng, our King, is waiting.'

'I'll be right with you,' says Mr Marr, 'I'm just packing a pair of *boxer shorts . . .*'

All the time his eye is on the phone. If he can call me or Purkiss or, preferably, someone better qualified than either of us, he is in with a chance.

I sat back on the bed. This great detective I once read about used to go to the scene of the crime, close his eyes and visualize. Very often it turned out that he tuned in to what had actually happened. I closed my eyes and tried to *see* the aliens with Mr Marr . . .

He brings them back to the house and plays for time. But they don't give him that chance. The clothes pile up. More and more drawers are opened. Finally the blobs tap him on the shoulder and say, 'It's time to go, Marr!' That's when he makes the toast. Will there be anything to eat in the Crab Nebula – you know? But he's nervous. He burns the toast. The blobs are getting restive. Their ship is parked up by the War Memorial and at any moment some local is going to start asking questions.

Come on, Simon. You need more than this. This is just guesswork. You need some sign. If he really had been spacenapped (I wasn't yet sure that he had) he wouldn't go down without a fight. He'd leave some sign, wouldn't he? He'd leave a clue. For me or Purkiss or Walbeck.

He'd ask to go to the lavatory. Of course.

'Lavatory?' say the aliens. 'What is this?'

The aliens have progressed light years ahead of us. They have no need of toilet facilities on their planet. Man gives them a GCSE lesson in biology and they laugh behind their flippers at how primitive we are. He explains the cultural need of humans to lock the door when they go to the bathroom. And then . . .

I was already walking towards the bathroom. The door was closed. I tugged at it hard. When it opened, the first thing I saw was the mirror. It was flecked with tiny white spots. Mr Marr had been spitting at it for years. On the washstand in front of the mirror were four or five tiny, deformed pieces of soap. But, in the middle of the glass, dead in the centre, someone had scrawled a single word: HELP!

They had used lipstick. My first thought was: *Where did Mr Marr get lipstick?* But then I realized. It was probably his wife's.

He keeps all his wife's things, just as they were. There are even pairs of her stout, sensible shoes in the back kitchen.

You see, I do think we *know* things before they actually happen. There has to be a sense beyond seeing or hearing or taste or touch or smell. Not everything they tell you down at the First Church is idiotic. Great scientists, like Einstein, for example, sort of *suspected* things like relativity before they had had a chance to prove them. He had an idea and found that the facts fitted it. I had had an idea, and it was looking as if the facts fitted it only too well.

Other stuff in the bathroom had been disturbed. The cupboard on the wall had been ransacked. Toothpaste and toothbrushes were on the floor. Someone had opened a bottle of shampoo and sprayed it around the place like it was champagne at a Grand Prix.

I pinched the bridge of my nose with my thumb and index finger and began to visualize.

Mr Marr is surprised at the mirror. The aliens follow him and catch him writing. 'This is going to the lavatory, Marr?' they say, their metallic voices sounding a bit like Flasher Slingsby at his most evil. There is a struggle. They cover him with poisonous slime or zap him with a laser gun. Then they have fun! They play with earthling cosmetics! Because, deep down, these aliens are just a bunch of kids. And then, suddenly bored, they tuck him under their flippers and saunter back through Wimbledon.

No one sees them. No one would blink twice if a 400-foot reptile wandered through Wimbledon Village after eleven at night. It is *dead*!

I was not jumping to any conclusions, but I thought we could well be talking spacenapping here. At least, it seemed as possible as any other explanation. Quite *how* this linked up with what I had seen outside 24 Stranraer Gardens the previous night I didn't know. But one thing seemed pretty certain. I had been wasting my time talking to Jesus about it. It was not His department. This was a very practical issue, with very serious implications for me and everyone else in the Wimbledon area.

I was just about to go into the living-room when I heard a sound outside. A kind of scratching at the front door. I had closed it. Hadn't I? I sat on the edge of the bath. Maybe I had. But Yale locks were not likely to present much problem to the heavies from the other side of the Red Shift. I stayed where I was, listening to my heart knock against my ribs.

Finally I went out into the corridor.

There was no sound coming from the front door. But someone or *something* was moving along the gravel at the side of the house. I inched my way towards the front room. If I could get down the path and out into the street, maybe I could at least warn someone before they dragged me up the old ladder and added a fourteen-year-old boy to their collection of souvenirs from the planet earth.

I breathed deeply and got ready to sprint.

Pathetic, isn't it? When they really do come in large numbers, we'll be out there putting up everything we've got and they'll wade through us. We'll be like those Aborigines faced with Captain Cook, the first white man they had ever seen. They thought he was the spirit of their ancestors and ran away.

I reached for the door handle. As I did so I heard someone try the back door. Two short turns and then a knock. It *was* burglars. They had done over Mr Marr, and now they had come back for me! I thought I heard steps moving away. They would try the front again. I almost ran to the back door and opened it in one swift movement. I found I was looking at Purkiss.

I gave a little squeal. I was inches from Purkiss's big, thick glasses, long, greasy hair and big, bloodshot eyes. I've never been able to find out what he does for the Parks Department. I think they just leave him around in open spaces to deter flashers. His mouth was twitching, the way it does when he has something to say.

'Where is he?' he said eventually.

'I don't know, Purkiss,' I said. 'I really don't know.'

At this point Walbeck emerged from behind a bush. He scurried across the gravel, waving as he did so, and scanning the sky for signs of alien craft. He looked, I have to say, very worried indeed. He had his piece of paper with him, but I think we all felt this wasn't a time for writing.

'They'll come for me next!' said Purkiss.

I looked at Purkiss. I didn't, somehow, think this was likely. I don't really think an alien would bother with Purkiss even if he landed on him on his way to somewhere else. And it seemed downright impossible that the said alien, having nobbled Mr Marr and got him halfway to Saturn, should suddenly stop, snap his fingers and *go back* for Purkiss.

Walbeck was hugging the line of the wall. Every so often he would point at the sky and shiver violently.

'He didn't show up for work,' said Purkiss.

'I know,' I said.

Purkiss opened his bloodshot eyes wide. 'There's no sign of him!'

'We don't know whether they have actually taken him,' I said. 'That's one possibility. They could be keeping him somewhere. They could still be here. You know?'

Then I stopped. What was I saying?

'We don't actually *know* that it's aliens.' Walbeck crouched down and put his hands on his head. He turned down the corners of his mouth, pointed up at the sky again and then gave us the thumbs-down signal. It was as well he hadn't been around when they did actually show up or he would have let the earth down pretty badly. The sight of these two had calmed me, however, and, when I spoke, I was surprised to find I was talking quite slowly and clearly.

'We just have to be careful. From what I've seen so far, guys, if these *are* extraterrestrials, they're not the "Hi, let's party!" kind.'

Walbeck was now curled up in a ball, whimpering. Purkiss knelt down beside him and started to stroke him as if Walbeck was a frightened dog.

'But, as yet,' I went on, 'we don't know. We don't know what they look like or what their methods are. They could look like . . . Purkiss for all we know!'

We looked at Purkiss. It lightened the mood somewhat. Even Walbeck grinned and indicated, as only Walbeck can, that he hoped they didn't look anything like Purkiss.

'Should we tell the police?' said Purkiss.

We all know the police are useless at dealing with non-earth-based crime. All they are good for is holding the crowd back around the saucer while the boffins get to it. Some of them try feeling the old alien collar, and they are usually reduced to a small heap of cinders for their pains. Visitors from other planets just do not fit into police procedure. And I had the feeling that if we told the police, it would all turn out to be our fault.

'Tell no one,' I said urgently. 'I am going to keep a careful watch for any other manifestations, and as soon as they happen we will move. In the meantime, who knows? They may bring him back!'

Purkiss nodded. 'In the case of the Poznan Twelve,' he said, 'Mr and Mrs Vrchlika said they had been enhanced by the experience. It was only the dumplings that experienced material alterations to their state.'

'Sure,' I said.

We didn't mention the twelve-year-old nun in Santa Monica, though. Or the experiences undergone by the director of the Lycée Municipale in the West Cameroon in the spring of 1981.

All of us knew enough about spacenapping to be aware that it could go either way. Some days it was all wet kisses and talk of mutual cooperation. The next minute it was out with the old steel scalpels, and heigh-ho for penetrating the earthling body in a variety of disgusting ways.

We were all pretty tight-lipped as I locked the back door and went out the front to join them. Say what you like, my friends, all the evidence seemed to suggest that a respectable engineer of amazingly regular habits had, suddenly and for no obvious reason, disappeared without trace.

As I headed, unwillingly, back towards Stranraer Gardens, I felt that I was the owner of a heavy and awesome secret. Something that I could tell no one. Not even the character I had found it so welcome to have words with last night. No, not Albert Roger Quigley – Jesus Christ. You remember? His writ runs from Galilee to Tuscaloosa, but in none of the texts do we find any mention of His having control over things far out in deep space, or of His voice having the power to command among the spirals of twisting stars.

13

'Why', said Greenslade as we sat at the lunch table, a few days after my dad had died, 'do you eat meat with a spoon?'

I didn't answer. I chewed a lot and gave him some of my village-idiot face. All around us, boys in black blazers were cramming food down their faces. Out on the rugby pitch, Mr Grimond was shouting at Extra Quintus. The sky wore the same blue it had chosen for the day I saw my dad for the last time.

'You could cut it,' said Khan, leaning over and studying me over his glasses, 'and *then* eat it with a spoon.' He gave me a shrewd look. 'Is it true that your parents are very religious?'

I gulped and said nothing.

Members of the First Spiritualist Church always eat meat with a spoon. They were commanded to do so by a geezer called Lewis, who was big in the church in the 1930s and who, for a time, posed a bit of a threat to Rose Fox. 'Forks,' he used to say, 'do the Devil's work. And knives grieve the spirit.' He had pretty definite views on cutlery, did Lewis. He gave out some heavy notes about the correct method of holding your spoon as well. And towards the end of his life he got into condiments. 'Do not pass the mustard' was the general drift. I still flinch if someone at school offers me the stuff.

'Didn't you say your mum was a nutter?' said Greenslade, looking at me keenly. I shrugged. Then Khan nudged him with his foot.

'I'm sorry, Britton,' he said. 'Your dad . . .'

'That's OK,' I said, getting to my feet. 'Actually, my mum and dad belong to this church, and you . . .'

I looked down at their faces. I realized that I wasn't going to be able to talk to them about the First Church of Christ the Spiritualist. And I felt sad, because I wanted to explain it, but I didn't even know where to begin.

I never have friends back to the house. You can just never tell whether anything embarrassing is going to happen. But Khan and Greenslade had met my dad a few times. Once when he came to pick me up after a school trip that is still known as *Die Screaming in Koblenz*. That was in the days when he drove a motor bike. And once when he made a spectacle of himself during Mr Hammond's production of *The Caucasian Chalk Circle*. Nobody could hear what he was shouting – I think it was about the death of Communism – but my mum said it was as well they couldn't.

'What's with the games bag?' said Khan. 'I thought it was a free afternoon.'

'I'm playing squash with a friend of my dad's.'

I don't know why I said Quigley was a friend of his. I tell lies, sometimes, for absolutely no reason at all – except to see the expressions on people's faces. Both Khan and Greenslade looked rather serious as I picked up my bag and headed for the sunlight.

I think I had agreed to play squash with Quigley because he was the only person I could think of to talk to about Mr Marr.

Mr Marr hadn't shown up at any of the places where he should have been. It was time I told someone.

Once, of course, I would have told my dad. I talked to him about the extraterrestrials quite a lot.

'What you've got to watch,' he used to say, 'is Krull of Varna. He's the boy to watch.'

He was not convinced by the evidence, I'm afraid. I had shown him the black-and-white photographs of a Pleiadean Saucer, taken by Albert de Roquefort of Autruches in the Rhône Valley, and he was not impressed. In fact, he laughed a lot.

'I'm not saying,' I used to say to him, 'that that is a genuine photo. But that doesn't prove they aren't there, does it?'

'I'm sure they are,' said Dad. 'But where?'

This was where it got sticky.

'Well, they're there. At the moment. But they're on their way here.'

'Well,' Dad would reply, 'call me when they show. I'd like to be there to see it . . .' Then he'd put his arm round me. 'What size do you think they run to? And do they have corkscrews on their heads? That's the thing!'

I could almost hear his gravelly bass voice saying this. I saw again his blue jersey with the food stains down the front and smelt his breath, acrid with garlic from the La Paesana Restaurant, Mitcham.

Quigley had been suggesting we play, almost as long as I had known him. 'Come down to The Club, young shaver,' he used to say on Sunday mornings. 'Do you know it?'

'No,' I'd reply. 'What's it called?'

'It's called,' Quigley would answer with ill-concealed pride and excitement, 'The Club. And it's one of the most exclusive squash clubs there is. It is *over the road from the All England Lawn Tennis Club!*'

I couldn't see why this was such a big deal. But Quigley always got a thrill from things like that. The whole family dine out at a hamburger place off Piccadilly just so that he can say they are 'off to a little bistro in Mayfair'. I wouldn't put it past him to lug a Thermos down Pall Mall so he could tell us all he had 'dropped in at the Palace for tea'.

When I got to it, however, I must confess I was impressed. It had smoked-glass windows and a character in a commissionaire's uniform outside. I couldn't think how Quigley got the money to pay the membership. In the car park, every third car must have cost more than our house.

I sauntered up to the desk and put my games bag down in a firm but casual way. The guy, who was in a sort of mauve serge suit with THE CLUB written in the top left-hand corner in discreet lettering, was looking at me rather oddly, so I pushed my glasses back up my nose and gave him one of my businesslike looks. 'Simon Britton,' I said, using a voice I had heard my dad use when on the phone to the bank, 'for Roger Quigley.'

'Roger' to the outside world. 'Albert' to those lucky enough to feel close to the great man.

You could tell from the man's face that Quiggers was pretty well thought of here. There was a ladder, Emily had told me, and Quigley was at the top of it. Occasionally some puny stockbroker who fancied his chances, just because he had played in the Olympics or something, would try and move in on The Boss, as Quigley was known. And the guy would have to be carried out by teams of paramedics.

As I said the word 'Quigley', the man himself appeared. He was wearing a loose cream shirt with a drawing of a hairy geezer and what looked like a signature underneath it. As he saw me, Quigley pointed to it. 'Alberto Loosali!' he said, as if I was supposed to know who this was.

'Right,' I said.

Quigley went to the desk. Stuffed into his bag was a racket that looked as if it had been tested at speeds of several hundred miles an hour. He was wearing a pair of green tracksuit trousers. Even his buttocks had a taut, menacing air. I was beginning to feel tired just watching him sign me in.

'Loosali,' said Quigley, 'beat Rumero in Athens!'

I had absolutely no idea who either of these characters were.

Hoisting his bag over his shoulder, Quigley jogged off towards a door marked MEMBERS ONLY. I followed him, marvelling at the change in posture he had achieved simply by wearing trainers that looked as if they were worth about £200. You knew, just from his equipment, that Quigley was the business as far as squash was concerned.

'I'll go easy on you, young shaver,' said Quiggers, 'for dear Norman's sweet sake!'

I'd played squash with my dad. He was banned from his club for smoking while playing. But before they gave him the boot, we did play. Just once. It was the funniest thing I can remember.

'Oh *no*!' he would shout, as he ran across the stone floor, waving his racket. 'Oh *no*! This is going to be a *disaster*!' His forecast was usually correct.

Quigley's approach was very different.

He was the only guy I've ever met who took a shower *before* playing. 'I like to be clean for the experience,' he said. He looked like a man who would not need to shower after the game.

I had to get in the shower with him, which was a pretty sobering time for me. Partly because he made very free with the old Quigley chopper, shampooing it and hosing it down as if he was about to enter it for some competition, and partly because he insisted on singing as we stood, man to man, under the steaming water.

'Praise God I am not blessed with pain! Praise God I am in bliss!' he carolled as he towelled himself down and sprayed talcum powder on what had to be the biggest cock in South London. No one laughed.

A thin guy in the corner asked whether I was Quigley's son. And Quigley, as he got into some figure-hugging shorts, said, 'I am all the father he has, Walter.'

Walter looked impressed. As we went out to the court, he said to me, 'Lovely man, lovely, lovely man!'

Maybe Walter had an account at Quigley's bank. I don't know.

Greatly to my relief, there were no spectators.

I was wearing a baggy pair of jeans, which Quigley had been pretty sniffy about. 'We must be properly clad,' he had said. But I knew, from the moment he closed the door to the court, that I was by no means underdressed for the event. About the most suitable garment to have worn would have been a suit of chain mail.

He started by suggesting a 'knock-up' and then, almost immediately, whacked the ball against the rear elevation at about the velocity of light. It came back at me with such force that my one thought was to find some quiet corner, pull a rug over my head and let the ball finish whatever it had to do.

But there is no place to hide on a squash-court. It is just you and the ball. And, when you're playing with Quigley, it doesn't feel like one ball. It feels like an angry swarm.

The ball snaked round like a heat-seeking missile, cutting off my line of retreat. As I stood there, my racket held out in front of me like a serving-spoon, it made contact with the wall to my left and ricocheted back towards me. It seemed annoyed that I had missed it.

'Move into the ball!' yelled Quigley.

I ran, hard, in the opposite direction.

'It's spinning!' he yelled. 'I've put top spin on it!'

It looked like he had done a lot more than that. It looked like he had brainwashed the thing. It was coming after me like a Dobermann pinscher. I swerved to my left and the ball hit the far wall of the court. It showed no sign of slowing up. After the way he'd hit it, it could be whanging around the four walls for the foreseeable future.

Quigley, his buttocks thrust out behind him, was bouncing up and down on the spot. 'Thar she blows!' he yelled. He seemed pleased with the way things were going. 'She comes on hard, me dearios!'

I have a pretty hazy grasp of the rules of squash. When Dad and I played, the idea seemed to be to keep the ball in the air for a few minutes and then award the points to the person who seemed to need them most.

Quigley and I hadn't finished knocking up yet, and already I was wondering if The Club kept an oxygen cylinder handy. The ball headed off in the direction of the service area, travelling waist height at about thirty miles an hour. With a kind of feeble cry, I set off in pursuit.

I was getting angry. You know? I was fighting back.

I caught up with it – or, rather, it caught up with me – as it was setting off from the rear wall on another leg of its journey south (or was it north? Or west? Or east?). I held out my racket, with my right arm fully extended, drew back my left leg and drove forward, hard. The ball hit me in the chest.

'Stretcher case!' yelled Quigley, in the grip of almost unbearable excitement. 'Give that man a jelly bean!'

With these words he danced up the court, his long legs waving elaborately, like a crane-fly's. When he finally got the ball in his sights, he swept it up against the back wall. My one thought

was to get as far away as possible from both him and it before he
started whacking me into play as well.

'Give it welly!' he shouted as I shambled to the nearest corner,
listening to the irritated whine of the ball. 'Give it welly, young
shaver!'

I did not, I have to say, give it welly. I did not give it any
kind of footwear. I gave it a kind of reedy sob as it slammed
into some other surface that I had not known was there.
How many walls were there in this court? And which way
up were we? I was beginning to feel as if I was in a space-
flight simulator. As if Quigley might appear above me at any
moment, grinning, as he slurped across the ceiling upside
down.

This time I stayed where I was. I tried to look like a man
waiting for his opportunity. I stood on my points. I held the
racket with both hands. I ducked. I weaved. I gave the ball some
pretty nasty looks. But I did not make the mistake of actually
moving in its direction until it had finished whizzing round the
court and was trickling towards the door.

It was time for a bit of conversation.

'Mr Quigley,' I said, 'did *I really* see my dad out in the street
the other night?'

This did, at least, prevent Quiggers from scooping up the
ball and sending it back into orbit. I was doubled up. My face
felt like a large, red balloon and my shirt was dripping with
sweat.

'How d'ye mean, m'deario?' said Quigley.

'I mean, was it *real*? Or was it like a dream or something?'

Quigley picked up the ball and folded his long fingers round
it. Up in the gallery a couple of members had come in to watch
The Boss humiliate me.

'Life,' said Quigley, 'is a dream and a passing show. Hallo,
Bertie!'

'Hallo there, Big Man,' said Bertie. He was a guy of about seventy, wearing a blue blazer and a yachting-cap. Had he, I wondered, come into the wrong club? Or was this a sort of special drinking outfit?

Quigley put a hand on my shoulder. 'You saw what you saw, Simey,' he said. 'You saw what God wanted you to see. You were led by God's will. Because he wants you, Simey. He wants you for Our Church and for Jesus. Make no mistake about that, young shaver!'

Quigley made these remarks in a loud, audible voice. A couple more spectators had come in behind the person in the blazer. One of them seemed to be wearing what looked like a sombrero. The other, a man of about eighty, nothing but a fluffy, white towel. They seemed to be nodding keenly. Maybe they were Christians, planted there by some committee of the First Church of Christ the Spiritualist.

'What I mean,' I said in a low voice, 'is that there are things in the world, in the *universe,* that we can't explain. Aren't there? About why we're here and what we're doing here and what it's all about.'

'Yes,' said Quigley. 'Yes, me laddio – there are things in the universe that are pretty hard to make out. There are!'

He thrust his face into mine. He did not appear to have sweated at all.

'Sin is one of them,' he said, 'and wickedness is another!'

This wasn't a lot of help. I wanted some basic questions answered here, not the usual stuff about being good or bad.

'I mean . . .' I said, 'suppose someone . . . well . . . disappeared?'

'Who's disappeared?' said Quigley, sharply.

'Well,' I said, wondering if it was safe to say this out loud, as I did so, 'Mr Marr.'

Quigley laughed. 'Oh, Mr Marr! Well, if *he's* disappeared we know where to look, don't we? It's simple. Eh?' He prodded me in the chest. 'Spacemen got him!'

He found this very amusing. So too did the guys in the gallery. There were all chuckling to themselves as Quigley handed me the ball and suggested I try to serve. He laid some emphasis on the word 'try'. I was about to suggest that I went to lie down for an hour or so. Instead I held the ball gingerly between the first and second fingers of my left hand and braced myself for more pain.

'Beef!' said Quigley. 'Beef in the service!' I wafted the racket backwards and forwards a few times. The air resistance was pretty rough. Before I hit it, I had one more go.

'But if you saw something weird, and you had an *explanation* for that. And it was aliens. I mean, that was the one that made sense, then . . .'

Quigley came over to me. He looked troubled. He thought I was still on about my dad.

'Norman has a lot of unfinished business here. He was a man very much in medias res . . .'

'Was he?'

'Look,' said Quigley, 'we've had messages through about Veronica. He's talked about the Veronica business a lot. And about Mrs Danby too.'

From the way he said this, it sounded like he and Marjorie had been giving the old man some retrospective marriage guidance.

'Who's Veronica?' I said.

He stopped. He looked a trifle cagey.

'There are some messages from the Other Side that are not suitable for young people's ears.'

He cuffed me. I think it was meant affectionately, but I staggered a few yards from the effect of the blow.

'I don't think the little green chaps have anything to do

with your daddy's continuing presence on the earth,' said Quigley, 'and I have to say to you that if I saw one of your aliens I'd go up to it and I'd give it a good hug! I'd say, "Cor lumme, Alien – haven't yer heard about the love of Jesus?" And I'd take its little green heart to my bosom. Because the love of Jesus isn't just for you and me, Simo – it's for Venusians and Droids and the old ninety-foot green monsters from the planet Zog too!'

I was getting nowhere with this. It would be hopeless to tell him about Mr Marr. I had been stupid even to try. Why had I ever imagined that Quigley would understand? I braced myself for the service.

'Your dad did some very, very wrong things. He didn't always do right by you, I'm afraid. But God will forgive him for that. What we mustn't do is shut Jesus out from our hearts, because for as long as we do we hang around the places we loved and the ones we cared for *like ghosts!*'

I hit the ball as hard as I could. It helped to imagine that it was Quigley's head. It sort of trickled down from the racket and dragged itself up to the rear wall of the court. It was already looking tired as it made contact. It came down, rather meekly, towards the Quigley feet.

Quigley looked at it sternly and did a sort of on-the-spot gallop. His long arms swirled his racket round in the air. The last movement was the sort of thing I had seen conductors do when they were in front of large orchestras that were playing loudly. There was a rush of air through the court and the squash ball was back in business.

It really had it in for me this time. It clearly thought I had no business to be on the court. It went straight for my head. I held up my racket, purely in self-defence. The ball hit it dead centre and whizzed back against the rear wall. With a stab of fear I realized we were into a rally.

'Good!' yelled Quigley. 'Whammo, whammo, whammo, good!'

He plunged after it like a man possessed.

'Beef in the service!' he yelled. 'Beefo, beefo, beefo, beefo, good!'

There was an ache in the whole of my upper body. Water was running off my hairline like snow in a heatwave. When Quigley made contact with the ball it howled back into play, and, to my surprise, I managed to spoon it back to him.

He was well away now. He was past caring how the ball had got to him. 'Just keep it going, young shaver! Last man to the ball's a cissy, eh?'

Quiggers didn't really need a partner. Once the ball was in motion, he just went. All I had to do was look keen and occasionally wave my racket at the ball. He would grunt as he ran past me to bash it back into play – 'Nice try, Simo! Keep it coming, eh?'

After a minute or so there was just him, the ball and the walls of the squash-court. He ran from side to side, grunting and thwacking and yelling, and I moved, very gradually, towards the more suitable role of spectator.

I can't remember at what point I stole towards the door. All I do remember is that Quigley was volleying and forehanding and backhanding and the spectators were cheering and waving. And suddenly I was tiptoeing back towards the changing-room. I could still hear him grunting and thumping as I made my way out of the front door of The Club, en route for anywhere that wasn't 24 Stranraer Gardens.

What had I seen that night my dad had died? And where had Mr Marr gone? None of the adults who made it their business to tell me things could tell me anything about this affair. The only person I could have talked to wasn't around. I thought about him as I slouched off down the road. I thought about sitting with him after our squash game, him with his head in his hands, me sipping a Coke. But, no matter how hard I thought about him, it wasn't going to bring him back or explain why the world had got so hard to understand since he died.

14

The afternoon had clouded over when I got out of The Club. There was a line of grey clouds, lying like boats at anchor, above the hill. I slung my bag across my back and walked back down Wimbledon Park Road. I headed away from home, towards the big main road noisy with lorries and bright with the signs of tobacconists and fast-food places that never seemed to close.

I felt low. I stopped just before I got to the main road and tried to see if I could see my right bicep. It was still acting cagey, even though I took off my blazer and rolled up my shirtsleeve. There was still a vague depression where my chest ought to be. Maybe that was why I was so hopeless at all forms of sport.

But I didn't really feel bad about being thrashed by Quigley. I think it's important to rise above such things. I'd rather people thought I was intelligent than superbly muscled and well co-ordinated.

I felt my bicep again. It seemed to have disappeared completely.

What I felt bad about was that I had actually wanted to confide in Quigley. That's how desperate I was. And it reminded me how much I wanted to have a normal family. You know? The kind that they have in that soap-powder ad where they've made a home movie and dad laughs when she gets the stains out. I mean, I know it's schmuck. I know they're only a bunch of dead-beat actors, but sometimes I wish I could step inside the screen and become part of them. Khan gets kept in to do homework most evenings. Greenslade's dad hit his brother with a cricket bat. And Richthofer's mum – who isn't really his mum – had an affair with a chiropodist. But, compared to my family, they are all *normal*.

I can't understand how my mum and dad ever got together. You know? I can remember dad coming in one day, when we were on holiday in Dorset, grasping me by the arm and saying, in the serious voice he used to talk about religion, 'Always remember, Simon, I love your mother very much.'

Why was he telling me? Why did I have to remember? It wasn't helped by his adding, as he went back out to start having another row with her, 'She hems me in, boy! She hems me in! But *by God* I love her!'

He should have been on the stage really. But he joined the First Church of Christ the Spiritualist as a substitute.

I mooched down the main road, games bag on my shoulder. Why couldn't we do the things normal people do, like go to bowling-alleys? Why did the First Spiritualist Church believe that the Charrington Bowl, Kingston, was 'unclean and filthy with the work of the whore'? Why did we have to eat fish on Wednesdays? Was it absolutely necessary to follow Ella Walsh's instruction to 'avoid Ireland like the plague'? I'd quite like to go to Dublin. You know?

For some reason I turned off left down Furnival Gardens. Thinking about it afterwards, I decided that it must have been exerting a strong psychic pull. It doesn't look like a road with any spiritual significance. It isn't on a ley line or anything. At first sight it's just another long, pointless South London street with too many cars parked in it. But, as I trudged up it, I started to feel weirder and weirder. It wasn't simply that I felt depressed, although, if I had had a guitar and been able to play, I'd have sung the blues. As my eyes wandered from the dirt-stained pavement to the greyer sky, I could feel a presence in the air. And it was *him*.

You always knew Dad was around. You knew it from his cough or his habit of breaking into song or his preference for bawling at people he wanted to go and see rather than walking around and trying to find them. Some people, like my mum, aren't really present and correct even when they're there, but there was never any doubt about Dad. The broken veins on his cheeks, the half-smoked tipped cigarettes, the low growl before he delivered an opinion about something – they were all so *vivid*.

I couldn't believe he'd died, you see. All I wanted was a middle-aged man with a big nose. That wasn't so much to ask, was it? Surely the spirits that arrange the world could lay that on for me? I looked hard across the street, in between the cars, up towards the road ahead that was rising to another main street running across it, watching for that familiar face and listening for that unforgettable voice.

In one of the houses on the other side of the street an upper window was open. Loud classical music was coming out of it. I imagined someone lying on the bed, staring at the ceiling and watching the breeze stir the grey lace curtains this way and that. Up to my right I could see the black railings at the beginning of the patch of waste ground, and, ahead, nothing but roads and houses and, beyond them, houses and roads, cluttered with people as lonely and scared as me. The suburbs are hell. They go on and on and on, like Sunday afternoons.

He came out of a house about 150 yards away. He looked up and down the street, as if he was frightened of being followed. Then he looked up at the front bedroom window. He wasn't wearing white. He didn't *look* in the least ghostly. But he was wearing the sort of clothes he would not have been seen dead in, when alive. For a start he was wearing a hat, which is something my dad never ever did. 'Headgear,' he once said to me, 'is an unnecessary indulgence, except when the temperature is below zero.' But, although I was a fair way away from him, I could have sworn it was my dad. If it wasn't him, it was an incredibly good simulation. He didn't see me. He turned and walked up the hill, past the waste ground.

I thought hard about what Quigley had said. Was it all my fault that my dad was forced to walk the streets of Wimbledon? I remembered him once saying to me, the year we went to Cornwall, 'I stay for you, boy. You know that, don't you? I'm here because of you.' And when they argued, which was a lot, it was often about me. I could hear them at the other end of the house, as I lay awake in bed. 'You don't appreciate him,' one of them would say, and the other would answer, 'No, no. It's *you*! It's you who doesn't appreciate Simon!'

Had I made them both unhappy, and was this why he couldn't be at peace? Or was I dreaming all this, making some poor, innocent, middle-aged person look like my old man, simply because I so much wanted to see him again?

The figure I was following – I still wasn't certain it was my dad – didn't look at all depressed to be hanging around South London. In fact, once it had got going, it looked pretty pleased to be here.

If it wasn't my dad, then what was it?

Supposing we weren't dealing with something as local as spacenapping. Supposing we were talking invasion. Suppose the extraterrestrials had moved beyond the initial, exploratory stages and on to one of their favourite ploys: full-scale invasion of planet earth. Method? Bodysnatching. Aliens, as I am sure you know, are no slouches when it comes to taking people to bits and reassembling them, programmed to do the will of the War Lord of Ro or the Headless Things of Jupiter.

Sure. Crazy, I know. I didn't, as yet, actually *think* this. But it was as good as any other explanation on offer.

The normal procedure is to pull a guy behind the hedge on his way to the office, strap him to a bit of Venusian technology and drain off the old cranium before you can say 'Bob's your uncle.' After this, the individual heads on into town – the only clue to the fact that he has been taken over by aliens being a slightly glassy look about the eyes and a tendency to give all words in any sentence a roughly equal amount of stress.

Why not dead people? You know? Dead people are perfect. We leave them lying around the undertakers' for days, just waiting to be reanimated by the guys from Orion or a highly developed corner of the Magellan Cluster. Stiffs from all over South London could be swarming towards some prearranged meeting point, their expressions devoid of all traces of emotion. Maybe what I had seen outside my window in Stranraer Gardens had come to me courtesy of the same firm that had lifted Mr Marr!

If it was a simulation, the extraterrestrials had done a fantastically good job. It even walked slightly to one side, the way my dad always did. It stopped, just as it got to Garratt Lane, and hitched up its trousers in exactly the way he used to do.

I still hadn't got a close look at its face.

It turned right into the next main road and headed off south. The funny thing was – they hadn't got the clothes to fit. The suit jacket hung limp and awkward from the creature's shoulders, and it was wearing huge brown boots. They were not the sort of thing Dad would ever wear. It's a standard mistake the aliens make. They run up a pair of trousers out there on some moon of Jupiter, and they never get it *quite* right.

They had also reckoned without human psychology. They probably didn't know about families and how humans sort of, you know, *like* each other. Their planet was probably not unlike the First Church of Christ the Spiritualist, and when people died they hung out the bunting. If my dad was alive, he would have let me know.

As I watched the entity tiptoe down the highway, I remembered Dad on the night I passed Grade Two Saxophone with merit. He was practically going up to people in the street on the way to the restaurant, grabbing them by the lapels and shouting, '*Merit! You hear me? Merit!*' in their faces. I remembered him at the table in La Paesana too, his face flushed with wine, his fists clenched aloft – 'Nail the bastards! That's what you've got to do, Simon! Nail the bastards!'

It's funny, when I think about any of these gatherings, although my mum must have been there, when I try to picture them I can't see her. It's as if she's been painted out, the way Trotsky was painted out of all those photographs after the revolution in Russia. It was my dad and me. It was always my dad and me.

Whatever was slouching down Garratt Lane, its hands deep in its unfamiliar earthling pockets, was something else again.

I started to feel angry.

Why had I believed that garbage from Quigley? Why had I ever assumed that any of this was my fault? How had I got into the absurd position of believing that, just because I occasionally pulled my wire, my dad had been forced to roam some of the least attractive parts of South London after his death? People will believe anything, that's the fact of the matter. It's all too easy to dismiss a new idea – like, things from the Crab Nebula are trying to take over the planet – simply because it sounds strange. Why is believing *that* any stranger than believing that God punishes sinners? Or that Britain is a democracy? Or any of the other crazy things adults ask young people to believe?

Steady on, Simon, I told myself. Let's sort out what's possible, here. What do we actually think, Britton?

Why shouldn't a take-over of the world begin in Wimbledon? It's as good a place as any other to start restructuring the DNA of earthlings. It's got the edge on northern Brazil, where, according to Bob Pratt, there is a phenomenal amount of this sort of thing going on.

I kept a respectable distance from the creature as it moseyed down through South Wandsworth. Was it headed for Tooting Bec and a quiet pint with some finned, semi-amphibious pile of green blubber with four heads? It wasn't an obvious monster. It looked, superficially, quite normal. But the more closely I looked at it, the shakier it looked as a human being. Everything looked a bit . . . *put on*. Very cleverly done and very neatly thought out. But missing the thing that divides us from the rest of creation: humanity.

I don't think I would have said anything if it hadn't started running for the bus. Sometimes you only *see* a person when that person does a particular thing. As it thrust itself down on its right foot, it jerked its elbows down at the ground as if it was going to use them to lever itself forward – exactly the way my dad used to do. 'In my youth,' he used to tell me, in a way I have to say I didn't entirely trust, 'I was something of an athlete.' It was the exact movement, I swear. I couldn't help it. I called, just once – 'Dad!'

Immediately I had called his name I regretted it. I felt that I had been ridiculously naive. If this thing was from the other side of the galaxy, it would be ready for such eventualities. It probably had a tape packed with all the things my dad ever said. In my dad's case it wouldn't need to be a particularly long tape, because he only ever said about thirty or forty things, in fairly strict rotation. It had probably got them all in there, stacked away neatly in its nasty little alien head. 'Mine is a pint,' and 'I am easy, old son!' and 'Have you seen the *Writers' and Artists' Yearbook* anywhere?'

But they never, as I said, get humans *quite* right.

It turned and looked towards me. Just for a moment I saw something behind its eyes I thought I recognized. But then it wasn't there any more. Its face changed and what I saw on its features was extraterrestrial panic, as if someone was getting on the line to it and calling, 'Re-turn to ship! A-bort mi-ssion! The hu-man-oid earth-ling has re-cog-nized you!'

It lowered its hat so that it covered its eyes and ran for the bus. The trousers really were *laughable*, my son. I mean, this was supposed to be my dad, right? The man for whom time stopped at some moment in the 1970s. This thing's trousers were trailing on the pavement, and were made of some coarse tweed, quite unlike anything Norman Britton had ever worn. It was bent over double as it reached the bus. Whether this was because it was still under orders to keep its face away from the light, or whether it was because it was finding our atmosphere difficult I didn't care to guess. The atmosphere in Garratt Lane is not great, even for humans.

'Dad!'

I couldn't help it. I called again. Not being a highly disciplined blob from a star system billions of years older than our own earth, but a flesh-and-blood boy of fourteen, I was a little at the mercy of the old *emotions.* But it didn't turn. It had to get to grips with the amazingly primitive transport devices still in use in the Wimbledon area, to look with some degree of confidence into the eyes of driver-conductors and tell them it had not got the right change.

It made the bus. The bus pulled away. I was left there on the pavement.

The real road-to-Damascus moments are the ones you work out for yourself. No one helped Archimedes, right? There was just him and the bath. What I went through on the pavement that evening was a revelation. I knew I wasn't crazy. I had never felt so utterly and completely sane. But I knew, the way you know the answers to a difficult exam when you've prepared the paper really well. These guys weren't buddy-buddy-give-us-a-football-pitch-to-land-on-and-let's-get-pally. They were devious. They were unscrupulous. They were unbelievably good at genetic engineering. And they were *here.*

I would have to be very careful who I started trusting with all this information, though. In some ways, the violent ward of the local mental hospital was an attractive alternative to number 24 Stranraer Gardens, and this was probably just where the extraterrestrials hoped I would be placed. But I didn't think I was ready for it yet. I needed a sympathetic audience. Not necessarily ufologists – they do not need convincing about *anything.* But people who would spread the word. People who would let me get through the details of this story without trying to take my temperature and asking me where I stood on mind-expanding drugs. I needed a fairly large body of people who were good at believing things. Who else, my friends, but the First Church of Christ the Spiritualist, South Wimbledon?

As I crossed back towards Wimbledon Park Road, a hymn from my childhood came into my mind:

> Tell them the word!
> Tell them the word!
> Why don't you ever just try?
> If you have some news
> That you really mustn't lose,
> Come along and Testify!

I found myself singing this out loud as I walked towards Stranraer Gardens thinking about the extraordinary things I had seen and heard since my father's death. And when I got to the chorus, I practically shouted it into the faces of the astonished passers-by:

> Testify! Testify!
> Take your troubles to the Lord!
> Testify! Testify!
> Dare to face the Fire and the Sword!
> Are you down and glum?
> Oh has the Saviour come?
> Have you news you really want to cry?
> Step among us brother!
> We're the ones! No other
> Will let you really Testify!

I thought about Old Mother Walsh's prophecies. I thought about Lewis. I thought about that snake with TWO THOUSAND YEARS GO BY on it. And I thought about all the crazy things people believe. Just to keep themselves sane.

> Step among us brother!
> We're the ones! No other
> Will let you really Testify!

PART TWO

15

One Sunday morning, about a week after I had seen my dad for the second time, I was lying in bed when I heard voices in the street below. They were singing. Not loudly, but loudly enough for half past six on a Sunday morning. Among the voices, I thought I recognized Roger Beeding's and Hannah Dooley's.

> Mother-life God she is calling Thee!
> Mother-life God she is calling Thee!
> Holla! Holla! Holla!
> Awa-a-a-y!

We have very patient neighbours.

I got up, staggered to the window and, while keeping my head below the level of the sill, attempted to close it.

My first thought was that I was 320 duck-jumps behind and if I was ever going to make the state of *shai-hai* I would probably have to spend a whole weekend duck-jumping. My second thought, which did not occur to me until I was crawling back along the floor towards my bed, was that today was the day when I was due to Testify. That was what the choir outside was for. I had been called upon to show my newly strengthened Christian

faith before the whole congregation of the First Spiritualist
Church. Praying with Quigley wasn't enough. I had to tell the
people. He was very emphatic about that.

I got back under the duvet and felt my balls, for reassurance.
These were probably one of the few things of mine not due to be
on show at the First Church of Christ the Spiritualist later that
morning. As Quigley had said to me last night, 'Speak the whole
truth of your heart when you testify, Simo!'

There is a sign outside the First Church that reads

> ARE YOU A CUSTARD CHRISTIAN?
> DO YOU GET UPSET OVER TRIFLES?
> JESUS ISN'T. COME ON IN AND JOIN HIM.

If I was a Christian at all – and I wasn't sure that I was – I thought
I was probably a custard Christian. Or maybe not even that.
Maybe I was a jelly Muslim or a sponge-cake Buddhist. *The
whole truth of my heart.* The thought of morning service is always
a pain, and the prospect of this one made me stick my head back
under the duvet to block out the already brilliant day.

I had also remembered that the Quigleys were still living with
us. 'We're having building work done,' Quigley had said, 'so we
can camp out with you!' He had said this as if he was doing us
all a big favour.

My mum came in at about 07.15, holding out my black suit
and a white shirt that she had just ironed. She stood looking at
me from the end of the bed.

'Oh, Simon!' she said. 'Oh, Simon!'

'Yes, Mum?'

She put the shirt and the suit on a chair by the window.

'I wonder if Daddy will come through today. I must say, I
hope he manifests himself. He'd be so proud!'

I thought there was a very good chance of his showing up.

Quite often there are more deceased members of the congregation present on Sunday mornings than there are living punters.

'Would he?'

She looked at me narrowly. She was rather less convinced about my conversion than the Quigleys. I had been doing my best to mime the odd prayer since my dad died, but I had a feeling she saw through me.

'You're not going to be silly, are you?'

'No, Mum. I just wasn't sure whether he *would* be proud. I mean, Mum, was he religious, or what?'

'He was . . .'

She stopped. I found myself wondering what exactly my dad *had* been. He had been religious. I knew that. Even if he wasn't always sure quite what religion he belonged to. She had told me how they met at a First Spiritualist Church 'Convert the Heathen' session outside the Anglican church in Putney. Pike, Quigley and Mum used to wait behind the hedge, rattling tambourines and waving placards saying ARE YOU REALLY GOING TO MEET THE LIVING GOD? as the congregation filed out and chatted to the vicar about the problems of British Rail.

Dad had had some kind of religious crisis later, but I didn't know too much about that. He had mentioned it to me, in a roundabout sort of way, but I could never work out when it had happened or how old I was when it occurred. It was funny I couldn't remember. But your own past can be a closed book, even at fourteen.

My mum, as mums tend to do, had divined my state of mind rather shrewdly and moved over to the bed in a thoughtful kind of way.

'Norman . . .'

At first I thought she might be addressing him directly. Then I realized we were into genuine past-tense mode. She sighed slowly.

'I very nearly married a man called Flugtermans,' she said ' – a dentist.'

Why was she telling me this?

'I met him at a tennis club, and he was a very, very attractive man indeed. And very fond of me. But I didn't continue the relationship are these your socks?'

'Yes.'

'They're stiff with dirt! And your father was not, I have to say, a handsome man, although he was . . .'

'Available,' I said.

She gave me a sharp look.

'Anyway,' she went on, 'then he went to Portugal and everything changed of course you should really have some new blinds but they're so expensive and they warp.'

I knew better than to interrupt. Sooner or later, out of monologues like this, some really vital piece of information was liable to emerge.

'Of course,' she said, 'I know you still blame me for what happened at Angmering.'

I kid you not, I had not a clue as to what she might be talking about. People assume that parents and children will understand each other. It doesn't work out like that. They share experiences, but they don't seem to share the same memories of them. Family business is strange.

I can remember my dad opening the newspaper once and saying, 'There is going to be a war in China.' And I can also remember him standing in the hall with my mum and her saying, 'I am going out!' and him, for some reason I will never understand, bursting into tears. Why did he cry? And was he even the same guy as the one with markedly dodgy views about the international situation in the Far East?

'Gorbachev is a genius!' was another one of his. Only to be followed, a few weeks later, by 'Gorbachev is an idiot!'

How could you explain this human stuff to Globo, Arch Lord of the System of the Blabbenoids? You couldn't. You know why? Because it doesn't make sense.

I looked at Mum as she moved towards the door. She seemed pleased to have got this off her chest. Whatever it was.

'In Angmering . . .' I said, cautiously.

She suddenly got angry.

'With Veronica, for Christ's sake!'

I still didn't get it.

She went to the window and looked down at our drab patch of suburban garden. She sighed. 'I'll never forget that night in Lisbon!' Then she turned to me: 'Always be faithful and true, Simon. Always be honest and faithful and sincere in your dealings with others where are your trainers?'

'On the floor.'

'Keep them out of sight!'

Then she puckered her lips and allowed her breast to heave one or two times. This is usually a sure sign that she is about to quote from the collected works of Old Mother Walsh, and this, indeed, is what she did: ' "Shoes are remarkable, warm, bright and neat. The best place to keep them is on your feet." '

And with these words she thumped off down the stairs, leaving me to collect my thoughts for the hard task of Testifying.

I rolled out of bed and, feeling I was doomed to the state of *hei-hei*, or eternal sloth and uselessness, I wondered whether I could find a pair of unstiff socks.

The choir outside seemed to have stopped, but downstairs I could hear the Quigleys. Marjorie, who has a carrying voice, was saying, 'Isn't Testifying the best thing? Mrs Danby says it's the *best thing!*' She sounded rather girlish as she said this. Then I heard Quigley's low bass, but couldn't make out what he was saying.

I took one last, depressed look at myself in the mirror above the electric fire and clattered down the stairs. As I reached the landing I heard Mrs Quigley say, 'We're having the patio done. Then we're getting a *completely* new roof.'

They were getting a good deal out of staying at our house. Some people have to rent places. And, while we were at it, how the hell were they managing to afford these improvements? My dad always used to say that *we* could not afford lunch, although, I have to say, this did not stop him eating it.

They were all in the clothes traditionally worn when people are going to testify. My mum was wearing a sort of large red sack and a conical hat that made her look like a gnome in a pantomime. Mrs Quigley was wearing a loose white robe with a hat and a veil rather like a bee-keeper's. She looked like a worker at a nuclear power station. Women at Testifying must be 'loose and bright', as Old Mother Walsh once said. The men are their usual uninspiring selves.

Mrs Quigley held out her arms as I came into the hall. 'Oh my darling, darling boy!' she said.

I had been getting a lot of this. I had so far managed to avoid being kissed by the old bat, but I had the strong feeling that, by the end of the day, she and I were going to be getting physical.

I stayed where I was. She decided against physical contact. Instead, she looked up to the ceiling from where she got quite a lot of her inspiration. Quigley was smirking next to her. *The whole truth of my heart!* How was he going to take the news of the hijacking of earthling bodies by extraterrestrial beings? I was going to have to be extremely subtle about this.

'Jesus,' said Mrs Quigley in sharp tones, 'can you see this boy?'

'Thee him,' said Emily. 'He'th blethed!'

My face didn't crack.

'Today,' said Quigley, 'is a very great day in your life. You're going to stand up in front of a hundred or so of your closest friends and tell them your deepest, most private thoughts.'

This seemed to me to be a pretty fair definition of hell, but I tried to look like a man who enjoyed such occasions.

'You're going to tell them,' said Quigley, 'what *you* think about . . . about . . . *everything!*' And then, with a kind of war whoop, he picked me up under the armpits and carried me out to the choir waiting outside. He was incredibly strong.

As we thundered along the road, he whispered in my ear, 'And after you've Testified, Simon, you'll be Confirmed in Faith. In ten days. Think of it! Cor blimey, mate, you're not just Simon, old lad. You're Simon pure!'

Bergman had a barmitzvah and I went. Everyone there was Jewish apart from me. There was a lot of chanting, and afterwards we went to a posh hotel and I got a free hat. Bergman, at the end of it, was officially a man. As far as I am concerned, Bergman has been officially a man since the end of the Upper Removes. He is one hairy guy. But it was nice to see all these old geezers with huge noses treating him as if he *was* a man. In the First Church of Christ the Spiritualist you are Confirmed in Faith, which means you are officially a berk. There are no free hats.

Quigley held me up with one free hand and opened the door of his car with the other. He threw me across the front seat, and the choir applauded – whether this was for my benefit or to register approval for Quigley's strong right arm was not clear.

He wanted me Confirmed in Faith did he?

Being Confirmed in Faith is the full masonic job. I've never been able to find out what goes on at the ceremony, but, from what I've heard, there is more to it than rolling up your trouser-leg. I know that the male members of the congregation 'play loudly on the organ and show their bodies'. I know a fair amount of water gets chucked around, and at some point I think you are expected to wear your underpants on your head. But in between all these things something happens which is only spoken of in hushed whispers. Maybe they paint your balls green.

All this stuff dates back years, to Old Mother Walsh and her Sisters. When they baptized people they stayed baptized. You know? There was none of this dip-the-finger-in-the-water-and-let's-talk-about-the-Test-Match bollocks. They used to run down into the Nerd, or whatever river it is that runs through Ealing, and throw themselves in, yelling about the love of Jesus. Water was cheap and unpolluted in those days.

He was really moving fast, was Quiggers. He couldn't wait to get me sewn up, could he? *Why the big hurry?* I wondered, as Mum, Emily and Mrs Quigley got into the back of his brand new car and he thrust it out into the traffic.

One of the areas where Quigley really needs a lot of help from the Lord Jesus is in the driving department. But I have never heard him confess his unworthiness in this field of human endeavour. He snarls at motorcyclists, accelerates hard at the back of buses and views the red traffic light as a challenge rather than a warning.

As we careered down towards South Wimbledon, I remembered other trips I'd taken to church. Mostly I thought about going with my dad. I thought about running along beside him as we came up to the main road opposite the church, about his taking my hand and singing, 'Hold my *hand* – I'm a *stranger* in *Paradise!*'

And, as I thought about that, another image came into my mind. A heavy, silver casket was swinging backwards and forwards and there was that smell in the air – a smell of old leaves and perfume and musty, clinging sweetness. There was music, too, and those long shafts of light that fell from a high window, somewhere over to my right. For the first time, I could feel my father very close to me, his face very dark and serious. He was talking to someone. Someone I couldn't see. I wanted to see who it was, but I couldn't. He was mumbling. The words he was using weren't English. They were some old, runic language I couldn't understand. But there was something even stranger than that about him. He was on his knees. Why? Why was he kneeling? And to whom?

'We are come to the Temple,' said Mrs Quigley, as Quigley reversed into a parked car.

The street was packed with members of the First Spiritualist Church. It was Day Release at the loony bin. Over by the door of the church I could see Meriel Viney, wearing a kind of white sack and a pair of what looked like tennis shoes. On her head was a hat that looked as if someone had dropped a large meringue on her head. She was chatting away to Roger Beeding and to Roger de Mornay. There were, I found myself thinking, a hell of a lot of people called Roger in the First Spiritualist Church. What was it about the name that made them want to funk on down and start praising the Lord? We had no Peters, no Colins, only one David and, though there had been a Kevin a few years back, we were now understaffed in that area too. But you just could not keep the Rogers away!

It's for old people, our church. Old people called Roger.

Right outside the church, directly in front of Roger Beeding, was a large Rolls-Royce. Sitting in the back seat was a woman in a long, cream dress and a hat the size of a toddler's swimming-pool. She was smoking a small cigar and sported a face that was a lot less elegant than the hat.

Quigley is down on smokers. Cigarettes are the work of the Devil. But smoking was obviously kosher as far as this old bat went. He rushed up to her as she got out of the Roller, took her right hand and thrust it into his beard. 'Oh!' I heard him say. 'Oh!'

Mrs Quigley looked pretty pleased as well. She had the air

of one who might head for the pavement and start writhing
at any minute. 'Mrs Danby,' she croaked, 'I'm so pleased! Mrs
Danby!'

So this was Mrs Danby. It was strange. I couldn't remember
ever having clapped eyes on her before. But she was looking at
me as if we were long-lost friends. She was smiling so hard the
gauze on her hat wobbled. And, as I met her eyes, I did have a
memory of something, although I couldn't have said what. It was
to do with a smell and some music and a steel thing swinging
out and back, out and back, like the pendulum in the story by
Edgar Allan Poe.

'This', Mrs Danby was saying, 'is one of the greatest days of
my life!'

She simpered at me. I was beginning to feel like a ritual
sacrifice. I mean, had the First Spiritualists moved on? Was I
going to have it off with this woman and a couple of goats?
Give me the goats any time, I thought, as I was shuffled towards
her.

'Has Norman come through?' I heard her say.

'We have been in *constant* touch with him,' said Quigley, as if
he was reassuring the chairman about the Exports Division.

The old bat beamed. 'How is he?'

'He is doing fine, Mrs Danby,' said Marjorie.

Who was this woman? And why would she not take her eyes
off me?

'What's he doing over there?'

Everyone looked at Mrs Quigley.

'Oh, he's been . . . jetting around,' she said at last.

'Yes,' said Mrs Danby, shaking her head winsomely, 'he was
always a busy soul, was Norman. Has he made new contacts?'

'He feels very, very fully occupied,' said Mrs Quigley, 'but we
are getting some very serious indications that he has been . . .
having a personal rethink.'

Mrs Danby nodded gravely. 'Yes,' she said. 'Oh yes. When we fall, how we do fall!'

I couldn't work out what she meant by this. In fact, I couldn't work her out at all. She was wearing high-heeled shoes – which is very unusual for a First Spiritualist – and she was smirking at people as if she was at a cocktail party rather than morning service.

Behind her I could see into what is rather optimistically known as the vestry – which is nothing more than a curtained-off area of the floor, rather like what you might see in a hospital casualty ward. Pike was standing by a wooden rack of pamphlets, including *What Has Old Mother Walsh to Say to Us?* and a large, colourful one for the kiddies entitled *Daddy isn't Dead, He's Just Gone Out for a Bit.*

Mrs Danby started up the steps, and we followed her. When she got to the large graph that shows the state of the church-roof appeal, she stopped and looked down at the waiting crowds as if she was a victorious politician looking down on her compliant voters. To avoid catching her eye, I looked at the graph. As far as I could tell, the roof seemed to be consuming money faster than we could give it.

She grabbed my hand and turned her wrinkled face to mine. 'You don't remember me, do you?' she said.

I didn't reply. I wanted to ask her if she was, by any chance, called Veronica, but I didn't dare.

She tossed her head and looked around at the congregation. 'I have not been to Service these few years,' she said. 'I have been in the Outer Darkness!'

Perhaps she had been abroad, to Africa or something. That would explain why I didn't recognize her. She was hard to miss, even among such a hand-picked collection of fruitcakes as the First Spiritualist Church.

'I was close to your father during his great crisis,' she said, 'and it was I who led him astray. Into other fields, other woods, other pastures that seemed sweet but were full, as it turned out, of stinking weeds!'

They had been on country rambles together, was that it?

'And now', she went on, 'I am hearing Norman again. I am hearing him loud and clear. You are helping me, Simon. And when you are one with us, when you have plunged your head in the cold, clear waters of baptism, then my great sin will be forgiven. I stole the father and gave Him back the son!'

I didn't like the sound of any of this – especially the bit about plunging the old head in the cold, clear waters of baptism. But there was nothing I could say. I still had this uncomfortable feeling that I did know her. That she belonged to some time, when I was a little kid, that had somehow been barred from my memory.

Down below, Roger Beeding was beginning the traditional question-and-answer routine that always comes before you go into the morning service.

BEEDING: Shall we go in and worship?
CONGREGATION: Let us.
BEEDING: How shall we go in and worship?
CONGREGATION: On our feet.
BEEDING: How shall we worship when we are within?
CONGREGATION: On our knees.
BEEDING: How shall we go before the Living God, if He appears before us?
CONGREGATION: On our bellies . . .

I used to have a friend, the only other boy of my age in the congregation, before he went to Nottingham. He and I had a version of the Introit that went:

BEEDING: How shall we stand in the church?
CONGREGATION: On our heads.
BEEDING: What may we hold when we are within?
CONGREGATION: Our penises.
BEEDING: How may we hold them?
CONGREGATION: Well and tightly . . .

I thought of him now – he was called Mike Jarvis and he was a great skateboarder – as the congregation swept up the steps, past me and Mrs Danby, and Pike triumphantly pushed back the curtain to reveal the inner sanctum of the First Church of Christ the Spiritualist.

It was a sight as familiar to me as my own front room. A large, empty room with high, narrow windows through which the bright day filtered slowly on to various shades of brown. Brown linoleum on the floor, brown chairs, arranged in neat rows, and, on the walls, pictures and photographs and testimonials from dead spiritualists, all of them, it seemed to me, written in faded brown ink and confined to faded brown frames.

At the back of the raised platform at one end of the hall was a wooden cross, about six feet high. That, too, was brown. As we trooped in for the service, the sun caught it and, for a moment, I had a vision of what it must have really looked like, all those years ago, when they nailed poor old JC up before the people, one bright day in Palestine.

At the far end of the hall, Quigley was showing Mrs Danby to what looked like a comfortable chair. There aren't many of those in the First Church. And, up on the platform, Roger Beeding was calling the faithful.

'How are we now?' he called.

'We are in the church!' called back the congregation.

'How are our voices?' he called.

And they replied, 'They are rich and fruitful!'

Mr Toombs raised both his arms. He looked like Dracula about to make a maiden flight. 'Let us,' he said, 'praise the Lord!'

We had started. There was no going back. And all I could think, as the service began, was *the whole truth of my heart! I am supposed to tell the whole truth of my heart!*

16

In the autumn of 1924, the young Rose Fox was visited by the spirit of Wolfgang Amadeus Mozart. He told her that, in a previous life, *she* had actually been the composer of *Eine Kleine Nachtmusik*, and, while she was in a trance, he dictated his new work to her – a Concerto in G for harp, oboe and string orchestra. The piece was performed in Wimbledon Town Hall in 1926, and the consensus was that, in 130-odd years, Wolfgang had not really developed musically. Some people were so bold as to suggest that he had now lost his grip and was writing pretty fair garbage.

It didn't stop at Mozart. It turned out that Rose Fox had been an awful lot of people in previous lives – mostly male, and all of them, apart from a rather dull-sounding galley slave in 34 BC, rather famous or important. These people have always Done Things in previous lives, perhaps to make up for their rather undistinguished efforts while being alive and in their own bodies.

Anyway, one of the people Rose Fox had been was John Wesley. And, from what I hear, her Wesley was a lot nearer the mark than her Mozart. He dictated to her many of the hymns that are still in use by the First Church of Christ the Spiritualist

– many of whose tunes are exactly the same – bar one or two
notes – as the ones the *real* John Wesley cobbled together in
the eighteenth century. Rose's Uncle Eustace, who lived upstairs
in her parents' home when she was a girl, was, incidentally, a
staunch Methodist.

The better Wesley went down, the more she did him. Mozart
didn't write much after the concerto for harp, oboe and string
orchestra, apart from an unfinished Requiem Mass, which no
one could be persuaded to perform. But Wesley went on to
write hymns, give advice and generally add shape, colour and
texture to the ritual life of the First Spiritualist Church.

He was pretty gnomic by all accounts. He didn't say, 'Right,
men – come in by twos, line up facing east and bang your
foreheads on the floor!' He would come out with lines like,
'Let your words to God be as the noise of Esau!' Which meant
that, for a couple of weeks, an amazing amount of shouting
went on. So much so that Wesley came back with, 'And yet,
softness be a virtue.' He did sound a bit Mummerset from time
to time.

One of the first bits of advice he gave the First Church was,
'Bend the knee, but not unwisely.' With the result that, to this
day, the guys spend a lot of the service in a kind of crouching
position.

He also said, 'Wave thine extremities and be joyful.' Which led
to all sorts of strange behaviour. People finally settled on a kind
of threshing movement of both arms, which, when combined
with the crouch, made the congregation look like a group of
canoeists on a particularly tough stretch of water.

But the most important thing Wesley told Rose Fox was, 'Let
there be constant movement in thy church.' He stuck to that.
In fact, he kept on repeating it. And he made it clear that he
wasn't talking about regular reallocation of senior positions in the
church. So, by the late 1980s, the services resembled the kitchen

of a fast-food restaurant during a busy lunch hour. People would get up, go to the opposite end of the room, jig about, go back to their seat (or, better still, someone else's), get up again and jog round the perimeter of the hall.

As Rose got older, Wesley's orders got stranger and stranger. Most people agreed that things had gone a bit far when he told the church, in 1982, to 'Face north-west whenever possible.' Did this mean when in the middle of the service? Or did it mean just what it said? Were we going to be looking at guys backing into the path of oncoming lorries in order to preserve the decencies? How about the old *sexual intercourse*? Were spiritualists going to be forced to do it in strange, and possibly overexciting, positions?

I'd love to be forced to do it in strange positions. It's my dream.

Most people ignored this commandment, although I have heard it said that Pike was to be seen with a compass on a number of occasions, trying to align himself correctly. It turned out the reason we all had to face north-west was because it was the direction 'from which Rose had come forth'! She was born in Liverpool. A year or so later she told everyone that they must make an annual pilgrimage to that city, where she had a cousin in the catering trade who was prepared to give them all cheap rates, but by that time Rose was losing her grip on the faithful.

We started with Healing. People are always being Healed down at the church. It is certainly easier to get the medical treatment dished out by Roger Beeding's wife than it is to get to see your local GP. She does patients in job lots, which is a system I could recommend to the Mayberry Clinic, Wimbledon.

'Stand before if you wish Healing,' said Beeding, and his wife – a short, dumpy woman called Clara – walked out in front of the congregation, her eyes tightly shut.

In a high, squeaky voice, she said, 'Come to me in Jesus' name!'

The usual bunch of hypochondriacs shuffled forward. Clara Beeding opened her eyes and looked quite relieved to see Jasper Lewens, Tracy Johnson and the guy with the wart. She had dealt with a case of peritonitis in 1985, and apparently it didn't work out too well.

'It's my neck,' Jasper Lewens was saying in a rather whingeing tone. 'It won't leave me alone!'

Before Lewens could moan on any longer, Clara Beeding put out her hand and touched the side of his head. 'Your pain,' she said, with fantastic confidence, 'is going!'

Jasper started to rub his neck furiously.

'O Jesus mine,' went on Clara, 'see the pain! See how the pain is going from this man! See how it leaves his body and becomes at one with Thy Word!'

Before he had a chance to respond, Clara had moved on to Tracy Johnson. Tracy has a thing I can only describe as Non-specific Pain. Some weeks it's in her head, some weeks it's in her chest and some weeks it's in her legs. This week it was in her womb. 'O Lord Jesus,' she kept saying, 'it is in my womb!'

Tracy isn't as easy to deal with as Jasper. She likes to make sure everyone knows exactly where the pain is, how long it goes on for and whether it's burning, stabbing, singeing or a combination of all three.

But, before she could really get under way, from one side of the church, the one that leads out to the dustbins, came a group of three or four people one of whom I recognized as Sheldon Parry, the born-again television director. Sheldon, who is a really nice bloke and very fond of children, was pushing an elderly lady in a wheelchair. She looked quite happy to be in the wheelchair. Or maybe she was happy at the fact that, in a few minutes, after a couple of minutes' contact with Clara

Beeding's right mitt, she would be skipping around with the best of them.

Clara did not look best pleased to see her. The peritonitis wasn't her only disaster. She had gone badly wrong – so my dad said – with a case of genital herpes. You could tell that she was looking forward to doing her number on the wart. She knows where she is with a wart. But she didn't flinch. She turned away from Tracy Johnson and went straight to the woman in the chair.

'O Lord!' she said, speaking extra loud to drown out Tracy mumbling on about her womb. 'O Jesus, who made the blind to see and the lame to walk, look down on this woman!'

The old lady looked up at her. Clara stretched out her hands and held them above her client's head. She was not going to back down on this one, you could tell. 'You can walk!' she said, in a throaty voice.

'No I can't!' said the old lady, sounding rather perky. 'I can't walk at all. That's why I'm here.'

Clara gave a little silvery laugh and stretched out her hand again until it was about an inch from the old lady's permanent wave. 'Rise up!' she said. 'Rise up and walk!'

The old lady struggled for a bit and then subsided back into her chair. 'I can't!' she said, sounding rather apologetic. 'I really can't. I'm sorry, but I can't walk!'

For a moment I thought Clara was going to give the old woman a piece of her mind. Didn't she understand? You don't get *better* down at the First Spiritualist Church. You get Healed. The two are not necessarily the same thing at all. And she hadn't said *when* the disagreeable old trout was going to walk. It might be next week, or a year next Tuesday. She might, at least, look a bit grateful at Mrs Beeding's taking all this trouble over her.

Before things could get really awkward, there was a movement from the other end of the hall. It was Quigley. He always knows when to provide a distraction. 'I have News!' he said. 'I have Great News!'

There is always News at morning service, and it is usually Great News. It can be news of a member of the congregation's promotion, or someone's marriage, or – even better – someone being run over by a lorry, but there is always news. On a slow day, Quigley just goes through the newspapers and rambles on about whatever comes into his brain. One year, I remember, he gave us half an hour on John McEnroe being slung out of the Men's Singles.

This morning, I had a horrible feeling that the news might be something to do with me.

Quigley pushed his way forward towards the platform as the woman in the wheelchair was hustled away and the man with the wart returned, rather miserably, to his place in the congregation. Quigley had with him, I noticed, a brown box.

'I have News,' he said, 'about one of Us!'

I coughed nervously. Quigley leaned down, picked up the box and, from it, pulled out something that looked like a waffle iron.

'This,' he said, 'is a paper-stripper!'

People nodded seriously.

'It strips off,' said Quigley, archly. Quite a number of heads turned in my direction.

'It strips off old wallpaper so that new paper can be hung. New starts can be made on old walls!'

Suddenly his face grew dark with anger. His voice climbed a couple of octaves. 'But stripping paper isn't the answer,' he yelled – 'it isn't the answer if the wall is basically *no good*!'

People nodded some more.

'This paper-stripper,' he went on, 'isn't doing God's work! Because God, like us, cannot work with substandard materials. We are going to throw it aside!'

The man next to me looked a touch apprehensive. The paper-stripper was about a foot long and nine inches wide. It looked as if it was quite solidly constructed.

'Away you go, old paper-stripper!' screamed Quigley, as he raised the device high over the heads of the congregation. 'You are only so much *rubbish*! Go forth!' And, suiting the action to the words, he hurled the metal object towards the opposite wall, narrowly missing Hannah Dooley as he did so. It crashed into the flowerpots on the whitewashed ledge under the window, raining pottery, bits of geranium and John Innes Number 3 Compost all over the congregation.

They loved it. You could hear them gasp as Quiggers reached out his arm to them.

'But in this church,' he said, 'is a virgin piece of wall. A piece of wall that is clean and firm and decent even when the paper has been stripped away from it!'

I had a nasty feeling that I was part of this do-it-yourself metaphor. I stood there looking up at him, wishing that someone would demolish me.

Mrs Quigley, as always, was on cue. 'Have you got News, Albert?'

He looked at her blankly. Yes, you could see him thinking, I have damaged a vitally important piece of domestic equipment!

'News for us, Albert?'

Quigley was still reeling from the impact of his great gesture. He was, of course, the man who had once brought in a cup, painted black on the inside and white on the outside, and, after pointing out its close resemblance to the soul of the average sinner, had jumped up and down on it, foaming at the mouth. But the paper-stripper! This was something that would be hard to beat.

'News?'

'News!' said Quigley, and then looked across at me. For a moment I thought he was going to get back to the DIY metaphor and start to try to get them to see me as undercoat or Jesus Christ as primer, but, instead, he recovered himself enough to say, 'Great News!'

There was a sort of rhubarb effect from the pit. 'What news?' 'Great news?' 'What be this news?' 'News, they say!' etc. etc.

Quigley looked in the direction in which he had hurled the paper-stripper as his old lady repeated, 'O Jesus, Great News!' She raised her hands above her head, trying to get this going. 'O Jesus Christ!' she said.

You could see that the temperature needed raising. A few people came back with 'O Jesus!' or 'Yes, Jesus!' but nobody was ready for talking in tongues or, indeed, listening to people talking in tongues, which I have often thought is much the more taxing of the two options.

'Is it News about a boy?' she asked, reminding me of an actor working with someone who has completely forgotten his lines.

Quigley was looking at her blankly. 'A boy . . .' he said, his heart still with the wallpaper-stripper.

'What's the boy's name?' asked Pike.

Short of giving the guy cue sheets, there was not much else we could do. Quigley's eyes shifted, weasel-like, from me, to Pike, to his old lady. At the far side of the church, old Mr Pugh, who had swallowed about half a kilo of compost, was coughing furiously.

'Yes,' said Hannah Dooley, who gave the appearance of one prepared to be genuinely surprised by the answer, 'What *is his name*?'

Quigley very slowly raised his right hand. I had the impression that if he didn't come through on this one soon his position was going to be in very grave danger. Life at the top end of the First

Spiritualist Church has a sharp, corporate edge to it. But, before our eyes, he seemed to find strength. The first two fingers closed together as if he was a little kid pretending he had a gun. He extended his arm fully and began to waggle it in an arc across the faces of the congregation.

'It's a very special name,' he said.

It was still hard to tell whether he had actually cottoned on to what the name was. But quite often Quigley will keep his audience in such a state of suspense that he forgets what it was he intended to say.

'O Lord!' said Mrs Q. She looked a bit happier now. Hannah Dooley was looking as if she might do something usefully hysterical at any moment. The woman next to Mr Pugh seemed to be in tears, but that might have been due to the compost.

'It's a beautiful name,' said Quigley. 'A beautiful and holy name!'

'Yes,' said Pike, his eyes glinting madly behind his wire glasses, 'but what is the name?'

He sounded, I thought, a touch peevish about this – although years of supporting Quigley might make any man edgy. I wasn't sure. A strange change had come over Leo in the last week or so. Of all of the First Spiritualists, he was the only one who seemed, in some way, to have been affected by this business with my dad. Why should that be?

'There's an S in it!' said Quigley, who was still keeping his cards pretty close to his chest.

'Ohhh!' said the congregation.

This was all getting a bit like the Paul Daniels show.

'There's an I in it!' said Quigley.

'Ohhhh!'

'And an M and an N and an E!'

I wondered who he was talking about. A new recruit called Smein, possibly.

'And an O!' said Quigley, sounding a bit perturbed.

Maybe he was talking about someone called Simone. Or a new Japanese Christian called Monsei. Not that it mattered. No one is liable to comment on a renegade E in the First Church. Quigley was now back on course, and you could feel the relief in the audience.

'It's a SIMON!' he said.

'Ohhhh!' moaned the punters.

The paper-stripper was forgotten. He could have flung fifty paper-strippers at them now and they wouldn't have minded. 'It's a SIMON!'

Or a Smonie or a Nemois.

I felt myself propelled towards the stage. Terry Melchett, the supermarket manager, whose wife left him for another woman, gave me a hard shove in the small of the back. Kate Melville and Sue d'Argy Smith, whose daughters left the church, as so many do, just before they became nubile, each took a hand and gave it a sharp pull, and over their heads came the long arms of Gordon the Bachelor, whose fingers stroked my hair, as countless other key personnel in the body of Christendom, South Wimbledon stroked, shoved, pulled and all but *carried* me towards the stage on which I was supposed to pour out the secrets of my heart.

'We're going to sing!' shouted Quigley.

There is no order of hymns in the First Spiritualist Church. You sing as the spirit moves. Sometimes two different sections of the congregation will be belting out two completely different numbers.

'What are we going to sing?' called someone at the back.

There was a lot more rhubarb, along the lines of 'Yes, what?' and 'What *are* we going to sing, brothers?' and then Mrs Quigley cut in over the top of this with a cadenza that would not have disgraced Dame Kiri Te Kanawa.

'Te-e-e-sti-fyyy!'

We all looked around. There was a hunting-horn quality to this which suggested that someone else was supposed to get up and answer. They did.

'What shall we Te-e-e-stify?' sang young Mr Pugh.

'We shall tes-ti-i-i-fyy,' sang Mrs Quigley, to a tune that seemed to be completely of her own devising, 'to-o-o the-e-e Lor-or-ord!'

'Give me a one!' said Quigley.

Over by the piano, Mary Bunn squirmed on her piano stool and gave him a one.

'Give me a two!' said Quigley.

Next to Mary Bunn, Big Louie the Jamaican, on drums, gave him a two.

'Give me a *three*!' said Quigley.

Next to Big Louie the Jamaican, Sylvia Margaret Williams, our seventy-nine-year-old bass guitarist, gave him a three.

Quigley leaped into the air like a monkey that has sat on a bunsen burner and gave a sort of primal grunt. The First Spiritualists needed no encouragement. They had done this before and they would do it again. As one voice they went into one of Rose Fox's greatest hits:

> Testify! Testify!
> Take your troubles to the Lord!
> Testify! Testify!
> Take your troubles to the Lord!
> Take your troubles—
> Oh take your troubles—
> Take your trou-ou-ou-oubles—
> Take your troubles to the Lord!

There is more, I fear. I don't think it was dictated to her by John

Wesley. But, when in doubt, it is the one we always reach for. Great truths are always simple, right? And, whatever else you might want to say about this number, you would have to admit it was simple. The tune sounds as if it was dictated to Rose Fox by a three-year-old child.

The band hit their instruments harder and harder and the congregation started to stamp in time.

> Testify! Testify!
> Take your troubles to the Lord!

The walls were shaking. On the roof above me, the shabby light-shades shook on their long flexes. The glass of the windows shook in its wooden frames. Mary Bunn, hitting the keys harder and harder for Jesus, lifted herself off the stool and brought her bum down with a crash as she laid down chord after chord. The congregation were like different parts of a huge engine, each one passing a movement on and the recipient taking it up and changing it. It was as if there was a wave of water and the wave turned a wheel and the wheel turned a cog and the cog turned a piston and the piston punched out a wave, bigger and more overwhelming than the first wave, turning a bigger wheel, a bigger cog, a bigger piston and then finally a wave that seemed enough to swallow everything in its path. The whole crowd was shouting, like some awful, natural machine.

> Testify! Testify!
> Take your troubles to the Lord!
> Testify! Testify!
> Take your troubles to the Lord!

As I got closer to the raised platform at the far end of the church, it was as if the sound was pushing me forward. The sound was shaking the roof and rocking the floor. It was rapping in my back as I was pushed past Roger Beeding and Roger de Mornay and closer and closer to the eight steps that led up to the low wooden platform on which was the gigantic cross and the large black-and-white photograph of Rose Fox.

It was only when I was actually up there and the music had stopped, and I found myself looking down at a hundred or so expectant faces, that I remembered the magnitude of the task in front of me. I had not only to Testify as to how, where and when the Lord Jesus had entered my heart but also to give the punters a detailed account of the innermost secrets of my heart. What I felt about life, my immediate family, the church and the wider issues facing society. Such as the full-scale invasion of SW19 by extraterrestrial beings.

I did not feel confident of my ability to do any of these things. But I was dead sure that the last item would take some getting round to.

'Hi, guys!' I said, eventually, 'I'm Simon Britton. Remember me?'

17

This got a laugh.

People do laugh in meetings of the First Church of Christ the Spiritualist. In fact, they do just about everything short of brushing their teeth, but this was what I would call a really *good* laugh, if you know what I mean. I felt they were really pleased to see me. They were genuinely amused.

Suddenly, Testifying didn't seem such a big deal. You know? I was just going to tell them about all the things that were on my mind, about my dad and about Jesus and about aliens taking over the . . .

I looked round at the faces. They didn't look ready for aliens. Not yet. Not in sw19, anyway. I must work round to the subject gradually.

'Basically,' I went on, 'I'm fourteen. You know?'

There was another laugh. A sort of happy, let's-all-be-friends-there's-no-problem kind of laugh.

'And', I went on, doing something a bit casual with my hands, 'being fourteen can be a hass! Right?'

'Right,' said a small, fat man in the front row whom I could not remember ever having seen before.

Sooner or later I was going to have to turn this conversation round to Jesus Christ. I figured it was better to start with Jesus. They knew where they were with Him.

'I'm at Cranborne School,' I said, 'and I'm doing GCSEs in two years' time.'

This didn't go down quite as well. I could feel them getting restive.

'In biology, chemistry and physics,' I continued, 'geography, IT, English, French, Latin, Spanish and maths. Which is not my best subject!'

They did not want to know this.

'But', I said, 'I haven't come here to talk about my exam prospects!'

'No,' said a voice from the back of the hall, 'you have not!'

I flung my arms wide.

'Right, too right!'

What had I come here to talk about? Jesus Christ.

'Jesus Christ!' I said.

'Amen,' said Quigley, rapidly.

'Amen,' said everybody else.

This seemed safe ground. It wasn't too committing. It was giving everyone a lot of pleasure. And it was certainly an improvement on my thoughts about the core curriculum. I tried it again.

'Jesus Christ!'

'Amen,' said Quigley.

'Amen,' said everyone else.

Maybe I should just go on doing this all night. You know?

'Jesus Christ!' I said.

There was a pause.

'Amen,' said Quigley, rather grudgingly.

'Amen,' said everyone else.

I was going to have to get to the point.

'The other day, my father died.'

They liked this. A sort of appreciative hush fell upon them.

'He went out to the . . . er . . . pub, and he had a heart attack and he died!'

'Alleluia!' said the strange fat man in the front row, who was clearly new to this sort of thing.

'But,' I went on quickly, 'very soon after this, he turned up outside our house at 24 Stranraer Gardens!'

There was a lot of nodding. This was par for the course, they seemed to be saying. You kicked off, you had the death experience and back you came to tell people about it.

'When did you make contact?' asked old Mr Pugh, who seemed to have recovered completely from the compost. I really was going to have to get round to discussing the extraterrestrial problem. We could be here all night rapping about the finer points of mediumship.

'It all depends what you mean by *making contact*. And who you're making contact with. We all talk about making contact, don't we? It's one of our big things as . . . er . . . Christians, which of course we all are. But this contact I am talking about is a terrifying, although of course in a way wonderful, but also terrifying, form of . . . er . . . contact.'

This was very well received. I've noticed that in sermons of any kind it is important not to state your hand too early, or too clearly. You have to dress it up a bit. You know? You may have come there to say something really basic like, 'Sin is Bad!' or 'God is Good!' but it is crucial to start by talking about your Auntie Renee's operation, or why your dog was sick in the back of the car on the M4. Were they ready for me to get closer in?

'What I have to say,' I went on, 'is *so* important and *so* . . . vital that at first it may be difficult to believe. You may say, "Oh no! That Simon's a loony!" You know?'

'We won't!' called Quigley, with what I feared was misplaced optimism.

'You may say, "Cart Simon off to the nuthouse!" You know?'

'Amen,' said Hannah Dooley.

'Alleluia!' said the fat man in the front row.

It was now or never. I had to go in, and go in fast.

'If I were to tell you,' I said, trying to look each one of them in the eye, which is not an easy thing to do with ninety-odd people, 'that Wimbledon was being invaded by alien beings from another planet, you would probably laugh and call me a lunatic. Right?'

They did not look as if that was the case, actually. If anything, they seemed rather receptive to the idea of talking about the invasion of the locality by monsters from deep space. The fat man in the front row was shaking his head vigorously. He obviously wanted aliens on the agenda of the First Spiritualist Church.

'But,' I said slowly, looking round the hall, 'I think I have evidence – *clear* evidence – that something of this sort is going on, right here, under our very noses in our . . .' I groped for the right word and found it '. . . Christian community.'

We were on course here. We had said goodbye to GCSE options and we were on course. The awful thing was that, as I said it, I began to have serious doubts about it. As if what I thought and what I said were two completely different things. But I found myself looking straight at Pike. And he was leaning forward on his chair, his hands clasped together. He was nodding! He seemed so attentive, so clued in to my every word, that I suddenly found the confidence to go on. In a kind of rush I went back to the main menu.

'Well, I can't be very specific about them. About who they are or why they are doing it or what they want. But all I can say is that I am *certain* that there is, as I speak, an extraterrestrial presence in the area. They are *here*, guys. As is, of course, Jesus Christ!'

I thought I had better bring things back to Jesus. And it certainly did help. People were nodding seriously, as they tended to do when you mentioned JC.

'I know that a lot of people find this sort of thing ridiculous. A lot of people dismiss it out of hand. But I don't think they should. Impossible things can be true. I *saw* my father, I am telling you – out in the street. And he's dead!'

At the back I could see Quigley purse his lips. He did not, I have to say, look at all pleased. *Jesus*, I thought to myself. *Work in Jesus. Now!*

'Jesus,' I said, 'healed the sick and raised the dead.'

'Alleluia!' said the fat man in the front row.

'And a lot of people found that ridiculous!' I realized as I said it that this could sound a little tactless. Especially in view of the fact that, in the far corner, the old lady in the wheelchair was making determined but unsuccessful efforts to get up and walk.

'Not,' I went on, 'the sick and the dead, of course. They were very glad to be helped in that way. But the cynics, who refused to believe the *evidence* of their eyes. People who scoffed. People who sneered at what others truly believed.'

This was good. Quigley was looking foxed. Everything I was saying was, so far anyway, completely acceptable Christian dogma. As far as I knew. Although what is and is not acceptable in the First Church of Christ the Spiritualist changes from minute to minute.

'Aliens,' I went on, 'are somewhere out there in the universe. It stands to reason that in such vast space there must be some other beings. Are we saying that God has absolutely no imagination at all? That all he can come up with is a few rotten old . . . humans?'

This was even better. The old direct questions seemed to be quite a good technique. You could see them struggling for answers and coming up with nothing at all. I tried a few more, in quick succession.

'Has something happened in your life that you can't explain? Have you seen something that just doesn't fit into the normal pattern of things? Do you have a feeling, for example, that you are being watched?'

'Alleluia!' said the fat man in the front row. He was on my side, guys. He could stay. I raised my voice slightly. At the back Quigley was looking very worried indeed. If he was going to interrupt, he had left it a little late.

'Are you,' I continued, 'unable to lay your hands on familiar domestic objects, and have you come to the conclusion that someone must be moving them?'

Hannah Dooley, who is notoriously absent-minded, was nodding furiously. I paused dramatically and raked the audience with my eyes the way I had seen Quigley do.

'Who do you think might be responsible for all these things you can't explain? Who do you think might be here, even as we stand here in Christian worship? Who might be walking among us even as we pray to the Lord Jesus?'

'Aliens!' shouted Pike with sudden tremendous enthusiasm.

'Aliens!' yelled Hannah Dooley.

'Alleluia!' said the fat man in the front row.

Quigley was white with fury. I saw him whisper something to Mrs Danby, but she didn't seem to hear him. But it was too late for Quigley. 'If you really want something, boy,' my dad used to say, 'then go for it!' I went for it.

'Aliens,' I continued, 'are right here at this moment! They have landed! And I have *conclusive proof* !'

There was more rhubarb. 'He has proof!' 'Conclusive proof!' 'He says he has proof, Mabel!' etc. I stopped for a second and tried to think what my conclusive proof was. The thought of describing it out loud to over a hundred people made it feel less convincing than I thought it had been.

'A close friend of mine called Mr Andrew Marr has *disappeared*!'

I saw Pike's weather-worn little face watching me with intense concentration. 'Aliens!' he yelled. He was getting the idea quickly, guys. Years of intensive training in the paranormal had taught him how to draw these kinds of conclusions with consummate speed.

'Aliens!' I said. 'And these same aliens have also . . .'

Here I paused again. I gave the next three words a great deal of lip and tongue work.

'. . . taken my father!'

Here I raised my hand to heaven and shook my fist at the sky. My voice rose an octave or two as I screamed, 'Give him back, you bastards!'

'Give him back, you bastards!' yelled Pike.

'Aliens!' yelled Hannah Dooley.

'Alleluia!' said the fat man in the front row.

Quigley made his move. But both he and I knew it was too late. He sounded positively mealy-mouthed as, with a great show of wonder and puzzlement, he started to say, 'These aliens . . .'

'Yes,' I said, sticking with the simple idea, 'Aliens! These aliens!'

'Aliens,' said Pike, dead on cue, 'are come amongst us, my friends! Hear! Hear the word of the Lord!'

If there had been any danger from Quigley, it was headed off, once again, by Pikey, who dashed into a space by himself and, springing up and down like a goblin, started to shout, 'Hear the word of the Lord!' at regular intervals.

I could see Quigley was about to make another move, but before he could do so I held out my hands, palms downwards, in a gesture much favoured by Mr Toombs in his last ecclesiastical campaign. 'Let us pray,' I said.

'Oh, let us pray!' said Hannah Dooley.

'Pray!' squeaked Pike. 'Oh, let us pray!' He looked up at the ceiling. 'Old Mother Walsh,' he said, 'prithee the snake be not come!'

This went down very big with the lads. When she was feeling down, Old Mother Walsh was always going on about how the snake was slithering in our direction. It was entirely feasible, of course, that it should be at the controls of an interplanetary vehicle of some sort.

'Old Mother Walsh,' Pike said again, 'let not the snake come out of the sky!'

There was much murmuring of assent at this. You would have thought, from the way they were all carrying on, that they were all closet members of the British Interplanetary Society. Quigley was looking at me in open horror now. You could see that my attack had taken him completely by surprise. Even if he had wanted to try unmasking me, he wouldn't have dared. This was the most exciting News the First Church of Christ the Spiritualist had heard in years. They were bored with all this let's-hear-it-for-Galilee-purify-your-heart rubbish. Even talking to the dead can pall. They wanted Simon Britton.

'Let us pray,' I said, 'that this . . . alien menace be . . . dealt with! By the . . . proper authorities and by . . .'

'Jesus Christ,' said Quigley, smartly.

'Alleluia!' said the fat man in the front row.

'Amen,' said Hannah Dooley.

'Because,' I said, looking straight at Quigley, 'don't let's kid ourselves. There are other planets and there *are* people on them, and from time to time those people may well want to get on board ship and head down here. And if we *refuse* to believe that, we're being like the mockers and the sneerers who refuse to believe in the Lord Jesus Christ. Because belief . . .'

Here I raised my right hand and pointed my index finger
straight at the bearded one. He didn't flinch. He looked straight
back into my eyes.

'. . . is the important thing in the world. And arguing for
what you believe, however stupid or illogical or plain mad it may
seem. And standing up for what *you* choose to believe against
those wicked people who just want you to believe what they tell
you. Who just want to take over your mind and not let you think
for yourself. Who . . .'

'Who welcome the snake!' said Pike.

I had a sudden vision of a reception committee for the snake.
It wasn't difficult to imagine it wriggling out of a cigar-shaped
object on Wimbledon Common.

Pike did a sort of wild leap and whirled round to face the
congregation. 'Aliens!' he said, sounding like the compère at a
Hallowe'en party.

What I had said had clearly got to Pikey in a major way.
Maybe I was more eloquent than I thought. It was only much
later that I remembered my speech had been more or less word
for word something my dad had said to me once. It was funny
– when my dad had said it to me it seemed like the rather tired,
friendly sort of thing that parents often say to you. Spoken, or
rather screamed, by yours truly in the First Church of Christ the
Spiritualist, it was *dynamite*.

It certainly put the wind up Quigley. He didn't say anything at
all as, led by his former lieutenant, the congregation swarmed up
to the dais and lifted me high on their shoulders. Yelling 'Aliens!
Jesus!' and 'Aliens are come!' and 'Prithee the snake not be here!'
in about equal proportions, they carried me round the body of
the hall. I shook my hair back and waved my arms above my
head as Pike mopped and mowed in front of me and the band
struck up an impromptu tune.

I could have been old JC himself, I tell you, riding into

Jerusalem on his donkey, ready to spread the Good News. I could have been one of those prophets who foretold him. I could have been almost anyone I chose that day. I had testified, all right. I had put Unidentified Flying Objects right back on the agenda where they belonged, and, from this day forth, the First Church of Christ the Spiritualist was never going to be the same again.

18

That, more or less, is how the First Spiritualist Church experienced its last and greatest schism. I mean, it was ripe for it. I sometimes like to think it was my eloquence, but the fact of the matter is that if I had got up on my hind legs and suggested a bit of karaoke instead of the morning service, they would have leaped at it. They were ripe for change, and, as it happened, I couldn't have chosen a better subject with which to widen the scope of the church's activities. Or, indeed, to discomfort Quigley.

There was, as I subsequently discovered, quite a high crossover between ufology and fundamentalist Christianity. Hannah Dooley knew a bloke in Birmingham who had been set on by a group of small 'pod-like' creatures while out walking his dog. They did a number of very unpleasant things to him and left him, dazed and confused, at New Street station at two in the morning. Mr Toombs had been a founder member of the British Premonitions Bureau in 1967 (it registered 500 premonitions, most of which were concerned with major transport disasters). The place was a powder keg.

It wasn't only ufology. There were six clairvoyants, four water diviners and nine people who had had direct contact with poltergeists. They all wanted space. Sheldon Parry, it turned out, was a life member of the Society for Psychical Research and had been deeply involved until he had lost his library books. They all needed to express what they felt.

All I did was get things started. There had always been schisms in the First Church of Christ the Spiritualist. There had been Lewis, the guy who was down on cutlery and condiments, and much earlier a bloke called Evans, who maintained that Old Mother Walsh was really a man in drag and that it behoved members of the church 'to wear the clothes of the other kind'. Evans was arrested in Piccadilly in 1908, wearing 'lace petticoats and stays and drinking from an opened spirit bottle'.

And there were a lot of memories. You know? Since the days of Ella Walsh, the real main event had been table-rapping, but people in the church still talked about Old Mother Walsh and her prophecies. It wasn't only the snake with TWO THOUSAND YEARS GO BY on it. There was a whole lot of other stuff scheduled for the beginning of the second millennium: green rain, black snow, animals learning to talk and a heck of a lot of red-hot hail. One guy had already arranged to sell his house and go and live in the Caribbean in 1998 because, as he said, 'You might as well have a decent last couple of years.'

I don't think I would have made quite so much impact, however, if it hadn't been for the fact that, while they were carrying me round the church yelling, 'Aliens!' 'Jesus Christ!' and 'The snake cometh!' the roof fell in. I say 'fell in'. In religion these terms are relative. You know? One minute Jesus is a sort of cross between Batman and Captain America, next thing he is 'just a bloke with a few special powers', and before you know it he is a deranged Jew with a no more than ordinary claim on our imaginations. A couple of sheets of corrugated iron broke loose and fell on Mr Pugh's head. That was all. But it was enough. In a week or so you would have thought a crowd of angels had wafted in from Putney singing my name and crying 'Hosanna!'

The burning bush, right? I mean, did it? You know? Or did it just look kind of . . . reddish?

Nobody said much to me after the service. As we trooped out of the hall, the old lady in the wheelchair was still trying to get up and Clara Beeding was kneeling in front of her. I thought I heard her say, 'Go on, you can do it!'

A couple of people came up to shake my hand as we got into Quigley's car. He stood back, a tight smile on his face, as Roger de Mornay said, 'A beautiful, beautiful, beautiful speech!'

Once we were inside the car, Quiggers allowed himself a full-blooded sneer. 'Well, well,' he said, 'little green men!'

I didn't speak. In fact, nobody said much on the way back. Just as we came into Stranraer Gardens, Mrs Quigley said, 'We have worked so hard to bring you to the Lord, Simon! You cannot know how important to the church this is. Mrs Danby . . .'

Here Quigley cut her off sharply. 'Don't let's talk about Mrs Danby. I'm sure we can manage Mrs Danby, Marjorie!'

There was something really horrible about the way he said this. A pure flash of creepiness. I missed my dad more than ever as I went into the house, ahead of the others, and climbed the drab stairs to lie on my bed, looking out at the bright blue sky above the street.

After a while, the door to my bedroom opened and my mum's head peered round it. Her mouth was turned down and her little eyes were beady with worry. She blinked at me for a minute or two and then said, 'Aliens!'

I didn't respond. She clicked her tongue in the way she does when I eat peanut butter straight from the jar.

'Spacemen!' she went on.

I sighed.

Mum went over to my window and looked down at the street.

In a small, faraway voice, she said, 'Mr Quigley's awfully cross with you and Pike. He's very worried. He's very worried indeed. And he cares about you, Simon. He thinks about you and prays for you all the time. He does!'

She went out then, and left me alone.

The next week saw a constant procession of spiritualists in and out of our kitchen. Some of them came to talk seriously with Quigley and to shake their heads at me. Rather more, including Pike, came to shake me by the hand and ask me detailed and unanswerable questions about the nature of the extraterrestrials who had landed in the Wimbledon area. Once or twice, at mealtimes, I thought Quigley was going to speak to me about the matter. But he didn't. Usually he likes to get you alone, as, I have noticed, a lot of Christians do. So, when he suggested that we all go 'to furnish the larder' on Saturday morning, I thought I was reasonably safe.

Normal people go shopping. First Spiritualists go to furnish the larder.

Shopping is a tricky one for them. You have to be very careful when prowling along the shelves. A First Spiritualist doesn't drink coffee, or eat white bread or cheese (apart from Gorgonzola – the Good Cheese, as it's called), and faced by a frankfurter is liable to scoot off into a corner, whimpering. Nobody quite knows who decided all these things were dangerous and evil, or why they did so. But they take the rules pretty seriously. Branston Pickle is 'harmonious and honest', but all forms of sausage are, basically, in league with Beelzebub.

One of the reasons they go shopping in groups is because not everyone agrees about which foods are OK and which ones are going to plunge you into hellfire. Someone will reach for a jar of fish-paste only to be brought up short by another member of the party reminding them that fish-paste is unclean, while someone else may get as far as the checkout with a year's supply of baked beans, when, across the crowded shelves of the supermarket, comes a voice reminding them of the danger they are facing.

There are a lot of scores paid off when shopping. My dad used to love chocolate cake, and, whenever they were having a row, my mum would remember that chocolate was 'a poisonous thorn in the side of Creation'. At other times the two of them would wolf down a whole packet of After Eight mints with no apparent difficulty.

This Saturday we went with the Quigleys, Hannah Dooley, Pike, the Clara Beedings (as Roger and Clara are known) and, to my surprise and dismay, Mrs Danby. She showed up in her Rolls in the car park of the supermarket, and, although there was a lot of nodding and smiling and remarks about coincidences, it was pretty clear that her presence had been arranged for someone's benefit. I suspected it might be mine.

I hate going around in groups. Especially groups of people from the church. I'm terrified we might see Khan or Greenslade on a day when everyone has decided to follow Mother Walsh's directions about placing the feet on the ground without damaging the old insect life. But on this particular day we looked almost normal. Everyone was very friendly, and there was much jolly laughter as we passed the frankfurters and Quigley made as if to ward off the evil eye.

He waited until we were browsing through the chilled fish before raising the issue: 'Do you really think that Old Mother Walsh's snake is *actually* going to wriggle down Wimbledon High Street when the time comes?'

I didn't ask what time he meant. The time of Snakes Wriggling Down Wimbledon High Street, presumably.

'Er . . .'

My mum was piling tinned ravioli into the trolley. She looked like a small animal that expected to be surprised at any moment.

'I don't think you do, do you?' said Quiggers. 'I think you think, as I do, that Old Mother Walsh wasn't talking about a *real* snake. She was talking about the snake that is in all of us all the time!'

What snake was this? A tapeworm perhaps?

'A lot of the simpler souls,' said Quigley, 'probably think a great big snake is going to slither out at them and start gobbling them up in a few years.'

You could see from Pike's face that this was exactly what he thought. If this snake did show, I thought, please God it liked the taste of men with beards.

'Cor lumme, young shaver!' said Quigley. 'Your little green chaps are no more than that snake, really, are they? They are a way of saying, "The world's in pretty bad shape, Jesus, and pretty soon someone will come along and give us pain and suffering and woe." '

I looked him straight in the eye.

'No they're not. They're just *there*, that's all. And I never said they were green. What I said was, it looks as if they're here. You know?'

Quigley laughed. He was still being Mr Nice Guy. My mum had finished shovelling the ravioli into the trolley. She and Emily and Mrs Quigley were headed for toilet tissue at a brisk pace.

'Little talk with Jesus?' he said, and, halfway through reaching for a tube of tomato purée, he closed his eyes and froze solid as if overtaken by a large quantity of molten lava. I waited for him to finish.

When somebody pressed his PLAY button, I said, 'People think I'm stupid because I think there's something in this alien business. But I'm not!'

Quigley grabbed my arm. 'No, li'l' Simo,' he said. 'You are not. You are special! You are favoured.'

He rocked to and fro, his eyes half shut. On the line to Jesus once again. ' "A boy will come 'fore the snake's unfurled, and preach the woman to save the world!" ' he said. A bloke who was trying to get at the tomato purée gave him rather an odd look, but Quigley was not bothered. I recognized another of Old Mother Walsh's rhymes.

' "Go to the river in ones and twos, but be sure you put on your overshoes!" ' I quoted back at Quiggers.

He became enormously excited and, as the rest of the party started back towards us with a huge mound of lavatory paper balanced on the ravioli, he hopped from foot to foot, clutching my arm. Only Pike, I noticed, had stayed with us. He was watching Quigley, a sour look on his chapped little face.

'That,' said Quigley, 'is the point. Old Mother Walsh didn't always mean what she said to be taken *literally*. But, by God, the end of the world is coming and, by God, a pure and holy boy will preach the woman who will *speed his coming!*'

With these words, he pointed dramatically at Emily Quigley.

If anyone was going to be chosen to usher in the end of the world, she could well be the girl to do it. She had the face for it. Was this the deal? Did Quigley see me as some kind of John the Baptist figure? If he did, it wasn't surprising he was trying to get me Confirmed in Faith. Anything to make Emily Quigley look good. I may not be pure in heart, but, since Mike Jarvis the skateboarder went to live in Nottingham, I am about the only fourteen-year-old boy in the First Church of Christ the Spiritualist.

It gave me a spooky feeling, actually. Maybe he had a point. Maybe what I was saying wasn't so very different from what Old Mother Walsh had given the troops all those years ago.

He could see I was wavering, and he held my arm tightly as the others came up. 'Extraterrestrials', he said, 'may well be on their way. I don't dispute that. Who knows what the Lord will send us on Judgement Day? But, cor lumme, snakes and aliens don't have to be taken literally. All we know is that, as Mother Walsh said, *when the pure boy preaches the woman . . .'* – here he gave Emily a meaningful look – '. . . something pretty nasty is going to be heading in our direction. Don't call it aliens, Simo, call it Sin. Call it Wickedness. Call it Pain and Suffering!'

Pike gave him a curiously malevolent look. 'Call it aliens!' he said in a rather spooky, hollow voice. 'I know it's aliens!'

Quigley looked rattled. But, before he could say anything, Mrs Danby emerged from round a large pile of tins of tuna-fish. She was carrying an armful of cat-food cans and smirking to herself. Quigley, with a short, convulsive movement that was halfway between a bow and a twitch, took my hand and led me towards her. 'Here's your boy,' he said. 'Shall we away the noo?'

This whole thing had a prearranged feel. What were they going to do to me now? Take me out to a patch of waste ground and kick my head in for spreading dissent?

'Where are we going?'

'We have a sufficiency of ravioli,' said Mrs Quigley, 'and . . . er . . . Norman has something to say to us!'

'What?' I said.

They all started to look at each other rather furtively. Mrs Danby dumped the cat-food in the trolley and came close to me. She smelt of dried flowers and pepper. There were bags of skin under her neck, and she had a deep, posh, drawling voice, like an actress in an old film.

'Norman has specifically asked to talk to us at Mr Quigley's house,' she said. 'Even though the kitchen only half-completed!'

'Maybe', I said, with a completely straight face, 'he wants to see how the units are getting on.'

Mum gave an eager little nod. 'Yes . . . yes . . . maybe he does!'

I marvelled, once again, at the rapid change in my father's attitudes after his death. The last words he had spoken to me on the subject of kitchen units had been really quite abusive.

I wasn't at all sure about this. Look what had happened at the last seance. And, since then, there had been Mr Marr's disappearance and my dad's own, frightening version of the Second Coming. I couldn't bear the thought of hearing that voice again – the low, small voice like that of a child alone in a house at night.

'Do we have to?' I asked.

There was suddenly a very, very tense atmosphere. All of them were looking at me. Mum started to sing, in a light, quiet voice – something she only does when she is nervous. They had clearly been leading up to this all week.

'Oh, Simon,' Mrs Danby was saying. 'I led your father down dark and narrow ways. Ways strewn with thorns and brambles and alive with venomous snakes! And now the whole church is in danger!'

Quigley nodded vigorously. 'I think,' he said, with a rather savage look in Pike's direction, 'that we are in need of Guidance. Splits in the church, Master Pike! Splits in the church! Remember the Lewis Doctrine! Remember the Schismatics of New Malden!'

I had not heard anything about these guys. But as, presumably, they had been wiped off the face of the earth by someone pretty close to Ella Walsh or Rose Fox, there seemed little point in asking about them.

There was nothing I could say. I am fourteen. I have no rights. I followed them out into the car park and sat, miserably, in the back of Quigley's car as, in a mood of forced cheerfulness, we drove towards the Quigleys' house behind Mrs Danby's Rolls. I was squashed between Pike and Hannah Dooley in the back seat. The summer still hadn't gone away, although we were almost out of September. Above us, great masses of cumulus clouds stood out in the sky like old-fashioned sculptures.

The Quigleys live further out than us. To get to their house you drive down arterial roads lined with buildings that are neither warehouses nor shops. They squat on ragged patches of grass like abandoned containers, painted bright colours, stuffed with more than anyone could want of Do-It-Yourself Equipment, Garden Furniture or, in one case, Pure Leather.

The Quigleys live next to a park. Their house is semi-detached. It is worth £300,000. So Mr Quigley keeps saying. I wouldn't live in it if you paid me twice that amount. It is a big, square box painted dirty white, and, although he is always knocking through, extending, repapering and spring-cleaning, there is something dead about the place. The furniture stands around listlessly as if it is waiting to be sold. In the garden, the flowers and vegetables are as neat as Mr Quigley's accounts. There is an apple-tree up against the fence that separates them from their neighbours, but it has been given a kind of Buddhist monk's haircut. It does not look capable of bearing fruit.

The sun was still bright as we approached the Quigleys' house, but it didn't seem to have reached their road, which was the same as it ever was: dank and green and desperately quiet.

The first thing I noticed was that the whole of the top half of the house was swathed in what looked like green plastic bandages. There was scaffolding rearing up the face of the house from the front garden and, next to the front door, a large notice saying:

GORDON BRUNT
GENERAL BUILDER
SINCE 1964 SERVING SOUTH LONDON

Next to the notice was a fat man in blue dungarees and a white hard hat. He looked as if he might well be Gordon Brunt. He also looked as if his mission might be to make South London completely and utterly miserable. As the crowd of us came out of the car, he leaned backwards over Mr Quigley's fence and spat, slowly and deliberately, into the geraniums.

'What do they do, Marjorie?' said Quigley, with sudden and violent passion.

Mrs Quigley was curiously calm as she replied: 'They take our money. They abuse us. They leave their *filthy newspapers in the loo!*'

When she actually spoke to the guy she was quite amiable. 'Hallo, Kevin. Are there problems?'

Kevin looked at her blearily. 'It's a bastard, this one, Mrs Q,' he said. 'It's a real bastard!'

Quigley coughed. 'We need,' he said, rather stiffly, 'to use the house for prayer.'

Kevin looked at him suspiciously. 'You what?'

'We need,' said Quigley, with deliberate, offensive clarity, 'to use our dwelling to talk to the Lord Jesus Christ.'

Kevin looked at him doubtfully. 'I'm not sure about that,' he said. 'The plumbers are in.'

At this moment, a loud banging noise came from one of the upstairs windows. Quigley, who seemed not quite in control of himself, grabbed the man by the ears. 'This is my house, wherein I dwell. And I would be grateful if you could get up there and tell that *oaf* Duncan to stop whatever it is he is doing!'

I hadn't understood, until now, why it was so important for the Quigleys to make contact with my dad at their house. Now it was clear. When he's at home, Mr Quigley is even more masterful than he is in other people's houses. The man shambled off into the house, and the rest of us picked our way across the front garden.

As we came into the front hall I heard Kevin yelling up the stairs, 'Stop the hammering! They want to pray!'

'You what?' said an invisible plumber.

'They want to pray!' said Kevin.

A large, hairy youth came out of the bathroom at the head of the stairs. He was carrying what looked like a huge steel club. 'Why can't the idiots pray somewhere else?' he said. Then he saw Mr Quigley, and his hand went to his mouth. Quigley clearly had a master–slave relationship with these people.

'We will be in the back room,' said Quigley in tones of quiet authority, and, watched by several more astonished employees of Gordon Brunt Ltd, we all filed through into Quigley's dining-room.

The ceiling had been removed, and we were looking up at where the roof of the house once had been. That, as I had seen from the outside, was shrouded in green plastic, and, as all the windows seemed to have been boarded up, there was scarcely any light at all. It felt as if you were in the middle of some enormous forest where the trees had grown together, blocking out the day.

Quigley pushed the seance table into the middle of the room, grinning at me over his shoulder as he did so. 'We're rough and ready, young shaver,' he said. 'But we're homey, aren't we?'

His confidence, which had slipped a little since my Testifying, was coming back. Here, surrounded by his family, his vast collection of Gilbert and Sullivan records, his several hundred bound copies of *What Car* magazine, his three watercolours of Wimbledon under snow and his collection of rare antiques, he was a man again. Even though all these objects were shrouded in heavy-duty plastic, he was a man again.

'Shall we pray?' he said, in an insidious voice.

'Yes!' said Hannah Dooley.

Mum sat at the table and pushed the grey hair back from her eyes. She pressed her hands together. They were red and raw from cooking and washing, and the lines on her face seemed to have multiplied since I last looked at it. 'Norman,' she said quietly, 'is very, very near.' Mrs Danby, who was dressed in sporty tweeds, as if for a shooting party, gave a superior kind of nod. I wondered whether there was anything in the teaching of Tai-Ping that could get me through the next half an hour. I thought about *sei-sei-ying*, or the condition of being a birch leaf in early autumn, but did not find it helpful. What was needed here, rather than a meditative technique, was a pump-action shotgun.

I had no choice. They were all sitting waiting for me. With a mounting feeling of dread, I went to a chair at the far end of the table from Quigley and lowered my head in the gloom. Quigley stretched out both his arms across the table and looked up at what was left of his roof.

'O Jesus, we seek Thy help. As our church is itself in a confusion Thee Thyself often experienced when on this earth in places such as, for example, Gethsemane, which was, by anyone's standards, a pretty tough time for You. Hear us now as we attempt to contact Simon's father, and help him in the great spiritual work that awaits him in this prime time of his boyhood!'

He shot me a quick look from under those bushy brows. I kept my eyes down. Emily was looking at me in a way I found frankly flirtatious.

Suddenly Quigley stopped praying. His old lady was bearing down in her chair and generally showing signs of getting off the psychic runway in double-quick time. She hadn't even frothed yet.

I was two down from her, but I could see Hannah Dooley wince as Marjorie started. Quigley stopped, clearly expecting her to give it a bit of movement, but, instead, she went into a sort of mammoth clench. She bound her brows and bit her lower lip and generally carried on like someone with serious constipation. After a quite incredibly long time she said, shaking her head wildly, 'No!'

Everyone looked a touch put out. In twenty years of psychic work, Marjorie Quigley had never yet refused her fence. I looked up and saw Emily looking at her mum in consternation.

Her mum shook her head again. 'No no no no no!' she said. She gave a huge sigh. 'There's no one there!'

Look. This was ridiculous. We're going out to lunch, or what? We *knew* there were loads of people there. We'd only just put down the phone to them. The woman was just not doing her job and getting through.

She started to tap herself on the forehead. 'Total blank,' she said. 'Nothing there at all!'

We did her the favour of pretending that she was not talking about her own lack of brains.

She bit her lip furiously. 'Damn!' she said, like a tennis player who has just lost a point. 'Damn! Damn! Damn! Damn!'

Mrs Danby leaned across and took her hand. 'Gently,' she said. Then she looked at me and sighed. 'Norman always liked to go gently.'

This struck me as amazingly suggestive. Why was she looking at me like that? I looked across at Mum, and found she was looking at Mrs Danby with an expression I did not recognize. It could have been fear or sympathy or irritation or a combination of all three. I thought about her and about Dad and the Danby woman. I had no idea, really, what any of them thought or felt.

Mrs Danby was simpering at Mum. When she'd finished simpering, she said, 'I blame myself!'

My mum looked vaguely hurt. She scratched herself behind the ear and said, 'Oh don't do that, Mrs Danby!'

'If it hadn't been for me,' Mrs Danby said darkly, 'Veronica would never have gone to that wine and cheese party. Or to Angmering, for that matter.'

Everyone started to sigh and shake their head. Mrs D held up her claw-like hand. Quigley started to ooze humility. He

bowed forward over the table. He got his head so low you could
practically see the cleft in his buttocks. 'Oh Mrs Danby,' he said,
in the tone of voice he usually reserves for Jesus Christ. 'Oh Mrs
Danby!'

Mrs Danby smirked. She didn't have to do a lot to get results.
But I've noticed that a certain amount of loot helps to invest
even your most casual remarks with a certain significance.

Mrs Danby shook her lizard-like head and pointed at me
dramatically. 'When all's well with the boy,' she said, 'we will
come into our own!'

I felt they had money on me. You know? Like I was a horse
or something.

Mrs Danby was well away. She broke her hands free of the
grip of those on either side of her and pressed her palms to the
table. 'Thou seest me, Lord,' she said. 'Thou seest this boy also.
Help him! Grant that he be not in Error! Help him back to the
circle! And may he be the healing of the things I wrought with
his father!'

'*Wrought*', eh! What had she and my dad wrought, I
wondered? Suddenly I was in Error! Error is pretty bad. If
you're in Error you are one step away from the thumbscrews.
If there had been less enthusiasm among the congregation for
ufology, maybe they would have devised a public punishment
for me.

People who fail the church are sometimes made to appear at
morning service 'as they were first made before God', which
these days usually means in their underclothes. If they have been
just very bad, and if they have someone to stand up for them, they
are given three strokes of the whip, usually by Sheldon Parry, the
born-again television director, and then made to put on a short
green smock for the duration of the service. If they have been
very, very bad and are not well connected inside the church,
the man with the wart gobs all over them, people chuck potato

peelings at them and then they are turned out into Strathclyde Road in their underpants.

I was moving dangerously close to the potato peelings. This much was obvious. I checked under the jeans to make sure I wasn't wearing the Donald Duck boxer shorts.

'Yes,' said Quigley, looking at me. 'Grant that what he has seen may not be a thing sent to tempt him!'

Pike made a kind of snuffling noise, and Mrs Quigley tried once again. She took the hands of those on either side of her, lowered her head and gave a constipated grunt. She grunted until sweat stood out on her brow. She grunted so hard there seemed a very strong chance she might drop a turd right there and then. But, after a minute or so, she shook her hands free, waggled her head furiously and said, 'Nothing. Nothing. Nothing.'

They were in a meeting, guys! Mozart was talking to Rose Fox. Rose Fox was talking to Vivaldi. My dad was tied up with Dickens or waiting for General Franco to turn up.

'Damn!' said Mrs Quigley, 'Damn! Damn! Damn!'

'Precious . . .' said Quigley.

'Fuck!' said Mrs Quigley. 'Fuck! Fucking arseholes!'

Everyone looked at her oddly. It was OK for her to do this kind of thing when in a mediumistic trance, but this wasn't quite that, was it? She was, allegedly anyway, compos mentis. If this kind of thing was allowed to continue, she might well start swaggering into Sunday service and shouting things like 'Bugger!' or 'Piss off!' if she found someone in her seat.

'My darling . . .'

It was then that it happened.

Leo Pike, in forty years of attending Spiritualist seances, had never made much impact on the spirit world. He had an aunt in Leicester who had died of double pneumonia in 1964, but she had never wanted to speak to him. In fact, none of the dead, famous or unfamous, had ever shown any interest in Pike. And, as far as I had been able to judge, the feeling was pretty mutual. In all the years I had been watching him, he had, as far as I could tell, absolutely fuck-all interest in them. You could wheel in Julius Caesar and Pike would just sit there, peering at him through his gold-rimmed glasses.

You can imagine my surprise, then, when Pikey, without prior warning, started to hum like a top. At first I think most of us thought it was some electrical appliance. Then we noticed that the Pike head was sort of pulsing backwards and forwards like a mechanical toy.

Nothing unusual in that. Pike's head quite often pulses backwards and forwards like a mechanical toy. In fact, he has an extraordinary repertoire of mannerisms, all of which could be reasonably mistaken for possession of one kind or another. There isn't a moment when the lad isn't twitching or jerking or going into spasm. So, at first, we saw nothing unusual in his bonce doing the rhumba on top of his neck.

Then his toupee started to slip.

Pike's rug was a topic of endless fascination in the First Spiritualist Church. I can still remember the day when it walked into all our lives. I must have been about nine, but I still remember my dad putting his back to the door, after Pikey had gone home from a seance.

'Did *you see* it?' he said in hushed tones. 'Did you *see* it?'

'Sssh, Norman,' said my mum. 'Don't let's talk about it.'

But it was impossible not to talk about it. One minute, there he was with a few scraps of grey hair plastered across his scalp – the next he looks like a prizewinner at Cruft's Dog Show. This wasn't just any old wig, you know? It looked like it had been grown in a tropical rainforest.

For weeks we had talked of little else. How was it held on? Was it stitched? Was it pure will power? Was it, perhaps,

Blu-Tack? One woman was prepared to swear she had seen Sellotape on the back of Pike's neck.

And now it was moving. The more his head jolted backwards and forwards, the further down his scalp it crept. By the time he had finished rocking, his fringe hung over his eyes. When he finally spoke, it was as if his voice was coming out of a large, brunette bush.

'O Lord,' he said, in a high-pitched voice. 'O Lord!'

We all just goggled at him. I mean, no one had ever seen Pike do this before. Right? Then he slewed round hard in his chair. His wig was now at a slight angle. He looked as if someone had just hung a mop on his nose.

From behind the toupee came a deep, deep voice. 'How y'all doin'? it said, in a strong American accent. 'An' how's little Nelly?'

19

No one had an answer to this.

For a moment I thought Quigley was going to tell him to snap out of it. But then my mum said, in a timorous voice, 'Do you mean Nelly Woodhouse that was with the Guardian Building Society?'

There was a silence. Then Pike said, in the same Texan drawl, 'Don't rightly know, ma'am. Don't rightly know.'

Mrs Danby was looking at Pike with a new respect. This all went to show just how far Quigley had slipped since I Testified. Time was when no one would dare open their trap in front of Mrs Quigley.

'The spirits wander,' said Mrs Danby, 'and find their homes in new bodies.'

Everyone nodded with fantastic respect. *'The spirits wander,' right? You heard Mrs Danby. She said the spirits wander, and she has a Rolls-Royce, guys! I* thought to myself that, however far they had wandered, if they ended up in the body of Leonard Arthur Pike they must be really desperate.

Pike started to sing 'Home on the Range' in quite a loud voice. I had never heard Pike sing in real life, so I couldn't tell how this spirit voice matched up to the real one. Whoever

was talking to us from Over Yonder, however, knew *all* the
words.

> Oh give me a home where the buffalo roam
> And the deer and the antelope play . . .

I thought there was a strong chance that some of the lads might
join in, but this proved not to be the case. Pike gave us all four
verses, including the one about the wagon train being painted
green, which I had never heard before. When he had stopped,
there was silence. Nobody could follow that. We all looked
at Pike. What was he going to do next? Would it be with or
without music?

'I'll mosey on down now,' he said, now sounding as if he came
from Alabama rather than Texas. 'I'll mosey, ah guess.'

'Stay, spirit!' said Mrs Danby. 'Who are you?'

Pike gave a deep chuckle. 'Tex,' he said. 'Tex is my name.'
Then he started to sing 'Home On the Range' again.

I don't think we would have worn all four verses again
(especially the one about the wagon being painted green) but,
when he got to the line about the deer and the antelope playing,
he burst into tears.

'What's the matter, Tex?' asked my mum.

'Little Nelly!' said Pike, now sounding vaguely Australian.
'Little Nelly Woodhouse died on the prairie!'

That was all we could get out of Tex. Mrs Danby tried.
My mum tried. Even Quigley abandoned his dignity and had
a go. But Tex had nothing more to say to us. I still wake up
at night and think about Nelly Woodhouse. It was haunting,
somehow.

There followed the longest silence I can ever recall at a seance.
Pike just sat there with a toupee and tears all over his face, and
we sat there staring at him.

After three or four minutes Quigley said, 'He's in deep, deep trance.'

'Yes,' said Mrs Quigley, 'he is very, very far away.'

Mrs Danby nodded.

'I have been where he is,' La Quigley continued, 'and it is a bleak and lonely place.'

'Yes,' said Mrs Danby.

Mrs Q was finding her way back into the action.

'It is a place,' she went on, 'where the soul is buffeted by winds and violent storms and feelings from the old, old time.'

'Yes,' said Mrs Danby.

Before Mrs Quigley could start drawing us maps of the terrain on the far side of the Veil, Pike gave an absolutely agonized scream. It really was scary – I kid you not. What was even weirder was, it sounded like his own voice.

'Mr Marr!' he yelled. 'Mr Marr!'

I leaned forward. 'What about Mr Marr?'

But Pike went on screaming. It was a horrible sound. As if someone was being hurt, badly. The sort of noise you imagine coming from a torture chamber. '*Mr Marr! Mr Marr! Mr Marr!*'

'What about him?'

Then a new voice came out of him. It was a mechanical, grating sound from deep in his throat. I'm not easily spooked, but I didn't like this voice. It reminded me of the voice that had started all this, the night my dad died. 'I serve a different master,' said the voice. 'I serve other gods!'

It was well weird. No one was holding hands any more. We were all staring at Pike. As we watched, his wig fell forward over his nose and landed on the table in front of him. No one tried to pick it up. Pike continued to stare ahead of him, but his eyes weren't focused on anything.

'Where are you from?'

Pike gave a glassy smile. His head turned to me, just the way

Mrs Quigley's had done when she passed on that first message from my dad. And, when he spoke, I'll swear it was my father's voice coming out of him. It sounded just like him.

'I'm a long way away, Simon,' said my dad. 'I really am a long, long way away.'

'Dad . . .'

Then the mechanical voice cut in on him, like a radio changing channels. 'Our planet is dying,' said the mechanical voice. 'We have no food or water. Help us, please! We have no food or water.'

Quigley's eyebrows drew in tight. He wasn't sure about this at *all*.

'Our sun is weak,' said the mechanical voice. 'Our canals are dying. The moon is in its last quarter. Help us, please!'

'How can we help?'

That's my mum. If she met an alien in Wandsworth High Street, she'd be telling it the way to the supermarket and offering it free babysitting before you could say 'flying saucer'.

I wasn't sure what Mrs Danby thought of all this. She was gazing at Pike in bewilderment.

Before Quigley could interrupt, I leaned forward and said, 'From which planet are you?'

I practically spelt this out. I wanted this thing to hear me loud and clear. It didn't, however, answer me directly. Which, if you think about it, isn't surprising. Anyone – even an advanced being from the other side of the universe – who is forced to use Leo Pike as a channel of communication is bound to experience transmission difficulties.

'From which *planet*?'

Pike's head was still facing me. At my last question there was movement behind the eyes. You could see a thought stirring, but you couldn't say if it was Pike's or not.

Then the voice started again, cracked and dry. 'Our planet is old and tired. The craters are dying. There is no night now. We need food and water.'

Whinge, whinge, whinge, eh? When we finally meet beings from another galaxy, all they do is moan! As I was thinking this, Pike started to laugh and the voice took on more colour. It didn't sound mechanical now. It sounded sneaky and mean, like a kid that thinks it's got away with something.

'We got Marr,' it said. 'We fixed Marr good!'

'Which *planet*?' I said again.

I was getting annoyed, as well as frightened. But before I could say any more, my dad's voice came back.

'Don't look any further, Simon, please,' he said. 'It's too dangerous. Please don't look for me any further. We all have to die, my darling. I didn't want to go! I didn't want to leave you! But I'm dead. You must stop looking for me . . .'

'Dad . . .' I almost shouted.

But, as I did, the mechanical voice came back, loud and clear. 'I am Argol, from the planet Tellenor in the constellation of the Bear. And I bring death with me. I am the bringer of death to your world!'

Pike clambered to his feet and tried to walk forward. The table was in the way, but he was still trying to move. Emily Quigley started to scream. Pike's legs went up and down like someone walking the wrong way along a travelator. He still stared straight ahead as he ploughed into the heavy dining-table.

Then, suddenly, he picked it up and flung it across the room. Pike isn't a big guy, but he did this like he had been in secret weight-training. As the table fell against Mrs Quigley and my mum (who started to cry), Pike just kept on walking, like a robot responding to an invisible signal. When he got to the wall, he didn't stop. He just kept trying to walk through it.

'Leonard . . .' whimpered Hannah Dooley. 'Oh Leonard . . .'

'I am not Leonard,' said a sneering, robotic voice. 'I am not

Pike. I am Argol from the planet Tellenor in the constellation of the Bear. And I bring death with me. I am the bringer of death to your world!'

We knew this. But we were still interested. No one had ever seen Pike express an opinion about anything. His job was to open car doors for Quigley. Now here he was, walking into walls! Mrs Quigley could roll. She could froth. Although she seemed not to be doing a lot of that these days. But did she walk into walls? We were looking at a very serious contender indeed.

Mrs Q was looking rather critically at Pike's performance. And he was certainly not getting the kind of back-up she got from her old man. He was just quietly walking into the wall, while the rest of us stood around in an awkward half-circle.

From a room somewhere else in the house came a loud gurgling sound, followed by a scream. It was hard to hear what was being said, but someone had put a nail through a pipe. None of us paid this any attention. I looked at Pike, my mouth open. How had he got hold of that name? Why 'Argol'?

I'll be frank. In a way, I thought he was putting it on. I mean, I thought there *were* aliens, or something like aliens, out there. But I wasn't sure they were the kind of entities that come from other planets. They could have been the kind you find here. It is easy to make up someone to look like someone, isn't it? And to play on someone's fears and hopes. Could they have got an actor to pretend to be my dad? It was possible. Somebody was trying to freak me out, and, from what I could gather, it might well have something to do with the Quigleys, with Veronica and this Mrs Danby.

But what I thought and what I believed had been moving further and further apart in the weeks since my father had died. What I was prepared to believe now, although it changed from day to day, was something frightening and surprising and new. Belief is spooky. It's something you use to get you from A to B,

I guess, and right now that seemed a long way to me. Besides, for reasons I will come to shortly, the name Argol was familiar to me.

'Look, Argol,' I said, trying to get the boy-to-alien tone just right, 'if that is your name. How did you get here?'

Pike's face was now pressed firmly into what was left of the Quigleys' wallpaper. He had stopped using his legs. He was just concerned with getting his nose as far into the brickwork as humanly possible.

'I think,' said Mrs Quigley, sniffing the stale parlour with her long, dog's nose, 'that there's a bit of *play-acting* going on here!'

Pike leaped into the air. He sort of bounced off the wall as if he was on a piece of elastic and someone had just yanked it from the other end. He whirled round, stood in a kind of ape-like crouch and started to swing his arms in front of him. Mrs Quigley backed away nervously. It was, I thought, the last time that she would make sarky remarks about a fellow medium's performance. When Pike spoke again it was in that mechanical voice. But there was nothing human about it at all now. It was 100 per cent artificial. It sounded like a menacing version of my Amiga 500.

'Why do you not believe?' it said. 'Why do you pretend you are the only beings in the universe? Why should that be, my friends? Why do you not recognize us? We are here. We are among you.'

Quigley folded his arms. He was starting to get annoyed with Pike, you could tell. 'Just in Wimbledon?' he said. 'Or are you all over the place?'

Pike started to walk towards him. His mouth was open and he was dribbling down his front.

'Leonard!' said Quigley, his voice shaking slightly. 'Don't be . . .'

Pike's face started to distort. One hand came out in a kind of claw and swiped at Quigley. My mum jumped and screamed. Hannah Dooley, her nostrils flared, was muttering something to herself. When the voice came back it was the full robot job – an awful, grating sound. 'We landed in Wimbledon,' it said, 'and soon the rest of the planet will be ours!'

With these words, the forty-eight-year-old accounts clerk leaped at Quigley's throat and, pinning him to the floor, started to bang his head on the dust-sheets that shrouded the household's £700 Persian carpet.

20

This was, I thought, just what Quigley needed.

He was not of this opinion. He got his hands round Pike's neck and started to squeeze. But Pike kept on banging his head against the floor.

'Look,' said Quigley, 'let's be reasonable about this, shall we?' Not an easy thing to say when someone in the grip of an alien being is trying to make scrambled eggs out of your brains. 'Let's . . . er . . . discuss . . .'

You had to hand it to Quigley. But Pike would not stop. His face was dark purple and there was that look in his eyes again. I didn't say anything, guys. I had remembered where I had heard that name before.

'Leonard . . .'

'I do not know of *Leonard*,' said Pike. 'I am Argol from the planet Tellenor in the constellation of the Bear. And I bring death with me. I am the bringer of death to your world!'

And death number one looked set to be that of Albert Roger Quigley. Mrs Q was pulling at Pike's cardy, and even Mrs Danby was weighing in on Quigley's behalf, but Pike kept right on banging.

'Argol,' said Quigley finally, 'I beseech you in the name of Jesus Christ – Argol!'

Pike stopped banging and a slow smile spread across his face. When he spoke he sounded more like Pike than anyone else. 'Argol,' he said, with childlike delight. 'Do we have to bang our heads on the floor before we understand? *Argol*. It isn't difficult to say, is it? You can say *Persil*, can't you? You can say *Daz* and *Flash* and *Bold*. You can say *Argol*, can't you? Argol is my *name*, lunkhead!'

Quigley remained cool. If he wasn't such a complete bastard he'd be a great guy. But, say what you like about him, he was probably the perfect bridge between us and a being from another world, especially when that being proved to be as mean and nasty as Argol looked to be.

'Argol,' he said, 'please let go of my head! OK?'

'All right,' said Pike.

Then the breath seemed to go out of him, like air out of a lilo. He fell forward on Quigley's chest. But, just as he did so, he gave us one more burst of the mechanical voice: 'Andrew Logan Manningtree Marr, born Glasgow 1946, died Wimbledon 1990. Marr knew too much. Andrew Logan . . . Manningtree. Manningtree Marr. Operation Majestic. Operation Majestic UK8.'

There was a clicking at the back of his throat. I stepped away from him towards the wall. What he had just said, if that was what he *had* said, was as frightening as anything else that had happened since my dad died.

He went on: 'Operation Majestic UK8. Marr knew too much!'

Then Pike, or Pike's body anyway, flopped all over Quigley as if the two of them had just been exchanging bodily fluids.

Pike did not move. After some time, Quigley said curtly, 'Get him off me!'

Mrs Danby, Mrs Quigley, Hannah Dooley, Roger Beeding and my mum rolled Pike off him. Pike curled up on the floor. He seemed, as far as I could tell, to be fast asleep.

'Let us pray,' said Quigley.

'Yes,' said Mrs Danby.

What a man! He has just been pulverized by a being from the other side of the galaxy, and what does he do? He is right on the line to Jesus. He didn't even get up. He just rolled neatly over on his side and commenced talking to the Big Man.

'Jesus Christ,' he said, as if he was an experienced soldier talking to a rather dumb general, 'there are many impostors in Thy world, and many of Us have failed to Grasp the . . . er . . . Meaning of these Things.'

He stopped. When he has those upper-case problems, you know he is running out of steam. Then he said, in a thick voice, 'Is he all right?'

'I think so,' said my mum.

I looked at her. It was weird. Since my dad died she had got smaller and smaller. If she went on this way, you'd be able to pick her up soon.

Everyone has their moment, right? And hers was the day he croaked. It was like he hadn't done anything really interesting until he kicked off. He couldn't surprise her. Maybe dying is the only honest thing we do. As I looked at her, I thought of her shrinking, like someone in a fairytale, and how one day I might hold her in the palm of my hand with her little voice squeaking commands at me as if she was a mouse I'd picked up in the garden. I didn't like that idea. I figured I ought to be the person to make her grow, but I just didn't know how.

'He was in the grip of some Force,' said Mum. 'I was reminded of that poltergeist in West Germany!'

Quigley shot her a glance. 'Let us pray,' he said again. 'Let us pray that Our Church, which We have built up through Thy Faith and trust, will . . . hold together . . . and that . . . although there are Beings that . . .'

There was a pause. Then a thin, hopeless little noise came out of him, like a half-hearted fart. To my horror, I realized Quigley was crying.

We were getting to him. We were getting to him. Me and the aliens were finally getting to him.

No one moved. We had seen a lot of people cry in our time, but this was the first time that Quigley had done us the honour. We let him finish. He did make a pretty thorough job of it. He started with a series of gulping sobs, went through to a noise like a drain emptying out and finished up with a sort of throaty sob.

Mrs Danby went to him and put her arms on him. 'Albert,' she said, 'I want to help you. I want to help. I promised the money to the church, and I want to give it. But I must see the boy's faith, do you see?'

'My dear . . .' began Quigley. But she was having none of it.

'We all know how I led Norman astray. How I led him out of the garden and into a rough and stony place where naught but thistles and brambles grow! How I made him betray what he *believed*!'

This whole thing was about what you believed. My dad and I had talked about these things so rarely. We just never seemed to get round to them. It was always the joke or the next argument or the next meal at La Paesana with my dad. And yet he must have believed in something.

He said to me once, when he was driving me to school, that there was nothing left to believe in these days. I said to him, 'But you believe in . . . well, in . . . in what Mum believes, don't you?'

He gave me a kind of bleak look. 'I'm not sure, old son. I'm not sure what I believe in any more. I thought I knew, but it's . . . it's so hard . . .'

I looked out at the school. The school he'd wanted me to go to so that I could be as clever as he had once been, and go to Oxford the way he'd done and not waste it as he had been foolish enough to do. I leaned across to kiss him goodbye and I said, 'Believe in me, Dad!' As a joke, right?

But he put a hand on my shoulder and said, in that philosophical, gravelly voice he had, 'All we have to believe in is our children. And yet we betray them!'

He said things like that, my dad. But not usually in the early morning. Usually when he'd had a few. Betray? I mean, be serious! Who said we trusted each other in the first place? It is nearly the year 2000, my friends.

I looked up. Mrs Danby was staring across the darkened room at me. Upstairs, the hammering and shouting seemed to have stopped. Her voice sounded shaky.

'You know . . . Simon was to be . . . was to . . .' She looked at me sort of pleadingly. 'And now he has *changed* us all! Hasn't he? He has made us think!'

You can say that again, was what I read on Quiggers' face.

'You know . . .' Mrs Danby went on, 'are there beings from other worlds? Here? In Wimbledon? It's perfectly possible, isn't it?'

She laid a hand on Quigley's shoulder. 'I cannot give the money until my doubts are resolved. I am deeply confused.'

She spoke for all of us here.

She shook her head wildly. 'Too much, Albert! Too many things that cannot yield their secrets!' And, with these stirring words, she went outside to her Rolls-Royce. Although why anyone with a Silver Cloud needs to worry about things yielding up their secrets is still a mystery to me.

Whatever they were talking about had had a very bad effect on the Quigleys. Mrs Quigley was hyperventilating and giving me some very dirty looks indeed.

My mum dabbed her eyes with her handkerchief and said, 'Arnold Bottomley had a seizure when he was on a canal boat and it took four of us to hold him, although he had been so

easy-going on other trips, especially the Greek one that I didn't
go on. He did quite well at Sussex University!'

Nobody responded to this. Nobody knew whether the seance
was over. Were we still talking to Jesus?

Very slowly Pike got up. He shook his head. Touched his face.
Realized he hadn't got his glasses. Then he said, 'Where am I?'

'32 Strathclyde Road,' said my mum.

'At the moment . . .' said Quigley ominously.

'You what?' said Pike.

Quigley too sat up now. The two men looked at each other
in silence. Somehow or other Pikey found his glasses and, in the
course of getting them hung on his ears, discovered his rug was
missing.

'Oh my *God*!' said Pike softly.

'Yes,' said Quigley, 'Oh my *God*!'

Pike, on all fours, started to pad around the floor in search of
the missing toupee. I could see it over by the wooden boards
that had been nailed across Quigley's windows. It looked like a
sleeping dog on the white sheet. I didn't like to point it out to
him. I just wanted to get out of there.

'Spacemen . . .' said Quigley, with a sniff. 'Spacemen . . .'

'You what?' said Pike.

'Spacemen!'

Pike's bum was in the air as he groped his way forward.
Suddenly Quiggers was on his feet and, before anyone could
say anything, he was taking a brisk run-up at the Pike bottom.
Moving like a man who has played more squash than he need,
he spun round, drew back his right and booted his wigless ex-
sidekick right up his grey-flannelled arse.

'Argol from the planet Tellenor,' he said. 'Argol from the
fucking planet Tellenor!'

'Who?' said Pike, as he fell face forward into his rug.

But Quigley was not to be stopped. He was raining kicks

into all the softer bits of the body chosen by the being who was to bring death to our world. If Argol had any bollocks at all, I thought to myself, this could well be the end of Albert Roger Quigley.

Rog did not, however, disappear in a white sheet of flame. He just kept right on kicking Pikey, and Pikey kept right on taking it. Their relationship was right back on course. There was absolutely no sign of Argol. Maybe he had zoomed off into another body. You know? Maybe he *was* in the body but he just liked getting kicked by earthlings. Maybe they were into S & M on the planet Tellenor.

Pike was curled up into a ball, like a hedgehog, clutching his wig to him the way a kid might hold on to its teddy before going to sleep. Rog just kept on putting the boot into him. Each time the toecap went into his stomach, Pike moaned quietly, his knuckles tightening round his toupee.

In the end, Quigley put his hand on his hip and stepped back a pace. 'Now,' he said, 'what was all that about, *please*! Argol from the planet Tellenor! And as for Mr Marr – did you ever see him more than twice in your life? Eh, "Argol"?'

'Who is Argol?' said Pike, evenly. 'And where is the planet Tellenor?'

If this was an act, it was a good one. It certainly threw Quigley, because he turned his attentions to me. Breathing heavily, he reached for my shoulder and pulled me towards him.

'We are going to bring you to heel, boy. You hear? We are going to stop your troublemaking. You hear? We are going to draw the reins in very, very, very tight!'

'Albert . . .' began my mum tentatively.

Quigley turned on her. 'There's something bad got into your son, Sarah, and Mrs Quigley and I are going to have to do something very serious about it. He is going to *have* to be Confirmed in Faith. You hear me? He *must* be. You hear?' Here he grabbed my arm and squeezed it, hard. 'Even if we have to drag him kicking and screaming before the Lord. Our Church needs funds. You understand, boy? Our Church needs you!'

I was scared. But not just by Quigley. I was scared because if what Quigley had said to Pikey was true and he really *didn't* know Mr Marr, how come he had access to his full name and date of birth? The only person in the world who knew those was me. For some reason he hated that middle name of his. It was almost as closely guarded a secret as Operation Majestic UK8.

Oh yes, there is such a thing. That was the real reason I was sweating as I went to bed that night. Operation Majestic UK8 is *dynamite.* Nobody else, apart from those directly involved – and, of course, Mr Marr – knew about that stuff. It's dangerous even to mention it to people, according to Mr Marr.

But Pike knew about it. If it *was* Pike talking. Not someone or *something* using his poor little body to give us a dreadful warning.

21

You may find this hard to believe, but Operation Majestic 12 really happened. You can look it up in *The UFO Report*, by Timothy Good, if you like. It's the most convincing evidence we have of an alien invasion of this planet, and a matter of public record.

In 1952, according to the American nuclear physicist Stanton Friedman, a top-secret briefing document for President Eisenhower was leaked to the public. It revealed that the wreckage of a flying saucer was allegedly recovered seventy-five miles north-west of Roswell, New Mexico, in July 1947. Admiral Hillenkoetter's report for the CIA noted, among other things, 'that the characteristics of the human-like bodies were different from homo sapiens; that there were strange symbols on portions of the wreckage which had not yet been interpreted'. And 'that it was strongly recommended that Operation Majestic 12 be kept accountable only to the President of the United States'.

There is objective evidence that something odd did happen near Roswell in 1947. We know for a fact that the area was sealed off and that army and rescue services were called to the scene. And that no one, not even the press, was allowed near. Stanton

Friedman, who has years of experience in the design, development and testing of advanced nuclear and space systems, concludes, in his 1990 report, that *the leaked documents are genuine.*

Before you say, 'Then he is barking mad,' think hard about this. There are plenty of things they don't tell us about. And Operation Majestic UK8, like its American counterpart, is one of those things. The reason you haven't read about it, even in the official UFO journals, is that it has been kept so secret that not even the ufologists know about it.

Operation Majestic UK8 refers to a set of documents shown to Mrs Thatcher *in secret* in 1984. These documents refer to a spaceship that crash-landed on the island of Jura in the Inner Hebrides in the autumn of 1983. (Autumn, as you will have noted from this manuscript, is a busy time for the extraterrestrials.) An alien who was brought from the wreckage in a container to the Mill Hill Medical Research Centre survived in our atmosphere for three days, five hours and twenty-five minutes. According to the UK8 papers, a full-scale invasion of the earth was planned, although, from what the creature told them, the research scientists concluded that it would be *eight or nine years* before the 'fleet' was fully prepared.

The alien, who was, according to the scientists, 'of humanoid form', was from the planet Tellenor in the constellation of the Bear, identified subsequently by scientists as probably belonging to star system BG4543/2221 in the Beta Principis cluster. Mr Marr reckoned that he conveyed 'certain information' to the scientists, including that his planet was controlled by a creature. The creature's name was *Argol.* Hardly anyone knew this apart from me and Mr Marr. How could Pike have possibly known? Wasn't it likely that the thing that had got into him at the seance was really from the planet Tellenor? It hadn't been like any other seance I had ever seen . . .

I thought about this the day after Pike went crazy. It had been a particularly bad day at school. 'Dummy' Maxwell had told me I had a 'hunted look' about me. I ask you! My dad always used to say that he didn't pay teachers to make personal remarks.

I was sitting with my feet up, watching a film about a Puerto Rican mass murderer. First of all Emily Quigley came in.

'All Daddy wantth you to do,' she said, 'ith to thay that alienth ith only an ecthpwethion! He thinkth tho highly of your thtwength!'

I ignored her. The Puerto Rican mass murderer was letting off a pump-action shotgun into a bus queue in downtown Los Angeles.

After a few minutes, she went out and Quigley came in, waving a piece of paper. He grinned madly at me and said, 'Well, young shaver! This should sort you out!'

He put his hands on his hips and gave me a kind of larky look. 'Why do you always look so *sullen*, fellow? Gosh! Jesus ain't arf depressed at seeing his children down in the mouth, me deario!'

I kept my eyes on the screen. I never look sullen. Especially when I am watching Puerto Rican mass murderers. This one was now sobbing over his attorney's shoes. Quigley waved the paper over my face.

When its flapping had started to irritate me, I snatched it from him and saw that it was ruled like a timetable. On it were written, in crude capitals, things like:

> 07.45–08.10 – HOOVERING
> 08.10–08.15 – CHRISTIAN WORSHIP
> 08.15–08.25 – BREAKFAST (optional)

I went back to looking at the screen. Events move swiftly in these films and it's very easy to miss things. The Puerto Rican mass murderer was now in bed, surrounded by a crowd of admiring listeners, lawyers, policemen, close relatives and beautiful women. Obviously the only way to get respect is to make with the pump-action shotgun. You know?

Quigley reached forward and turned it off. I turned it on again. I was quite calm. At this moment, my mum came in.

'Do you think,' Quigley said to her, 'that the little bloke should be watching this . . . ?'

'Oh . . .' said my mum. She sounded scared.

Behind her came Mrs Quigley, who was holding a frying-pan. 'It's only some rubbish about a Puerto Rican mass murderer . . .' she said. 'He's got off by the blonde one in the wig, anyway!'

I knew she had psychic gifts, but I could not work out how she was so clued in to this film. Surely there was no way she could have seen it before.

Quigley started to pace up and down the room as the mass murderer, who had now leaped out of bed and on to the window-sill of his hospital suite, announced his intention of travelling the sixteen floors between him and the pavement without the aid of lift or stairs.

'You, me laddio,' said Quigley, 'are on pindown! You will be picked up from school by Marjorie or me or your mother or all three of us from now on.'

I kept my eyes on the screen. I tried to imagine Greenslade and Marjorie Quigley together. I just could not do it, somehow. It seemed hard to believe they were in the same universe.

'Golly, Simo, you are making it hard for us,' Quiggers went on. 'We want a pure boy that we can hold to our bosoms and we get a kind of . . . I dunno, matey . . . a kinda *monster!*'

The Puerto Rican mass murderer had decided to jump. His attorney's girlfriend was holding on to his legs as he went through the things that were wrong with his life, in broken English. 'Itta steenk!' he was saying. 'It alla steenk, thees life!' I knew how he felt.

My mum and Mrs Quigley were now sitting on the arm of

the sofa, their eyes glued to the screen, as Quigley paced around
the room.

'There is to be no hanging around the High Street and staring
into shop windows,' he went on. 'There are to be none of those
"hamburgers", either.'

You could really hear those inverted commas click into place.
What was he trying to do to me? We were talking Colditz here,
guys!

'There are no phone calls in or out. There are no little
"subs", and there are no trips to the newsagents' either, me
deario. Until you stop this upsetting talk and this . . . divisive
rambling about . . .'

'Aliens,' I said, rather irritably. I knew he was trying to rile me,
but I was determined to keep calm. I thought about *sang-sang-
dang*, or the state of being a rose bush in early May. It helped.

On the screen they had let go of the Puerto Rican mass
murderer's trousers and he was on his way to the sidewalk, head
first, at about seventy miles an hour. It was better for him, really.
He didn't look like the kind of guy who could have taken a long
prison sentence.

' "Sin is a busy old thing when out! See how it travels, Lord,
all round about!" ' said Quigley, who often reaches for the wise
words of Old Mother Walsh when things are getting tough.

After the mass murderer hit the deck, I got up and, resisting
the temptation to fold my left forearm over my right elbow,
make a prong of the middle finger of my right hand and then
lift it in Quigley's face while telling him he was a motherfucking
asshole, I went to the door. 'And don't look so sullen, me laddio!'
he called after me.

Sullen? I wouldn't know *how* to, my friend. I had risen above
him and was now in the state of *dung-hai*, or complete and utter
superiority to Quigley.

What was really getting to him was the fact that alien-fever was proving hard to eradicate in the First Church of Christ the Spiritualist. I thought about his notion that 'alien' was just another way of saying 'devil', or that Old Mother Walsh and her snake weren't, actually, any more real, although just as powerful, as Argol and the things from Tellenor. It didn't stand up. I don't say I knew what was happening, but, whatever it was, it was *real*. You know? I hadn't even dared go near Furnival Gardens since I saw my old man for the second time.

I would have to go down to Mr Marr's house. And, with this new regime in force, tonight would probably be the last chance I had to do it. I decided to wait until they were all asleep. I lay on my bed with a computer magazine and, from time to time, went to the window and looked down at the darkened street. I could make out the spot where my dad had stood that night.

Down below, Quigley shouted goodnight at me and I shouted back, and, at last, my mum tiptoed to the door and, looking fearfully around her in case Quigley saw, blew me a little damp kiss. 'You can be so sweet, Simon,' she said, 'but you're such a stubborn thing!' I didn't answer. I might have provoked even worse charges. Then she said, 'You're so like him. You're so like poor, poor Norman!'

Quigley was always the last to go to bed. His routine was monumental, guys. When everyone was in bed he would go round to every window, double-check if it was locked and then, before he came upstairs, place a few key obstacles in the path of any potential intruder. I swear he was obsessed with burglars. He spent a lot of time swaggering about the place, flexing his muscles and telling everyone what he was going to do with those 'foolish little feller-me-lads' if they showed up.

I had to wait for what seemed like hours. But, eventually, after several tours of inspection of the windows and much talk of the need for Banham locks, Quigley, exhausted by his own vigilance, staggered to bed. Minutes later he was making a noise

like a pneumatic drill. I slipped out of bed, got into a pair of
jeans and a T-shirt and headed down the stairs.

It was like a slalom down there. There was an ironing-
board, two kitchen chairs and a couple of broken wooden
boxes snaked around the front room. In the back kitchen was
a dresser, three pails of water a yard or so apart and a small
scattering of drawing-pins. In the front hall – in case any
burglar should choose to throw himself through the fireproof
glass in the window or slice through the mortise lock with a
flame gun – was a selection of things to trip over. There was a
rubber ball, a few of Emily's textbooks and a sort of forcefield
of nails resting heads down and points upwards towards the
unseen burglar's face. As I discovered this arrangement, I began
to feel almost sorry for any potential thief. After fighting his
way through all this, he would have to face an angry and almost
certainly stark-naked Quigley.

The street was empty. In one house, on the corner, there was
a light on in the front bedroom. A middle-aged woman, wearing
what looked like a turban, was looking out at the night. I don't
know what she was looking for, but she didn't see me. There was
a warm wind on my face and hands as I made my way towards
Mr Marr's place.

I didn't look up at the sky. But I really felt they were looking
at me. Like you do in the supermarket sometimes, when you
can sense something behind you and you turn and there's this
camera, mounted at the edge of a shelf, swivelling its one black
eye this way and that, like some malevolent goblin at the door
to a secret cave.

I didn't look behind me either. They were *here*, weren't they?
They could be keeping pace with me, along Forrest Avenue,
down Gladewood Road and across up through Park Crescent.
Maybe they had got people in every third house. Maybe Mr
and Mrs Lewis at 119 Cedar Avenue were not in their usual

positions, snoring back to back in the bed they bought twenty years ago. Maybe they were out in the garden, walking around stiffly, expressionless as vacuum cleaners, as they prepared the Giant Pod for Argol of the planet Tellenor.

I had a feeling that, when Argol finally showed, he was going to look a lot more scary than Leo Pike. I had heard his sound-bite, and he sounded like a man who meant business.

Looking in front wasn't really safe either. Suppose Argol, or someone like him, suddenly leaped out of someone's driveway to give me a taste of his galaxy's latest in combat weapons? The Jura alien had had a lot to say about Tellenorean life-forms. Much of it, Mr Marr said, was just too horrible to tell me. He didn't want me to have nightmares, he said. I thought about what they *might* be like. In a way, not knowing made it worse. I used to feel that way about Old Mother Walsh's snake when I was a little kid. Now it's something to laugh at, but then . . . I was feeling more and more like a little kid with each day that passed.

As I turned into Mr Marr's I was shaking. I had to force myself down the street to his house. I had to force myself up the path to his front door. And, when I fitted the key into that lock, my hands were trembling.

Listen – no one could have got into Mr Marr's. I had the only key. No one had forced any doors or windows, because they didn't need to, did they? On Tellenor, according to the Jura alien, they have mastered the technique of passing through solid objects – one of the things Mr Marr said was worst about the Tellenoreans was that you never quite knew when they were there.

If it was them, they had been through the house very, very carefully. Since my last visit they had had another go. Someone or something had been through the fridge and taken away a few samples of earthling diet – a chilli con carne and a cold lasagne that was probably even now being scoffed by a load of blobs up in the ionosphere. They had also started to take away literature. They had been pretty systematic. Most of the stuff missing was from Mr Marr's extensive collection of material dealing with invasions from other galaxies. And the huge file dealing with Operation Majestic UK8, which had taken pride of place in Mr Marr's top-secret collection of UFO papers (in the cupboard under the stairs) was nowhere to be seen.

I thought about the police. But if these beings had left any fingerprints, I had the strong feeling they wouldn't be the kind you get down at Scotland Yard.

He had kept the file under a pile of back numbers of the *Wimbledon Guardian*, because, as he said, 'there were a number of people who would be only too happy to see all documents in the case suppressed'. At one point, I seem to remember, he'd kept the papers in the fridge – which is why the top sheet had a large blob of sweetcorn in the top right-hand corner.

Our Tellenorean friends had taken the *Wimbledon Guardian* as well as the UK8 papers. I didn't like to think why they needed the local paper. By now, probably half the small ads in the current issue had been placed by aliens.

I was scared, though. I was really terrified.

And then, as I came out from under the stairs, I heard something moving upstairs. Two creaking boards, and that was it. I stopped. I listened hard. I could hear my heart tap against my ribs. My face suddenly felt very hot, and then, just as suddenly, very cold. There was silence. I wanted the silence to go on, but, as I listened, it felt as if I was racing it. That the thump of my heart was challenging it to go on and not to be broken by a . . .

Crrreak . . .

There was something up there. And, while I was not in possession of definite proof, my money was on it coming from

somewhere a little further away than the Fulham Palace Road.
As I changed from listening to walking mode, I tried to work
out whether it had feet or flippers or ran on rollers. The noise
had an insistent quality – like a small animal gnawing away at
something or gathering food and stopping every few minutes
to listen, as hard as I was listening in the dark of Mr Marr's
house.

I did not want to find out if it was friendly. If it was friendly,
how come it was scurrying around stealing magazines and
not coming out into the open and asking who was in charge
round here? Everything seemed to indicate that it was our
friend Argol, or some flunkey of his. I tried to remember if
Mr Marr had ever said anything about how Argol looked.
Was he a thing or a person? Hadn't someone said something
about his teeth? I was almost sure they had. His *teeth*! My
Christ! The gnawing was starting again. Not content with
stealing Mr Marr's library, the bastard was chewing up his
bedroom furniture!

Then I heard the humming. A high-pitched noise that seemed
to come from the head of the stairs. It wasn't the kind of sound
an engine made – or a dishwasher or a television or any of the
things I was used to seeing round the house. I only realized what
it was when I got to the front door. It was a human sound, but
unlike one I had ever heard before. It was more like the noise
dogs make sometimes – a see-sawing musical phrase, as if it was
talking to someone you couldn't see. That was it. Human and
yet definitely *not* human.

I looked up at the bedroom window as I closed the door
behind me. I saw Pike's face pressed to the glass. He looked as if
he was lit from below, and his nose and cheeks were spread out in
a white, lifeless slab against the window pane. But his eyes were
glinting, as if he was looking at something no mere human could
see. Or – and this thought only occurred to me when I was out

on the street and running for the hill as fast as I could – as if there was something else behind his eyes, looking out at the world, waiting for the awful moment when it would start to take apart our little corner of the planet, piece by shabby piece.

22

They had done something to my dad. And now Pike was under their control.

The only comforting thing about this was that, although they were well placed to take over my brain, they had, so far at any rate, declined to take up the offer. Maybe I secreted some hormone that gave the average Tellenorean a violently unpleasant feeling. Or perhaps Argol had an enlightened policy towards young people. Maybe it was going to be like the Cultural Revolution in China, and we were all going to be given the chance to team up with the aliens. Certainly, if offered the choice between Quigley and an eighty-foot beige monster with a corkscrew head, I knew where my allegiance would lie.

I tried to remember what else the documents had said. A lot of them, of course, were so secret that Mr Marr couldn't even show them to me. They were, he said, the kind of documents you eat rather than read. The guys at Mill Hill who had worked on the Jura alien had been very cagey about this, apparently, but I think Mr Marr said there was a lot of stuff about mind control. The Tellenoreans don't talk the way normal people do. They just sit there by the fire projecting their thoughts into each other's brains, like me and Greenslade. In fact, it was rumoured that one of the Mill Hill guys had had his brain messed around with by the visitor who screwed up the landing in the Hebrides.

The trouble with this alien business is that you cannot trust your senses. As Jenny Randles says in *Abduction* (according to Mr Marr, the only really reliable guide to the spacenapping phenomenon), 'Of course I am making no assumptions about what it means to have been abducted [by aliens], but if some researchers are correct, *many of you reading this book might have undergone an abduction experience without consciously realizing it.*'

It was possible that all this business with my dad was a deliberate ploy by Argol and his pals to destabilize yours truly. After all, I was close to Marr, wasn't I? And he was the only guy on to them. Maybe my dad was really and truly dead and what I had been looking at, in the road outside our house and in Furnival Gardens, had been a hologram put out by the Tellenoreans. Maybe it was me they were after. Maybe the reason I had Testified the way I did was a kind of double bluff on Argol's part. Maybe *they had already got to me.*

I was running now. Putting one foot after the other in a style I have developed during cross-country runs organized by Cranborne School, I allowed my head to sort of loll forward and my legs to patter after it, leaving the middle bit of me completely free for inflation and deflation. At any moment I expected one of the masters, placed at strategic intervals to stop a guy taking short cuts or lighting up a Havana cigar, to leap out from a place of concealment, brandishing *The Times* and bellowing, 'Come *on,* Britton! Come *along* there!'

As I panted into Stranraer Gardens, following the no-hopers' rule for cross-country – *never run in a straight line* – I was flailing my arms left and right and zigzagging at an angle of about ten degrees to the horizontal.

Everything in Stranraer Gardens was as still as I had left it. The trees in the street were shamming dead. Every last bit of unkempt hedge in our front garden was taking the same attitude it had always taken. In whatever street we live, our garden is always the shabby one. 'Gardening vexeth the spirit,' my dad used to say to me with a broad wink whenever my mum asked him to get out and cut the lawn. Whenever she said to him, 'But, Norman – don't you want to sit in it, like other people?' he would reply, rather grandly, 'A garden, my dear, is a place for passing through as quickly as possible on the way to the pub.'

I stopped a few yards from the house. All around the fences, the parked cars and the neat roofs was that weird stuff you get just before dawn in the suburbs – it isn't light or darkness but some other thing entirely – shadowy, ghostly, but so much itself you feel you could reach out and run it through your fingers.

I got my breath back. With that stupid feeling of relief you get when you're home, I pushed open the door, tripped over what felt like a set of billiard balls and fell headlong into a carefully arranged selection of this week's vegetables. As I went face first into about two kilos of potatoes, a large hand seized hold of my T-shirt from behind. The hand pulled me up towards the ceiling.

'Where've you been, my laddio?' said Quigley's voice, quiet but deadly. 'What have you been a-doing of?'

'I've been . . .'

That was as far as I got.

'It's been on the *Common* looking for little green *men*, has it? And holding their little green *hands* and having little green *drinks* with them and having little green *chats* about their little green *planet* . . .'

'Listen . . .' I said.

He was hitting me really hard. It was only when I swung to the left and broke free for a moment that I was able to observe that he was wearing my dad's grey towelling dressing-gown. My dad wasn't a tall man and it only just covered Quigley's enormous willy. It made him look as if he was wearing a mini-skirt.

'What are you trying to do to our church, Sonny Jim?' he hissed. 'Why are you trying to split us in two? After all I have done for you!'

I could not think of a single thing that Quigley had ever done for me. But now was not the time to tell him. He hit hard.

'Do you know what hangs on Mrs Danby's covenant?' he said. 'Have you any *idea*?'

I had an idea what the covenant was. It sounded as if all this was as much about money as it was about religion.

From upstairs I heard my mum shout, 'What is it? What is it?' Quigley went mad. He started to clout me around the head, yelling, 'Burglar! Burglar! Burglar!'

'Burglar?' came a cheeping from the back bedroom.

'Burglar!' yelled Quigley. 'Burglar!'

Pronouncing the word seemed to bring him to his senses. He stopped, looked over his shoulder and put both his hands up to my face. 'O Jesus Christ,' he said, looking over my shoulder as if JC had just wandered in from the garden, 'did you die for this boy?'

I kneed him in the balls as hard as I could.

'Jesus Christ!' he said, doubling up in pain.

'Oh, screw Jesus Christ,' I said. 'Screw him. And screw his mother Mary too!'

Quigley gave what I can only describe as an eldritch screech and came at me with both arms, legs and the front bit of his head. 'Blasphemer!'

Mrs Quigley was now at the head of the stairs. 'Burglar!' she screamed.

'What is it?' called my mum again.

What indeed? A burglar who blasphemed? Who broke into your house in the middle of the night and, after paying the usual compliments to your stereo, got on with the job of pouring scorn on your most cherished convictions?

Quigley beat me through into the back kitchen. I heard my mum's voice. 'Simon!' she called, in feeble tones. 'Is that you?'

'It is!' I yelled. 'The one who was in your womb for nine months and a day, remember? And, if I didn't think this bastard who's making so *fucking* free with my dad's house would follow me there, I'd jump right back in this minute!'

'He called Albert a bastard!' yelled Mrs Quigley.

'Well he is,' I said. 'He is a bastard. He's a complete and utter bastard, if you want to know.'

'He thaith Daddy ith a bathtard!' came Emily's voice.

Quigley clouted me smartly across the side of the head. I fell to the floor and crouched, Pike fashion, in a corner of the kitchen, covering my face with my hands. Quigley went to the door to check there was no one around, then, unable to stop himself, ran back to me and twisted my ear hard. 'Stop play-acting,' he said. 'I didn't hit you hard!'

'Let go of my lugs.'

He started to shake my head about. It was not going to be long, I reflected, before I made my contribution to discussions in 24 Stranraer Gardens via a Ouija board.

I sensed, rather than heard, my mum come in. Quigley had made sure he had stopped hitting me as soon as he heard her on the stairs.

'Mum . . .'

'Oh, Simon . . .'

Quigley leaped back, pulling down my dad's dressing-gown with a surprisingly prim gesture. I looked up at my mum. I noticed that she was crying. Those little eyes of hers were red and angry, and her chin quivered helplessly above her neck as she came towards me.

'Why do you let him do this to me, Mum? Why don't you stand up for me? Don't you love me, Mum?'

My mum dabbed at her eyes. She didn't answer.

'If Daddy was alive he wouldn't let him do this to me! Why do you? Why do you let him? You don't love me, do you? You don't even like me, do you? Why don't you like me? What have I ever done to you?'

Unable to answer this to her or my satisfaction, my mum started to cry. But they weren't her usual tears. Usually she cries like the rain we had on a holiday once, up in Scotland – a soft, grey drizzle – but this time her body shook with real sobs.

Quigley joined in. He's a big guy, but he seemed to have got to like crying. It was him, not me, that went to her and got hugged. He needs a lot of help. I don't think he finds himself any easier to live with than the rest of us.

'Help me through it, Sarah!' he was saying. 'Help me through this!'

Help me through the hitting-Simon experience! Why won't you?

I could see my mum's face on the other side of Quigley's shoulder. I could also see something I had absolutely no wish to see at all, which was Quigley's bottom. It was long and sausage-shaped and coated with fine, black hairs. It peeked out from under the rim of my dad's dressing-gown with a horrible sauciness. Mum's eyes were signalling to me – something far-away and desperate. I could not work out what it might be.

Eventually Quiggers rounded on me. 'Now, Simon, apologize to your mother for that disgusting, manipulative little display. Could you?'

I was obviously not taking the punishment right. I was not observing the Christian decencies for getting thumped. How tactless could I get?

'I'll never apologize to you, Quigley,' I said. 'I hate you. And I hate your creepy wife and your creepy daughter and I wish you were all dead. I wish you were dead and my dad was alive. I think you stink. I think all religions stink, actually, but Christianity stinks worse than any of them.'

There was silence.

Just in case I hadn't made this absolutely clear, I added, 'I'll never forgive you and I'll never apologize to you, and I'll never do anything you say.'

He was still looking pleased with himself.

'Why is it so important to get me back in your rotten little church, Quiggers?' I said. 'Is there some grubby, horrible reason? I bet there is. Well I tell you, Quigley, by the time I'm through with it there won't *be* a fucking church. The aliens are here, Quigley.'

He twitched slightly, like a lizard's tongue. I pushed on, sensing a weak spot.

'They've got into your congregation, Quigley, and they're going to wreck the church. They are. You're finished here, I tell you.'

It was then that my mum came over to me. She knelt next to me and, peering into my face, she said, 'Testify, Simon. Please. Come back to Jesus. Please. I don't want you to be damned. If you'll be Confirmed in Faith, I'll never ask you to come to the church again. And Mr Quigley will go. He will.'

She stroked my hair then, very gently, the way she used to do when I was a little kid.

'I want you to be saved, that's all, darling. And then we can get on with our lives. Please, Simon.'

I looked up at her.

She put her hand to my cheek. 'It's like Mr Quigley says – you're a pure boy! You are!'

I remembered some of the nice times we'd had. Me and Mum and the old man. Laughing at things or sitting together round the table and my dad making jokes and . . . Why is life such a bitch? Why does it lay these things on you? Why does it pull your heart two ways? And why do feelings always surprise you?

I wish we were machines. You know? People go too far.

23

'Why,' Greenslade whispered to me, 'isn't semen an element?'

Up behind the desk, 'Pansy' Fanshawe was preparing to see how sodium reacted with something whose name I could neither remember nor pronounce. Pansy had a far-away expression on his face. He looked a bit like a sorcerer as he stirred the mixture in a small clay crucible.

'It's a pretty big element in my life,' I said.

On the other side of me, Khan sniffed. He doesn't like us talking like this. If Khan ever whangs off, it is probably for the purposes of spectroscopic analysis.

Pansy looked up wildly. He is about sixty and they should have retired him years ago, but he has nowhere else to go. I sometimes think they may not be paying him. 'Now,' he said, in a quavery voice, 'molybdenum is . . .'

He stopped in mid-sentence, as he often did. I stared at him intently. It was about a week after my showdown with Quigley and I should have been at Harvest Festival. I have to avoid the last period on the second Friday in October, which is when the First Church of Christ the Spiritualist celebrates 'the rich goodness of God's vegetables'.

I was supposed to be there. But I wasn't. Outside, on the

sun-soaked Common, they were piling up French loaves and
bottles of Beaujolais. But I was staying inside, learning about
what the world was really like, or, rather, what Pansy Fanshawe
thought it was like.

After the night Quigley had kicked my head in, I had finally
seen something I should have seen a long time ago. I didn't have
to do any of these crazy things they made me do. I didn't have
to stand up and tell the whole truth of my heart unless I wanted
to. I didn't have to say shit to Jesus Christ if I didn't feel like it. I
had stayed in bed on Sunday morning, even though Quigley had
nearly kicked the door down and then burst into tears all over
my duvet. 'We need you, Simo,' he said. 'We need your deep
love! We need your purity!' I was lying there thinking about
fellatio at the time. How did they actually *do* it? Did it hurt?

He didn't need my purity. He needed me to sweeten Mrs
Danby. But I didn't need him. You see, it was really my dad that
made me go along with the church, even though he didn't really
involve himself. Somehow he managed to make it fun, the way
he made so many things fun, and, now he was either dead or else
taken over by some force I could not even begin to understand,
there was nothing whatsoever to keep me in the church.

'Now,' said Fanshawe, 'stand well back, because there may be
a bang!'

Pansy's chemistry lessons are mainly a question of lobbing
stuff out of the cupboard into a crucible and trying to get an
explosion going. Most of the time he doesn't even know what
elements he is trying to combine. He's closer to a mad chef than
a chemist.

Khan was trying to say something. He looked worried. 'Sir,'
he said, in his precise, slow voice, 'under certain circumstances,
compounds of the substances which you are attempting to
combine may have a reaction in which, say, the sodium . . .' He
did not get to the end of the sentence. With a mad gleam in his

eye, Pansy lobbed a small chunk of brown rock into the crucible. There was a colossal bang and the sound of the clay crucible hitting the desks, walls, windows and members of the Fourth Form. Thackeray started screaming.

Greenslade and I had hit the floor early. We know Pansy. When we raised our heads above the desk there were clouds of smoke blowing across the chemistry laboratory. Fanshawe was giving a kind of war whoop as, through the grey fumes, I saw the unmistakable figure of Quigley.

He stepped in front of the class like a demon king making his appearance in a pantomime. Behind him I could see my mum, Emily and Mrs Quigley, who appeared to be carrying a large sheaf of corn. It was, I think, the worst moment of my life so far. I was absolutely terrified that Greenslade or Khan might discover that I was anything to do with these people. How had they got in here? I seriously thought of crawling through the smoke to the door.

But it was too late. Quigley was pointing at me dramatically. 'I think this boy must come with us,' he was saying.

Fanshawe clearly thought that Quigley was the product of the chemical reaction he had just engendered. He was goggling at the First Spiritualists like a medieval alchemist who has just raised the Devil. 'Are you . . . er . . . a . . . parent?' he said feebly.

My mum stepped forward as more smoke billowed across the laboratory, circling around the faces of pupils, master and visiting religious maniacs. 'I am his mother,' she said, in a quiet voice, 'and he is excused today's last period of chemistry to attend a Christian service.'

Pansy looked at her as if he was trying to work out how to combine her with deuterium and to calculate the effects of the resulting explosion.

'It is,' said Quigley, with quiet dignity, 'a festival of the faith to which Simon belongs.'

Greenslade gave me a sideways look. I raised my eyebrows, resolving, as I did so, to let him know my side of the story as soon as possible. There was no point in fighting this one. Not in front of twenty-three members of the Fourth Form. I got up and walked, with some dignity, towards the door. When I got level with them, I rounded on Quigley. 'This is the *last* time, scumbag!' And with that, I stalked out into the corridor, as Pansy, still dazed from the effects of the explosion, meandered feebly after my mother, muttering about notes and the headmaster's policy on being excused important school activities.

'Where's Pikey?' I asked, as they marched me towards the car. Quigley did not answer this. Since Pike's behaviour at the last seance, he had been banished from the Quigley presence. I noticed that the assistant bank manager was biting his lower lip and grinding his right fist into his left palm.

As we got to the car, I stood back from them and said, 'You can do this to me once, but you can't go on doing it. I don't believe, you see. I don't believe any of that rubbish you talk.'

Emily Quigley looked really distressed. 'Thimon,' she said, 'it'th like in *Narnia* when Athlan thaith to Edmund that he mutht have *faith*!'

'Narnia,' I said, 'is bullshit. Give me Wimbledon any day.'

I looked straight at her. 'Why do you believe all this rubbish? It's crazy. You all know it's crazy. It's only habit keeps you doing it. If you once stopped and thought about it rationally, you wouldn't believe any of it.'

I looked back at the school buildings. I was amazed at what I was saying. And yet I knew, as I spoke, that this was what I had always thought but had been too frightened to express. Silently, we all got into the car.

There was a mood of quiet desperation about Mr and Mrs Quigley. As we drove up towards the Common, they looked at each other briefly, then looked away.

'Has Pikey left?' I said. 'Has he joined the true cause? Is he out looking for the bastards who stole my father?' They didn't answer this, but my mum leaned forward and patted my hand absently.

In the boot was a large pile of tins of tuna fish and a harvest wreath that had clearly been designed by Marjorie Quigley. We were coming to the end of the day, and the light was starting to fade.

The First Spiritualists were camped out at the edge of a grove of birch trees. There weren't many of them. When I was a child I could remember gatherings of two or three hundred people, but there were fewer than a hundred out on the dry grass. Someone had told me that no fewer than twenty people had left the church after my speech, many of them to join the Raelian Society, a group that exists to set up embassies on earth for alien intelligences wishing to make contact with earthlings.

'What's keeping them away, Quiggers?' I said. 'Is it the weather, or what?'

Quigley twitched, then decided to ignore this remark. As we walked towards the circle of Spiritualists, he turned to me and said, in a high, pleasant voice, 'I know you will come back to us, Simo! The Lord Jesus will make a way for you!'

'Listen, Quigley,' I said, speaking in a clear voice, 'Jesus Christ is out of the picture. When beings from another planet get started on you they will *laugh* at your beliefs. You'll be like some savage to them, clutching a wooden idol.'

Although they could all hear me, no one responded to this remark. Quigley looked more than usually Christian.

The First Church of Christ the Spiritualist was arranged in a huge circle around a large pile of groceries. The produce did not seem to be of high quality. The recession seemed to have hit Harvest Festival rather badly, I thought. I saw a lot of tins of spaghetti. Old Mother Walsh had urged her followers to 'bring living things and offer them to the Lord', and there is an account somewhere of the Sisters of Harmony sacrificing a sheep. These days people bring hamsters and terrapins and rabbits and dogs, but nobody quite has the nerve to pin them down on a slab and cut their throats. As we sat down a little way away from the rest of the group, I saw a small girl waving her hamster's cage at the sky. 'There You are, God!' she was shouting. 'There's Hairy! You can have him if You want!'

There are a lot of children at Harvest Festival. It's quite a jolly occasion. Looking at it now, I suddenly started to feel old. Older than anyone else there. A group of little kids were doing what is called the Carrot Dance, over by the groceries. It's a crazy thing where one child pretends to be a carrot and the others top and tail him and put him in boiling water. As I watched them, I thought about all the crazy things the people I've grown up with believe and do. How we bury people, how we marry people – First Spiritualists are always married as close to 3 February as possible, and, when the bride has made her vows, someone pours a bottle of milk over her head ('to feed her young') – how we pray, how we hang sheets out of the upstairs window to celebrate a birth, how we seem so utterly and completely deranged and yet feel so utterly and completely sane.

For a moment I wondered whether the First Spiritualists are any crazier than other people. People who pride themselves on being rational won't walk under ladders. Famous physicists talk about God without really knowing what the word means. Much of the faith of my mother and father's church would seem bizarre or laughable to Greenslade and Khan. But to me, standing there in the autumn sunlight, it suddenly seemed natural and comforting. Maybe because, at last, I had finally lost it. I was no longer part of the First Church of Christ the Spiritualist. My dad was dead, and he was never coming back.

Over by the birch trees, Mervyn Finch had started to play his squeezebox to Vera 'Got All the Things There' Loomis, and a few

of the adults were dancing the old dances that have been passed
down for nearly 200 years. Old Mother Walsh's 'Rabbit, Skip
O'er the Lump of Bacon' and, my personal favourite, 'Who's
Away to Jesus?' Hannah Dooley was pressed close to Sheldon
Parry, the born-again television director, crooning softly to
herself. Clara Beeding was chatting amicably to the man with
the wart. The sun was over the rim of the Common now, and
there was the beginnings of darkness in the tangled trees.

'Danth with me, Thimon,' said Emily's voice at my elbow. I
looked down at her as the music grew louder. She was so full
of hope and decency and trust. And that voice! Emily was,
according to her mother, an absent-minded girl, but she never
forgot to lisp. *Why not?* I thought to myself. *This is the last time
I'll be part of these people.* I took her hand and led her into the
centre of the dancers, as the light failed over Wimbledon.

24

We went through every dance in the book that night. We even did 'Goodbye to Clonakilty' (a title no one in the church has ever been able to explain), and, when it was quite dark, the group over by the trees lit a fire and we went into 'Ella Walsh's Foxtrot' or 'Bless the Lord and Shame the Devil'. You grab your partner by the waist and sort of waddle for a bit, then stamp four times, hard with each foot, on the ground. It's a dance designed for fat people who are not light on their feet. After you have stamped, you raise your right hand and, for some reason, shout, 'Shame the Devil!' Except at Christmas, when some people yell, 'Stuff the Turkey!' I usually try and say something different from both of these. Such as, 'Rinse the Saucepans!' or 'Phone Your Auntie!'

In the slow bits, I moved away from Emily and waggled my ears. It's something I have only recently learned to do, and she seemed to appreciate it.

As the music pounded on, I pulled Emily this way and that across the baked earth. It was almost dark. Over to our left, in the field that lay between us and the road, was the shape of a horse. A solitary man walked his dog home, up in the direction of the Windmill. And, all around us, people were swaying and shaking, clapping and singing as the beat grew wilder and wilder.

Emily cannoned into me, her face red with pleasure. 'Why do you believe in alienth?' she said.

'Because I think they're there,' I replied.

She grinned. 'Thatth why I believe in Jethuth!'

I grinned back.

'Why believe in alienth, though?' she went on. 'Alienth are thuch a complicated thing to believe in!'

I thought this was rather a shrewd point. Maybe away from her mum and dad she was capable of being a human being. I shrugged. 'You've got to believe in something,' I said, 'and I believe in aliens.'

I couldn't stop dancing with her. I moved with her, close, towards the centre of the circle and that crazy pile of groceries. I took her by both hands and I started to swing her in a circle, singing as I went, shouting the words of the song over and over again.

Quigley wasn't dancing. I saw him by the camp-fire, standing next to my mum, watching me hungrily. Maybe he thought he was going to get me back into the church, but what I was doing was strictly pagan. I was dancing for dancing's sake, not for Jesus'.

I was almost at the centre of the group when I saw the light in the trees. It was a reddish glow, moving unsteadily towards where we were at a height of about fifteen or sixteen feet. It would weave towards us then veer away crazily. Sometimes it would stop and shine downwards, as if it was scanning the earth for something. Then it would move off on course again. I could see a vague shape behind it.

I was the first to notice it. Then Emily, following the direction of my gaze, watched the light, or lights, as they swayed through the trees towards us.

Mr and Mrs Ian Gilliemore, who were taken from their Hillman Avenger on the night of 24 September 1958 and subjected to scanning by a 'big light' from a group of midgets in the traditional green cloaks, reported seeing 'a sort of dancing light' just before the midgets struck. They said the light moved in just the way this one seemed to be doing.

Other people had seen it now. A guy next to me was nudging his friend and pointing at the trees. My arm was tingling, like it's supposed to do when the Neptunians come at you through the undergrowth, foetal implants in hand. I went hot, then cold.

Word was spreading among the crowd. Even Mervyn, whose hands were flying across the keys of his accordion, was seen to gape up towards the thing dancing like a huge firefly in the dusk. The music slowed and then stopped. People stopped dancing and stood in silence looking over at it. They looked just the way they did when they turned to the altar on Sunday mornings. There were whispers, too. 'They're here!' I heard one man say. And another, 'It's true! They've come!'

Quigley, who was now standing next to Mrs Danby, a little away from the rest of the congregation, was watching open-mouthed. Next to him, I saw my mum push her grey hair from her temples. There was an expression on her face I hadn't seen in a long time. She looked hopeful. She was eager to welcome whoever was coming to her out of the darkness. She was going to exchange knitting patterns with the Visitors, and ask them if they would like a hot drink after their 17-million-light-year journey to Wimbledon. That was the most common look on people's faces. Hope. Stronger than you saw it in church. More various, shifting, fading, like the light at the end of a day, as the lights came closer and closer towards us.

Maybe they wanted the groceries. You know?

Were they lights, or was it just one light? It seemed to have changed colour. It was white now, and behind it you could see the shape. It didn't stop but came on towards us out of the trees.

Next to me a woman gasped, 'It's here . . . It's . . .' Emily clutched my hand and stepped back. Now it seemed at least twelve feet in height, roughly humanoid in shape and wearing what looked like a plastic bucket on its head. Its legs – if it had legs – were covered in what looked like a large brown sheet, and the light seemed to come from a kind of lamp attached to the back of what could, or could not, be its head.

As it came on across the grass, quite a few people dropped to their knees and pressed their palms together in prayer. Emily held my hand even more tightly. 'Jethuth . . .' she was saying, 'Jethuth . . . Jethuth . . .'

I held my ground. Even at this distance, in the gloom, I could see that the thing on its head that looked like a plastic bucket actually *was* a plastic bucket. In fact, I thought I recognized the bucket. The large brown sheet was quite clearly a large brown sheet, and the thing at the back was none other than my bicycle light.

'*Roughly humanoid in shape*', was, too, a fairly accurate description. Because, as the creature swayed around in front of us, it was becoming obvious, even to the more short-sighted of the congregation, that we were looking at Leonard Pike. 'I come', he said from inside the bucket, 'from the planet Tellenor!'

There was quite a good reverb effect on his voice. The woman next to me was quite clearly not at all sure whether this was Pike. From the look on Quigley's face, it was obvious that Pike was soon going to wish that Pike was not his name.

I couldn't figure this. If the Tellenoreans *had* got into Pike's body, wasn't this a slightly odd thing to make him do? Were they not as bright as we had supposed? Were they complete idiots? Or were they, perhaps, a nation of satirists? Perhaps they had come all those billions of miles for the purpose of taking the piss out of us.

As I waited, Pike started to fall, jumping clear of the stilts that had been holding him up. The bucket, miraculously, remained on his head. 'I come,' he said again, 'from the planet Tellenor.'

He was losing his audience. 'And I come from Epsom, mate!' said a voice at the back. There was a gust of laughter.

Pike, aware that the bucket was not helping him, removed it. The effect was startling. In the darkness, Pike's face, illuminated by the bicycle light, looked positively ghoulish. He was breathing rapidly, and his pinched, chapped little face was urgent with venom. He looked crazy with fear.

'He *was* taken,' said Pike. 'He was taken from the grass. Here on the Common. And I can prove it.'

With a shriek, he pointed his finger at Quigley. 'He's lied to you,' he said. 'He's a liar and a fraud. He's a cheat.'

Quigley looked white.

'Ask him what he's done with the money! Ask him what he *plans* to do with Mrs Danby's money! Ask him where it's gone!'

Quigley didn't speak. He started to open and close his fists, but he didn't say anything.

'They are here!' said Pike. 'Follow me! Don't follow the liar and the cheat! Follow me! I'll take you to the spot where they took him! I've looked through the accounts! Follow me!'

If Quigley had ever had a chance of regaining his grip on the First Spiritualist Church of South Wimbledon, he had lost all hope of it now. There was an awful conviction in Pike's voice. You just knew that what he was saying about Quigley was true. You knew.

Quigley just stood there, his immense arms loose at his side as the mass of the congregation, murmuring among themselves like extras in a bad production of a Shakespeare play, swept after Pike as he turned and, bucket in hand, ran off across the Common towards the spot where Mr Marr had been sitting the night the aliens came.

25

He was yelling something as he ran. Something about somebody dying. I couldn't tell who. Something about how he, Pike, was guilty. Guilty of what, though?

As we got to the narrow road that runs past the spot where Mr Marr used to watch the night sky, he turned and held up his hands towards the stars. '*Help!*' he screamed. Once.

I'd heard (or was it seen?) that cry before. Where was it?

'*Help!*' yelled Pike, again.

Of course. On the mirror in Mr Marr's bedroom. HELP! scrawled in lipstick.

The First Church of Christ the Spiritualist was, as its leading members were fond of saying, on the move. It was, literally, going places. Every single member of the congregation was haring through the bushes of Wimbledon Common in search of flying saucers. If ever there was a flight from the true religion, this was it.

We stopped on one side of the narrow road. Pike was on the other, jumping up and down like a man with a swarm of bees in his underpants. It was as if he was on the other side of a river that no one knew how to cross. And the road had the look of water, silvered under the rising moon.

Pike was pointing to the grass near to where Mr Marr had been sitting that night. 'Look at it!' he yelled. 'Look at it! It's where they landed!'

One or two of the braver spirits moved closer to the road and peered across at the grass. You didn't see it at first, but you saw if you held your head at the right angle. About twenty yards from where Mr Marr had been sitting, the grass had been flattened. It lay as if some giant hand had combed it out and then blow-dried it, in a perfect circle.

It was curious. No one wanted to cross the road. It was as if there was a force field there. As if Pike was behind an imaginary glass wall, cut off from the rest of the church. As he railed on at us, more and more people came up to the edge of the tarmac, looking across at him, helplessly, in the moonlight.

'I'm guilty,' Pike was saying. 'I'm guilty too. Jesus, forgive me. Oh forgive me, Jesus!'

'Jesus forgives you,' said someone over to my left.

This was standard with the First Church. You went out – you had a good time. You drank gin. You coshed old ladies. You embezzled church funds. And Jesus forgave you. But Pike looked like a man who would not, could not, be forgiven. As if whatever he had done had cut him off from the mercy he had been seeking for so long.

'It was here,' yelled Pike, 'on the road! Here!'

I looked at Quigley, who was standing well away from the crowd. His face was still that dead white colour. He was looking at Pike as if he expected him to change shape, to flower into some awful creature.

'I'm a murderer!' yelled Pikey.

He moved towards us across the road. Instinctively – as if faced by some poisonous animal – people moved back a little. Pike stopped in the middle of the tarmac. Somewhere, over on the other side of the Common, a truck moved up from below the hill and, headlights hooded, started across towards Parkside.

'I'm a murderer!' yelled Pike again.

'Leo,' came a voice that I recognized as my mum's. 'You're not a murderer!'

Pike's face reddened with fury.

The truck turned right by the big houses at the south edge of the Common and started along the straight stretch, where we were standing. Pike turned and saw it. For a moment I thought he was going to stand there facing it, daring it to stop. Then he moved back towards the circle in the grass on the other side of the road.

'Who did you think you murdered?' called my mum, in a bewildered tone.

The truck was coming closer. You could feel the earth shake as it changed down, ready to turn out into Parkside.

Pike's face was distorted with anger. 'Marr, of course. I murdered Marr, you morons! Right here I murdered him!'

His lips puckered up. 'It was . . . it was like spacemen took him. It was. He was lying here. He was dead in the road. I wasn't driving fast, honestly! When I came back, he was gone. He was lying here.'

He gestured towards the centre of the road. He seemed very intent on showing us the precise spot where Mr Marr's body had lain. That was all that seemed to matter to him. Then, with a blitheness I had never associated with Pike, he stepped two paces back into the path of the oncoming truck.

It hit him in the chest. The guy was quick on to the brakes, but not quick enough for poor old Pikey. By the time the truck had stopped, Leo was under its offside wheel and starting the long, complicated journey to the spirit world.

It's some consolation to reflect that of all the UK citizens undergoing the death experience, Leo was probably the one most prepared for it. He had spent nearly all of his forty-eight years in the First Church of Christ the Spiritualist, and during that time he had witnessed literally thousands of encounters with people from the Other Side. He had never missed a seance or a service, and he died, as Mr Toombs said the next Sunday, a 100 per cent, fully operational Christian.

But his death and the mystery surrounding it spelt the end for the church in which he had worshipped for so long. It wasn't the Wimbledon Crop Circle, as the shape in the grass came to be called, that destroyed it. Most people agreed that Pike had been out the night before working on it with an industrial fan. It was tiredness that finished the First Church. That, and the fact that it lost faith in the nearest thing to a charismatic it had had since Rose Fox. In fact, people seemed to be losing interest in aliens. One by one, over the next few weeks, they just drifted away. You could see it in their faces, minute by minute. They were getting that worried look you see on people's faces on the Tube. They were becoming, at long last, ordinary.

The elders started to investigate Quigley and the church funds the day after Pike's death. The Quigleys were still living with us. Gordon Brunt and his friends had taken away a wall without putting in the proper structural support, so the whole of the left side of Château Quigley had collapsed. They had also done something terrible to the boiler, and discovered dry rot in the airing-cupboard.

I heard a lot of the commission of inquiry. One night I heard Quigley shout, 'Would you bleed me dry?' All I heard of the answer was the low bass of Mr Toombs and the nasal falsetto of Roger Beeding. But, from Quigley's face when he came out, I gathered that that was precisely what they were intending to do with him.

Sometimes, in hushed voices in the evenings, I heard my mum and the Quigleys talking about money. But nobody said anything to me about that, nor about where Mr Marr's body had gone after Pikey ran into him with Lethal Weapon III.

One evening, after he'd been answering more questions from Toombs and Beeding, Quigley came into my room when I was doing my homework. I didn't look up. There was something scary about him these days. He just came over to my desk, looked down at what I was writing and whispered, almost to himself, 'You're as bad as your bloody father!' Then, with the back of his hand, he hit me, hard, across the side of my face.

One day, towards the end of October, I came home from school late to find my mum, Marjorie and Emily sitting in Quigley's car outside the house. My mum looked as if she was in the middle of being kidnapped. She gave me a weak smile and a fluttery little wave. It gave her, suddenly, the helpless look of royalty.

I tapped on the glass, and she wound down the window. 'What's going on?' I said.

'We're off to write prayers,' said Mrs Quigley, answering for her, as she tended to do these days.

'Do come, Simon,' said Mum.

The back wall of the First Church is littered with scrap pieces of paper on which are written things like PLEASE HELP AUNTIE JOAN THROUGH THIS PHASE OF THE TREATMENT, or DEAR GOD, HELP ALL THE PEOPLE I SAW ON WATERLOO STATION THIS WEEKEND and PRAY FOR ALL, ALIVE AND DECEASED, AT 110 HOLDEN ROAD, FINCHLEY. I wasn't sure for whom they would be praying. Under the present circumstances it could equally well have been me or Quigley.

'Where is he?' I said.

They all looked shifty. 'He's out the back,' said Marjorie. 'With Danzig.'

Danzig! It sounded as if Quigley had passed beyond the reach of prayer. Who the hell was Danzig? A German missionary, perhaps. I turned my back on them and marched towards the front door.

'Danzig,' called my mum, as I disappeared into the house, 'looked as if he might do it. So Roger stayed with him.'

This was getting even more mysterious. As I went through the drab little hall, I wondered whether there was an overseas branch of the First Church of Christ the Spiritualist and, if so, whether it contained a man called Danzig. He sounded like a guy with a problem.

As I came to the door that leads out to the garden I heard Quigley's voice. 'No, Danzig,' he was saying in a coaxing sort of way. 'No, no, no. Not there, Danzig. There! There! See? There!'

Had Quigley finally come out of the closet? Was he trying to get Danzig to do to him what no other man had ever done? I suddenly had a clear mental picture of Danzig – a hairy-chested man with a gold medallion and tight, white trousers.

I walked through on to what my dad used to call 'the wide green spaces of 24 Stranraer Gardens' and heard Quigley's voice again, this time low and thrilling. 'Yes, Danzig,' he gasped. 'Yes, yes, yes! There! Good! Good! Good!'

I turned to my left and saw a large Labrador. It was squatting on the flower-bed. Its back legs were straining furiously and its face wore a fixed and glassy expression. It was almost certainly going through the final stages of the digestive process. Quigley peered down at its bum. He looked pleased. 'My dog,' he said. 'Hundred and ten quid!'

The animal gave a final grunt and expelled whatever it had to expel. There was certainly a lot of it. When it had finished, it hared off across the garden as if it had done something clever.

'So,' I said, 'they're off to pray.'

He was wearing one of my father's ties. My dad always claimed to have gone to public school, but he was never precise about

which one. The ties all looked as if they came from a jumble sale.
I never liked him wearing them, but I liked them even less round
Quigley's neck.

'To pray for you, Simo,' he said.

'They needn't bother, Quigley,' I said.

He came over to me then. He was breathing heavily. I could
see everything about him very clearly. The black hairs on his
hands. The ridiculous, wiry neatness of his hair. The pallid,
clammy surface of his skin. 'You need help, boy,' he said.

'Listen,' I replied, 'pretty soon the whole of south-west London
is going to be under the iron heel of Argol of the planet Tellenor.
I should move on out if I were you.'

Quigley sneered. 'You never believed any of that rubbish, did
you? It was just a stick to beat me with, wasn't it?'

I didn't move back, although he shoved his face close to mine.
'No,' I said. 'The really pathetic thing about all of this is I did.
I still almost do believe it. That's how badly you bastards have
fucked up my brain!'

Quigley started to twitch. 'I'm not leaving, Simon,' he said.
'I'm going to be here for the rest of your *life*.'

I still didn't move.

With a sort of grunt, he wound his hand back and again
clouted me, hard, on the face. It hurt a lot, but I didn't let
him see that. I just stood there. After a while he didn't seem to
see me. He turned to the dog and said something to it. For a
moment I looked away, and when I looked back he was gone.
A minute later I heard the car engine start. I was alone in the
house.

My dad was dead. There were no aliens. Or, if there were,
they were playing it so cool as to be almost unnoticeable. There
were no ghosts or gods or any of that stuff. There was only the
unlimited prospect of Quigley. It was time to go.

I went back into the house and, when I was sure no adults had sneaked back in to spy on me, I went upstairs to my bedroom and started to pack.

I didn't take much. A few computer magazines, some cash I pinched from Quigley's drawer and my Abbey National card. I have £300 in there, which is quite a lot of money. My dad always said it was for when I got married. If I hung around here any longer, it would all go on a nose job for Emily Quigley. I took two paperback books, a toothbrush, my Ventolin inhaler and a copy of the repeat prescription, four T-shirts, two pairs of jeans and my other pair of trainers. Everything I really care about fitted into my games bag, which, according to the principles of Tai-Ping, is how it should be.

I looked round at the picture of Bruce Lee, the travel poster of Malaysia my dad gave me, my certificate of merit for Grade Two Saxophone, my 320 computer discs, my colour picture of an iguana and the tattered remains of a portable snooker table we got when I was twelve.

I thought about Mum and wondered whether to leave her a note. I decided not to – simply because I couldn't think of what to write.

Outside, the October day was darkening. I headed down the stairs into the silence of the early evening. When I got out on the street, I would just keep going. The sun was almost gone, but that was OK. I'd find a field or a park bench, and early next morning I'd head on down to the sea. Somewhere or other is a place my dad took me once, where there are tall stone buildings huddled above a blue sea, donkeys, and guys in grey suits with open white shirts and faces that look like their owners have had time to consider every move they make. Somewhere there's somewhere that isn't Wimbledon. Some place that isn't full of narrow grey streets and closed-up lives and people like Albert Roger Quigley.

I had one call to make before I hit the road.

There's a pub about four streets away from us where I used to go with my dad. Sometimes he'd look across at me, when my mum was deep in a copy of *Psychic News* and there was nothing on the television any time from May to October. He'd say, 'Fancy a pint?'

'Don't mind if I do.'

Not that I ever drank beer. I'd sit with a Coke and some crisps and watch him drink. Watch him sip in that amazingly slow way that adults do. Watch him stretch, yawn, look across at me and come out with those perfect forty-year-old cliches they use to make the time pass easily and without controversy.

'It's a hard road, Simon.'

'It is, Dad. It is.'

It is.

I wasn't going to drink, or anything. I'm not one of those fourteen-year-olds who go to pubs. I look my age. You know? I'm a straight-down-the-middle, ten-plus-four wonder. One of those aimless youths you stumble over on their way from the pinball machine to the nearest shop that sells electrical equipment. A blurred, white, not-quite-grown-up face in the crowd.

The garden there, where we used to sit, has a swing and a slide and is framed by a huge chestnut-tree. This mother was in the terminal stages of yellow. From time to time, a leaf would detach itself and sashay down to join its friends, slicing sideways, plunging headlong and then ripple-dissolving to the damp grass. There was dew on the white steel tables and a feeling that, at any moment, a man would come out of the bar and start stacking the chairs away. It was just dusk, when things start to look not quite themselves. I watched the light drain away and felt the cold clawing at the earth between the tables. The end of the year.

I sat at the table we used to use and tried to think what I really believed. I felt I ought to be thinking something momentous. It isn't every day you run away from home. Surely I had got some things clearer since he died?

I hadn't. I was just as confused as that day she came in and told me the news. Did life go on like this, I wondered? Did it offer absolutely no solutions? Is it all punishment from now on in?

There were a couple of drinkers in the far corner, but no one noticed me. I was just getting up to go and make my way on down to Greece when I felt a hand on my shoulder and heard a deep voice. 'Hi, kid!'

I looked up. It was my dad.

26

I jumped. For a moment I was right back in my bedroom that first time. I blinked. I closed my eyes and opened them again. He was still there. Viewed from close up, he showed absolutely no sign of being controlled by an extraterrestrial intelligence. The guys from Tellenor were probably so good that they had overreached themselves and programmed free will into him. You know?

He was holding a pint of beer in his left hand, and, when he smiled, I could see the fillings in his teeth. The dentalwork was a perfect match. They had worked wonders on the timing, too. He drank, wiped the froth off his mouth, put the glass on the table, readjusted it, dropped his hand and then put it behind his head.

I sat there, waiting for him to dematerialize. He didn't. Instead, he did a couple more fortysomething things. He pursed up his lips, looked at me, then away, and then, after shifting carefully on his seat, he farted.

What more do you want? It drinks beer! It picks its nose! It farts! We will never catch up with this galaxy, no matter how hard we try. They mimic our greatest achievements in a way that puts our own selves to shame.

'I was not as surprised as I thought I was going to be,' he said eventually, 'to hear myself pronounced clinically dead!'

I goggled at him.

'I hadn't been feeling terrific,' he went on, 'since I got into the hospital. A coronary thrombosis doesn't exactly leave a guy feeling perky!' He yawned. 'They don't really check on you very closely. It's very much a wing-it *oh-he-looks-a-bit-stiff* situation. I mean, they don't hold a mirror to your lips or anything.'

'They don't?'

'They do not, old son. They thump your chest a few times and call the old crash unit and then they grope around for your pulse, but it's a very amateurish affair really.'

He wasn't wearing the suit he'd been wearing in Furnival Gardens. He was wearing jeans, a sports shirt and a cardigan. For some reason I found the cardigan really offensive. It wasn't the sort of thing my dad would wear at all. Maybe the aliens had got into shopping.

'I don't think that your average British doctor is very good at diagnosing death,' he went on. 'I don't think it's taught at medical school. I wonder the mortuaries aren't full of people banging on the doors and trying to get out!'

'Do you mean,' I said, 'that you weren't dead?'

He grinned. 'I didn't experience myself as dead. Although that was the medical profession's analysis of my condition. At first I thought I might be having an out-of-body experience. Then I thought it might be an in-body experience – that my soul was to be confined to my body for some sinister theological reason.'

I reached out across the table to touch him. He took my hand and held it in a very un-Tellenorean way. This was him, all right. This was my dad, just as he had always been.

'What did . . .'

'I think the first clue I had that I might still be on the team was when your mum pitched up to inspect the body.'

'You mean . . .'

'They got me out of the ward and put me under a sheet in this side room. I lay there, quite quiet. I could hear everything that was going on, but I couldn't move or speak.'

I tried to picture him under the sheet. The light filtered through. Like lying in bed in the morning when they call you to get up and you lie there, listening to the noises in the street below, wondering whether you'll ever get up and join them.

'I heard the nurse ask her if she wanted to take a last look at me. She said she didn't think that would be necessary.'

'Typical!'

'I was a bit pissed off,' said my dad. 'I mean, it isn't every day you get the chance to view your old man's corpse, is it? It's an experience, isn't it?'

There was a pause. Then he sucked at his teeth and went on.

'She was actually surprisingly complimentary about me.'

'I know,' I said glumly.

'They all were. The nurse said I had been a very good patient. Christ, I'd only been in the hospital for about ten minutes before I snuffed it!'

It must have been weird lying there. Presumably trying to move a leg or an arm or get your mouth to move. And hearing these voices from a long, long way away. Voices that had been chattering away at you all your life.

'The nurse said I was very good company, which I thought was praise indeed for a guy who had just had a coronary thrombosis. Then your mother went on about how I had always wanted to be buried at sea.'

'That's what she said to me.'

He scratched his head. 'Did I ever say I wanted to be buried at sea?'

'Not in my hearing.'

'She seemed very convinced of the matter. From the tone of

her voice, I thought I was not going to be able to avoid being slung in the box and slipped off the Isle of Wight ferry. I just couldn't *move* or *speak*. You see?'

I could picture my mum and the nurse, who, for some reason, I had decided was Irish. A short, plump woman from Galway.

'She said I was an interesting and sad man in many ways.'

'Who? The nurse or Mum?'

He gave me a strange look. 'Your mum, of course. Do you think I'm a sad man?'

'No,' I said, rather shortly.

He took another deep draught of his beer. He looked up at the pale white sky above the half-ruined trees. He looked like a guy glad to be alive. With each minute that passed he was getting less and less extraterrestrial. But, at the same time, more and more *alien*. I didn't recognize some of his gestures. He'd got a new one where he crossed his feet, and a new version of his smile. It seemed to stay on his face for slightly longer than was necessary.

'Anyway,' he said, in a conversational tone, 'then they took me down to the morgue.'

'Christ!'

'Indeed. Ganymede, they call it. I mean, the guys who took me down were *real* incompetents. They treat the dead with absolutely no respect.'

He sounded rather civic about this. As if his experience was going to lead to a campaign for the rights of corpses, or something.

He looked at me thoughtfully. 'She didn't cry or anything. It was just sort of, "Shall we take him down then?" and Bob's your unc.'

'She was . . .'

'She was pretty calm about the whole business. I could have

done with a bit of weeping and gnashing of the old teeth. We got a very low-key response.'

Well, that wasn't how she had behaved at home. Hadn't she said she'd gone wild? I didn't feel like finding out whose version of events was true. I was too busy holding on to the edge of my chair and waiting for him to rise twenty feet in the air.

'We had our problems, but . . .' He sucked his lower lip. 'It makes you think, being in a mortuary.'

I could see that this might well be true.

'It makes you think, when you hear people call you Charlie as they sling you on the slab.'

'Why did they call you Charlie?'

'I think they call all the stiffs Charlie. I mean, they're dead. They don't count, do they? That's it. Sling them aside. You know? Pickle the bastards in formalin and donate their remains to medical research.'

We were on to Dead Lib again. He looked quite morose at the treatment handed out to cadavers. Then he took another long drink of beer.

'We don't understand life, do we?' he said. 'I mean, it's here and it's so *sweet*, and we don't understand it.'

'I don't understand it,' I said. 'I haven't got a clue, I tell you.'

It was amazing, really, that he had managed to recover from the heart attack so easily. He looked, I have to say, absolutely great. Still, I suppose this was what happened in the Middle Ages. You rolled around, went blue and your eyes shot up into your head. And then, if you made it, off you went to till the fields or whatever. I had heard the National Health Service was in a bad way, but I didn't realize that do-it-yourself, take-your-own-chances medicine had reached this level of intensity.

'I started to come round when they put me on the slab. I was lucky not to go straight in the fridge, I tell you.'

'I bet!'

'The word "autopsy" kept running through my mind. You know? But they were at the end of their shift. They closed the old door behind them and there I was, alone with a few dozen stiffs. Assuming they *were* stiffs, and not a fresh consignment of medical mistakes.'

He narrowed his mouth into an O shape and pushed his eyebrows up into what was left of his hair. There was still foam from the beer on his moustache. I watched the bubbles wink in the ghostly light, glisten, and then die. You could see the pulse beat in his neck. You could smell him too – a whiff of new soap and old changing-rooms. You could see the broken veins on his nose and see the puffy skin above his eyelids, bunched up like old crêpe curtains. And you could watch those little blue eyes that never quite met yours. It was my dad, all right.

'I don't know how long I was in there before I sat up and looked around. I know I banged on the door, but no one heard. And when I looked down at my ankle they'd put this label on me.'

'What did it say?' I asked. 'FRAGILE? Or, THIS WAY UP?'

He grinned. 'You are a witty little bastard, aren't you?' Then he yawned. I could see the red trap of his throat.

'Actually, it said NORMAN BRITTON, C OF E.'

'Did it?'

'It did,' said my dad. 'Not NORMAN BRITTON, MA OXON. Just NORMAN BRITTON, C OF E. After forty-odd years of being a good boy and paying the mortgage and . . .'

I could see that it had been an upsetting experience. But what did he expect them to write? NORMAN BRITTON, NOVELIST AND TRAVEL AGENT?

'Anyway,' he went on, 'I wandered round and checked out the corpses. They all had labels on. You know? And there was one just next to the door that must have come in while I had been lying there, unable to move. It didn't have a name on it. Just a ticket that said UNIDENTIFIED RTA. It was a real mess, I tell you. Looked as if someone had been practising three-point turns on its chest.'

He shuddered. I said nothing.

'And I thought to myself: *What's it all for?* You know? Did I want to go on being NORMAN BRITTON, C OF E? What's so great about my life?'

I couldn't, for the moment, think of an answer to that. So I still said nothing.

'There are big pluses about being dead,' said my dad. 'You don't have to take the dishes out of the dishwasher and put them in the dish rack and then take the cutlery out of its little plastic box and then put it in the cutlery drawer making sure that the *spoons* go in one compartment and the *knives* in another compartment and the *forks* in another compartment, except there are always *forks* in the *spoons* compartment and *knives* in the *forks* compartment when you get there, so it's hopeless it's always too late to get things right, it's a total frost, honestly, is life, you are a lot better off dead, in my opinion. Do you know what being dead felt like?'

'You tell me, Dad!'

'It felt like a good career move.'

Of course. That long white robe I had seen him in that night was a sort of hospital gown. They dress them up like ghosts. But how had he got down to Stranraer Gardens?

'They brought some other poor sod in,' he said, as if in answer to my question, 'but I was over behind the door and they didn't see me. I just slipped out, walked down a corridor, out through a side exit and came down to home. I just stood there looking up at it. You know? Wondering whether to take up my life or walk right out of it.'

He put one hand on mine. 'I changed the labels,' he said. 'I put my name on the road-traffic-accident victim and I walked out with UNIDENTIFIED clutched in my paw.'

He seemed to find this next bit difficult to say. His eyes were watering as he started it, and he looked away from me again, towards the deserted white tables around us.

'It was so *strange*,' he said. 'Sometimes I think there's something at the back of all this that's so . . . so bloody bizarre. You know? Roots of coincidence and all that . . .'

'What, Dad?'

He looked straight at me.

'The body they brought in during the night. The one on the slab. The unidentified traffic accident. I saw the face. It was your mate. Mr Marr. The guy who sat out on the Common, waiting for the spacemen to come. I walked out free, you see. And the undertakers buried him.'

27

It was at that moment that Mr Quigley passed the entrance to the pub garden. He stood under the street light, looking back from where he'd come. He shook his head and clucked to himself like the White Rabbit in *Alice*. He was carrying a bag of shopping. He looked annoyed about something. I got the impression he was looking for something to hit. Probably me. He didn't see me.

'What's up?' said my dad.

'It's Quigley, he's after me!'

'Quigley!'

It was now quite dark in the garden. For some reason we were both whispering. Out in the street, Quigley shouted off to his left. He was calling to someone, but I couldn't hear what he was saying. It sounded as if he was calling a dog.

'What's going on with Quigley?'

'Oh,' I said, 'he's had a lot of heavy conversations with you. Apparently you've repented of your wicked life.'

'I have!'

'Sure,' I said. 'I've been talking to you myself, you know?'

Dad looked away.

I said, 'Quigley's a bastard. He's living with us, and he treats me like shit.'

My dad looked back at me. I tried to think of the worst thing that Quigley had done.

'He's gone and bought a dog!'

I wasn't asked for any more information. But I gave it just the same. I told him about how he'd hit me. About how I was some kind of prophet as far as he was concerned, and he was desperate to have me Confirmed.

There was a bit of a silence when I'd finished, and then Dad said, with a grin, 'Quiggers is right about one thing, old son. I had a really wicked life, and I repent!'

Somewhere in the distance I heard the growl of thunder. I looked up at the sky and saw that the clouds were one dark, lurid, compact mass. My father looked really ghostly in the light from the street, and for a moment I found myself thinking: *He is a ghost. He really did die. This is all a story.* As I did so, he got to his feet. His face changed suddenly. There was none of the humour you usually saw in it, and there was a fixed look about the eyes that I found almost frightening. He rose, slowly and mechanically, staring ahead of him and beyond me. Then he lifted his right hand with the index finger extended.

Behind me I heard a kind of yelp. It wasn't a sound I ever remembered him having made, but certain things about it made me think it came from Quigley. There was a thump as his shopping hit the floor.

My dad still didn't say anything. He just stood there, staring past me, his arm flung out in front of him and his attention fixed on what had to be the assistant manager of the National Westminster Bank, Mitcham. Dad didn't speak. He didn't need to. I could hear Quigley give a sort of low whimper, but otherwise he said nothing. The silence in the garden was as loud as Marjorie Quigley's trousers. It went on and on and got louder and louder.

And then, finally, my dad spoke. Not in his normal voice but in a low, throaty baritone that reminded me of Vincent Price in *The Haunted Palace* – my dad's favourite picture: 'Albert Roger Quigley, do you remember me?'

It was fairly obvious from the noise coming from behind me that the man in question did remember him fairly clearly. In fact, as far as I could judge from the old hearing system, the effect on Quigley was fairly stupendous.

I mean, look at it from his point of view. My dad had recently been cremated. Quigley had sat there while the good people from the Mutual Life Provident Association had come round and told my mum the news about her death benefit. He had, in fact, been in close personal touch with the guy's spirit via one of the finest psychic talents in south-west London. He just *did not* expect to come across the late Norman Britton in the garden of the Ferret and Firkin at half past six in the evening. And he certainly didn't expect the said Britton to be pointing at him in a manner usually affected by people like Darth Vader or Banquo.

I turned round in my chair.

Look, I have seen people surprised in my time. I have seen people very surprised. I have, on occasions, seen very, very, very surprised people. But I have never seen anything like the expression on the face of Albert Roger Quigley that evening. He looked like a man who has just stepped into an empty lift-shaft. His mouth kept opening and shutting like a mechanical shovel, but no words – not even a direct appeal to the Lord Jesus Christ to be excused this experience on health grounds – passed his lips.

It was, in one sense, a stupid question. I mean, how short did Dad expect Roger's memory to *be*? But the way he delivered it would not have disgraced your average member of the Royal Shakespeare Company. It wasn't just that he was pitching it lower. He gave each word an incredibly fruity emphasis. When he got to the R in Roger, he vibrated the old tongue on the palate with the brio of an international string player. The finger, too, seemed to be going down fantastically well with Quigley. He was staring at it the way a cat looks at a dinner-plate. Would he ever get over this initial shock period? Was he going to have a thrombie right here on the spot?

Come on Quigley, pull yourself out of it! Deal with the situation! This sort of thing should be right up your street. Think of the articles. Think of all the hands-on psychical research that is just coming at you free of charge. Make with the sketch maps of the area. Measure the ambient temperature. Get down the witnesses' names and addresses. This is a one-off, my friend. If you move quickly you could bag this one – jam it into the specimen bottle and whip it off to the Society for Psychical Research *prontissimo*!

He did not, I fear, seem to be prepared to experience the phenomenon in a truly objective, scientific way. He was kind of staggering, with one hand held to his temple, and from time to time making a noise like water running out of a bath.

Dad, warming to his role, moved a couple of steps forward, his arm still flung out in front of him. He looked, I thought, a touch over the top. 'Quigley,' he said in a spectral voice, 'repent!'

There was another growl of thunder. Behind Quigley, Danzig appeared at the entrance to the garden. He lowered his head and, whimpering, sidled towards his master. Quigley looked ready to repent. He looked ready to tear his clothes apart. He looked rather less rational than his dog. 'Oh!' he said finally. 'Oh! Oh! Ohhhhh!'

He gave me a quick look to check that I was really there, and an even quicker look round the garden to see if there were any other responsible local citizens around to witness this triumphant affirmation of an afterlife. But the drinkers at the far end of the garden were gone. There was only me and this spirit in the gloom of the garden.

'Oh!' said Quigley, again. 'Oh! Oh! Ohhhhhh!'

'Quigley,' said my dad, moving into the shadows away from me, 'I am in hell! And you will join me here!'

Quigley stared at me. It was weird. Once my dad had got started, I had started to believe him. To believe his act. You know? When I think about it now, he *was* an actor. He was a guy who could *be* something for a brief period of time, and then he vanished like the spirit he was impersonating. When I looked at him in the darkness, I began to wonder if all of what he had told me earlier could be some trick on me, played by the spirits who had sent him.

'How can you sit there?' said Quigley. 'How can you *sit* there?'

I opened my eyes and gave him a puzzled look. 'What do you mean, Mr Quigley?' I said. 'What are you staring at?'

'*That!*' said Quigley, 'That . . . that *thing!*'

Quigley gestured feebly towards my old man. Then he turned to face him. Dad was flaring his nostrils and giving him a wild stare. I thought he was going well over the top, actually. But Quigley was not in a mood to ask why my dad had returned to earth. He was not in the mood to ask rational questions. I don't think he'd have noticed if someone had dropped a set of kitchen units on his head from 30,000 feet.

Dad took a couple more steps towards him. Quigley started to whimper. 'No,' he moaned, 'no!'

'Yes, Quigley,' said my dad. 'Yes, Quigley! Yes! Yes!' He looked as if he was all set to strangle the forty-four-year-old assistant bank manager.

My dad always was something of a ham. The sensible thing to do, having made the initial impact, was to walk off in a slow and menacing way, leaving Quigley to gibber. But Norman was determined to give full value for money.

'Do you know what hell is like, Quigley?'

'No,' whispered Quigley.

'Hell is being blown across vast empty spaces with the wind at your back and dust in your eyes. Hell is the taste of your own vileness, Quigley. The sour smell of your own wickedness and wrongdoing.'

If this was the kind of stuff he had put in his novel, it wasn't surprising that he hadn't found any takers for it. But it was still kosher as far as Albert Roger Quigley was concerned.

'Who are you talking to, Mr Quigley?' I said, in what I hoped was an awestruck tone. 'Who is it that you can see in the garden?'

'O Jesus!' said Quigley, suddenly remembering who was supposed to be in charge around here. 'O Jesus Christ, help me! O Jesus Jesus Jesus! Jesus Christ!'

'There is no Jesus Christ,' said my dad, in solemn tones. 'There is no God of the Christians. There are no prophets in your world, Albert Quigley.'

I hoped he wasn't going to start rubbishing the Koran. You never know when those Muslims might be listening.

Quigley dropped to his knees, his face white and shaking. 'Oh Lord,' he whimpered to himself. 'Oh dear Jesus Christ!'

'There is no Jesus Christ, Quigley,' said my dad, in a very authoritative way.

Quigley looked up at him, dog-like. 'Who is there?' he asked, pleadingly.

'There is no one!' said my dad. 'There is no one beyond this life. Those who return, return as themselves, condemned to live out the circle of their lives again and again!'

Thunder broke again, and this time there were two or three brief flashes of lightning. The chestnut-trees opposite me were suddenly vivid green and, as suddenly, dark again. The brick wall round the garden broke into focus and faded to black. Once again I had the feeling that what my father had said to me in the garden could all be some horrible trick. That he really had died, and that what he was telling Quigley was the truth. Not what he had told me.

Quiggers was gibbering. 'What . . . There must be . . . What is . . .' It was almost as if he'd stopped seeing Dad at all. That made it all scarier. Because I started to believe that I wasn't seeing him. That the familiar switchback nose and scraps of grey hair were going to melt *away* into the darkness. 'There must be . . . *something*!' Quigley said. 'There must . . . God . . .'

My dad came back well. He raised his hands above his head and then stretched them both out at the unfortunate First Spiritualist. He was now doing quite a lot of acting tormented. His head was wobbling violently, and there was dribble down his chin. Whatever he did would have gone down well with Quigley. The presentation was right. Albert Roger was very involved with the performance. He had suspended disbelief completely.

'There is nothing,' said my dad. 'There is nothing. No faith. No light in the darkness, Albert Roger Quigley! Nothing but the smell of your own loneliness and guilt!'

This was very much the kind of stuff that Quigley was used to dishing out. But it didn't look as if he was capable of taking it. He hunched up his shoulders. He looked as if he was about to cry.

'What's the matter, Mr Quigley?' I said again. 'Who are you talking to?'

There was no stopping my dad. I wanted to say to him: *Get off! Quit while you're ahead!* And a bit of me wanted him to stop the way you want an actor in a film to stop. Because he is so damned real that you think this pain and suffering is *really* him. You know?

'Death,' said my dad, 'is not a journey to some pleasant place. Death is simply the stopping of your heart. The end of sensation. The not being able to smell or taste or screw. Death is death.

And there are no spirits. There are things. Fleshly, heavy things that come back to mock and torment you!'

'Argol,' cried Quigley, who was, rather gamely I thought, trying to make some radical alterations to his cosmological system. 'Argol of Tellenor!'

Dad laughed. The laugh was really horrid. It was low and cracked to begin with, then it rose up the scale, eerily, and shook out its top notes across the damp, half-lit glade until I really did think that my father had come not from the hospital but from some horribly cold, empty region that lies in wait for us instead of all the heavens we have dreamed up to make things bearable.

'I am not he of Tellenor,' said my dad, who was always good at bluffing. 'I am he that was Norman Britton when on the earth, now returned to haunt you, Albert Roger Quigley, and to tell you that you are an evil man and that you will fall as I have fallen! Down and down, until you can fall no further!'

There was another roll of thunder, and once again the lightning lit up the garden and the surrounding trees.

As the sky's noise faded, my father moved into exit mode. He walked, slowly and stiffly, towards the ramp that led from the garden to the street. As he approached Quigley, Quigley started to sob. Then my dad paused.

'What must I do?' asked Quigley – always a man anxious for instructions.

My dad gave him the sort of look that only someone declared clinically dead can manage. 'I will come again, Quigley,' he said, 'when you least expect me! I will haunt your dreams and yea, your waking moments!'

'What must I *do*?' said Quigley, understandably keen to get on the right side of this spirit.

'Touch not my son, Quigley,' said the old man. 'Leave him be!'

I found myself wondering who we could haunt next. There

were a few members of staff who could do with a visit from beyond the tomb.

Dad did a bit of sneering, then he said, 'Farewell, Albert Roger Quigley!'

'Farewell,' said Quigley, clearly anxious to keep up the tone necessary for spirit dialogue.

My dad started off again towards the street. From the back he looked even better. He kept the shoulders stiff and he rolled a little, like a sailor back from a long voyage.

Quigley ran towards me like a kid let out of primary school. 'Can't you see him? Can't you *see* him?'

'See who, Mr Quigley?' I said, widening my eyes just a touch. 'See who?'

My dad was almost out into the street. I had the strong impression he might be tempted to come back and give us a bit more front-line colour from the other side of the grave. I leaned closer to Quigley, who, in a kind of transport of enthusiasm, grabbed me by both ears and squeezed my head hard. 'Oh my God!' he said. 'Oh Jesus! Oh God!'

You see how hard it is to get people to adapt? If he thought about it rationally, on the basis of the evidence presented to him, he had no basis for trusting Jesus Christ any further than he could throw him. But there he was, reaching for familiar things, as we all tend to do when scared out of our brains.

After a while he let go of my head and started to cross himself furiously. He was doing quite a lot of this, I noted. And it wasn't exactly the kind of thing endorsed by the First Spiritualist Church. Perhaps all this was going to push Quigley towards Catholicism – often, so my dad used to say, a good port of call for those on the way to a nervous breakdown.

'I have been a bad person,' he said.

This was no more or less than the truth. I had been telling him so for the last few weeks. But would he listen to me? Would he hell!

'I have done awful, awful things . . .'

Yes, Quigley. I know.

'. . . To you, li'l Simey, and to the church I love.'

He pushed his face close to me. He smelt of garlic.

'I have embezzled church funds!' he said.

Sure. We gathered. What we really wanted here was a tape recorder. I mean, where did he think I thought he *got* his new car and his loft extension and his fridge-freezer?

'I masturbate,' he said, in thrilling tones.

I did not want to know this. Not at nearly seven o'clock, in the garden of the Ferret and Firkin. Not anywhere, actually. I mean, we all do it, Quiggers. We get down in the darkness and from time to time we pull the wire. But we don't boast about it.

'Your father,' he said to me in a kind of sob, 'has just appeared to me in this garden!'

I tried to look impressed.

'He has told me some very important things.'

'Are you feeling OK, Mr Quigley?' I said.

'Oh Simey!' he gasped.

Then he did something really vile. He flung his arms around me and pushed his beard in my face. Something soft and dry touched my face. I realized, with some alarm, that these were the Quigley lips. The bastard was kissing me!

'I think', I said, trying to duck, 'that you should go and lie down.'

Preferably not on top of me! I knew nothing of Quigley's sexual life, but it was entirely possible that Marjorie and Emily were not enough for him. He was a red-blooded assistant bank manager. Up at the pub window I could see Mr McIvory, the owner. He's a tolerant man, but I just wasn't sure how he'd take me being frenched by a middle-aged man in the garden of his public house.

'Look,' I said eventually, 'fuck off and leave me alone. OK?'

'Fuck off and leave you alone!' echoed Quigley, as if I had just taken pi to sixteen decimal places off the top of my head.

'Yes,' I said.

'Yes,' said Quigley.

And then do you know what he did? He started to back away, just as he had when he saw my dad. He wound his way back over the leaf-strewn grass like a toy duck. His mouth gaped and his hands flapped. I held up my hand very much in the manner of Salvius the tribune greeting Glabriolix the slave and giving him news of the Emperor's dog, Pertinax.

'Quigley,' I said, 'wait!'

He waited. He was in a suggestible mood.

'Oh Simon!' he said, looking at my face as if he was trying to memorize it for some exam. 'Oh Jesus, young shaver! Oh me deario!'

He put his hand to his mouth. 'I must tell the world!' he said.

This might work better for me than his lying in a darkened room, which was what he really needed to do. We had to get him telling his story as soon as possible. Preferably to a tough-minded clinical psychiatrist.

He turned on the balls of his feet and spread his arms wide. He was keen to tell everyone the Great News about my dad coming back to life to expose Christianity. With a man of Quigley's energy and commitment behind him, I decided, it would not be long before Norman had a cult all of his own in south-west London.

'Tell the world!' he almost shouted, and ran, swiftly, out towards the street.

After he had gone, I sat back at the pub table. My dad's glass of beer, half-empty, was still there. But Quigley, if he'd noticed it, would have seen nothing unusual in a spirit getting outside of a pint of Young's Special. If you were a ghost and you could choose who you could appear to, Quigley would be a good bet.

I don't know how long I was sitting there, but eventually my dad came back and sat down in his chair opposite me. He looked the way he looked when he had been telling jokes and there were no more jokes to tell. His face looked old and crumpled and sad, and, as he picked up his glass again, I had the strong sensation he was about to tell me something I didn't want to hear.

28

'I'm in love with somebody else.'

I didn't say anything.

'There's another woman in my life. Has been for six years. I love her, you see? I just can't . . .'

He paused. I didn't help him out.

'I can't live without her.'

It was, I decided, a *ridiculous* cardigan. Had she bought it for him? He just didn't look himself at all. He was sort of smirking as he said all this stuff. In a way I found very irritating. I tried not to listen. I thought that, if I didn't listen, soon he would stop and then we would go home and life would start again, the way it had always been before. But he kept on talking, and I couldn't stop myself from hearing.

'She's called Veronica,' he said, 'and your mother knows about her. Has known about her a long time. And it's why she and you and . . . and why we . . .'

He stopped.

'I don't love Mum any more, you see?' he said. 'I don't love her.'

I looked up at him. Straight in the eyes. 'Is that where you've been? With this Veronica woman?'

'That's where I've been, and that's where I want to stay.'

He drank again. But this time as if he wanted to get the beer over and done. As if he suddenly didn't want to be here at all.

'I met Veronica at the Anglo-Catholic church in Putney – St Mark's. When Mrs Danby took me there. The old bat led me astray in more ways than one. After I started with Veronica, Mrs D went back to the First Spiritualists.'

'But you kept going to these Anglo-Catholic geezers?'

A lot of things were becoming clearer. That smell of oil and candles and that light from a distant window and him on his knees, mumbling. He must have taken me there.

'She seemed pretty keen to get me on the team,' I said.

Dad leaned forward and tapped me on the knee. 'She felt guilty. She offered a covenant to the church if I came back or you were Confirmed in Faith. A lot of money. But I wasn't going to go back . . .'

He looked away. He had that look he used to get on Saturday mornings after he had come back from the shops. As if he was looking at his life and not enjoying what he saw. As if there was a whole load of things behind him and nothing in front but age. You know? As if the night was coming in and he couldn't stop it.

'In the end, Veronica and I packed in Christianity.' He tapped me on the knee. 'Make up your own mind,' he said. 'Look at the world and make up your *own* mind.'

I kept my eyes on his face. 'Do you believe there is a God?' I said. 'Yes,' he said, slowly.

From the way he said it, he might have been talking about Krull of Varna. The thought didn't seem to bring him any comfort. Or make the prospect of that long night any easier.

'But I don't know what I mean when I say that word. It's just something I say . . . because I have to say it . . . Because it brings me some comfort.'

'Like Veronica,' I said. I had to say it, guys. I could not help myself. I just did not like the sound of this woman. She was young, probably. Younger than my mum. Nearer to my age than his, I felt sure. She sounded fat and self-important, I thought.

'I know you'll be OK, Simon,' my dad was saying. 'You're very tough and very smart and you're your own man. You always have been.'

He put his hand on my hand again. I moved it a little way away.

'Will this Quigley guy be finished now?' he said. 'Now they've rumbled him? He will, won't he? I mean, if he causes trouble you can call on me, you know?'

I just looked at him, blankly.

'If I thought you couldn't look after yourself, you see . . .'

I wasn't sure I cared for this 'look after yourself' stuff. I never like it when people say that to you. It was the same as this 'make up your own mind' line. I wasn't sure I *could* make up my own mind. You know?

'What are you telling me?' I said, in a flat voice. 'I don't get you.'

'I'm going away, Simon. I'm going away and I'm not coming back.'

It's funny. I knew he was going to say that. Just the way I knew my mum had bad news when she came in on me in Dad's study all those weeks ago. The evening he died.

'Where are you going?' I said, evenly.

'Veronica has a place. It's a long way away from here. We can start all over again. You know?'

'How can you start all over again?' I said to him. 'It doesn't make sense. You only get one life, don't you? How can you start it over again? It's started already, hasn't it?'

'Darling . . .'

I didn't like him saying that. He sounded like Quigley. He reached for me again, and this time I moved even further away from him. I'd had enough middle-aged men slobbering all over me for one day.

'I'm sorry, Simon,' he said. 'I'm sorry.'

And they were all apologizing!

'I didn't realize that Quigley . . . I mean, if it's that bad, of course I'll. . .'

'I can handle Quigley,' I said in a steady voice.

'Are you sure?'

'If I can handle you, I can handle Quigley.'

'Simon – sometimes I don't know . . . I don't . . .'

'Look at life,' I said, nastily, 'and *make up your own mind, guy!*'

He changed tack then. He gave up trying to grab me. He started going on about the life insurance. He knew just how much he was worth. He said that his not coming back was much the best option for all of us. He was insured with four different companies, he said, which was probably another reason Quiggers was hanging round. 'Dying on your partner,' he said, 'is much fairer and more financially beneficial to them than divorcing them.'

He put his head in his hands then. He was a bad man, he said – a weak, bad man.

'You're not bad,' I said – 'you're really nice!' It wasn't true that he was bad.

He cried a lot, but I didn't cry. I didn't see why I should. I'd done my crying for him the day they told me he was dead. Funnily enough, that hadn't seemed at all real. It was only now it was like he was really dying.

When he'd stopped feeling sorry for himself, he handed me a piece of paper with a number on it. 'If this Quigley gets too much,' he said, 'write here. Give me a bit of time to get settled. It's a box number.'

'What's wrong with your address?' I said. 'I won't tell anyone. You can trust me, guy!'

He looked at me. He looked all crumpled now. Those new clothes she'd bought him looked even more stupid than they had before. He said something – I forget what, but it was pretty clear he didn't trust me. Or maybe Veronica had got to him on the subject. I thought about how I'd walked around all those weeks, and what I'd felt about him and the crazy things I had found myself believing. And I thought: *Where were you when I needed you, Dad? Where were you when you died on me? You know?* He had done nothing.

There was a lot of stuff about his life too. About his novel and his business. That was in all sorts of trouble, apparently. If he did come back to life, he was in real problems with the bank. Although isn't that what life *is*? Being in trouble with the bank? He went on about Mum. How she had always held him back. How he had never really been able to write because of her. I couldn't figure this. What did she do? Start banging on the ceiling every time he took out his biro? I mean, she goes on – but what the hell? They all go on, don't they?

'When you're my age,' he said, 'you'll understand.'

'I won't,' I said. 'I understand now.'

He pushed the glass along the table. 'Come with us,' he said. 'You'd like Veronica. Come with us!'

'To Box 29? You reckon?'

As I said this, I realized it was too late for me and him. That I wasn't going to leave. Ever. And that he didn't really want me to. He had said that just to be polite. Oh, he was polite. He was polite and good fun and a hell of a laugh at parties. But, at the end of the day, you couldn't trust him.

'Your mum needs you,' he said.

I'd noticed. But I hadn't noticed him clocking the fact until the day he decided to bugger off to Box 29 with Veronica. I was almost ready to tell him I couldn't face Quigley on my own. But I couldn't find the words. And they wouldn't have had any effect.

When it comes down to it, grown-ups think about themselves. After that they think about other grown-ups. And a long way after that they think about children. Children really are on another planet as far as they are concerned.

'I want you to look after her,' he said.

'Well,' I said, '*you* don't seem to be intending to do it, do you?'

Then I looked back at the table. I was giving that table a lot of attention. Suddenly I felt I was talking to my mum. Because it was feelings and stuff. Me and Dad never talked about that much before. She did all that. But, now we were talking about it, I felt this great weight on me. As if we would never have the time to say all the things we needed to say to each other. As if we just didn't have the words for them. You know?

'Well,' I said, in the end, 'you'd better bugger off. You're taking a risk being here really, aren't you? Someone from the Mutual Life Provident might drop in . . .'

'Veronica's got the car . . .' he said.

She had a car and everything! He was made up!

'Look, Simon . . .' he muttered, as he got up, 'I'm sorry. I am so sorry!'

'Don't be,' I said.

He came at me again and I could tell he was going to make another stab at a heavy masculine embrace. I just sat very still, waiting for him to go.

'You're very angry with me now,' he said, 'but one day . . .'

'I'm not angry. I'm fine. Just fine! OK?'

There was a pause.

'What's she like?'

'Veronica?'

'Yeah.'

'She's . . .' Another long silence. 'She's funny.'

He looked at me. His eyes seemed to be coming from a long way away.

'Like you, Simon.'

He was wearing jeans. That was my dad – always trying to keep up with things. But I figured the jeans wouldn't last long. Veronica would be working on something to go with the brown shoes and the cardigan. She would reshape his whole wardrobe. And when she'd finished that, she'd start on him. He wouldn't be allowed to fart or pick his nose or put his feet on the table. After a while he wouldn't be my dad at all. He'd be Veronica's husband.

'Write,' he said, 'won't you? Because I can't. Write. OK?'

'Sure,' I said.

Then, at last, I looked him straight in the eyes. 'I won't give you away,' I said. 'I promise you that. I won't tell anyone anything about any of this as long as I live. I swear it.'

'I know, Simon,' he said.

He made a half-hearted move towards me, but I gave him no encouragement. I didn't even look up as he went up the ramp into the street, so I'm still not sure when he passed out of the garden and into the rest of the world. Sometimes I picture him walking out with his head held high and his step straight. Other times I see him sort of shuffling, as if the world had finally got to him. As if he was suddenly old and tired and defeated.

But mostly I try not to think about him at all.

Quigley never recovered from that evening. He told quite a lot of people what he'd seen. He even told the people at work, who were most impressed. He went through a brief period of chatting to the customers down at the bank about how he had seen someone come back from the dead. In a garden at twilight. But, although they were amused at first, I don't think they liked it and, after a while, he was sent for treatment. He told the doctors all about how my dad had come back to life in his grey cardigan and had told him the secrets of the universe.

Nobody's bothered about Pike or how or why he went through Mr Marr's pockets, cleaned out his ID, took his keys and squatted in the house to acquaint himself with the principles of ufology. It is as if Marr, Pike, my dad and Quigley had never been. As if they were all part of some troubled dream I was having.

Quigley's in a mental hospital near Tooting. He went in just before Christmas last year. Mum and I go to see him sometimes, and we agree that he is a much nicer person than he used to be. He tells us about Old Mother Walsh and how the snake is coming for him. It has five heads, apparently, and is from the planet Tellenor. Lewis set it on him. It has a number on it, but not the number of the second millennium. It is marked with a 24, the number of our house. He's worked Argol in there too. Argol is on his way in a kind of steel tub, apparently, and when he gets here we are *for* it. The only thing you have to be careful not to mention is the First Church of Christ the Spiritualist. I don't understand the details, but apparently Mrs Danby got her lawyer on to him about some financial thing. She herself left the church, and is going to leave all her money to the Battersea Dogs' Home. She wrote my mum a long letter saying that I was a Devil Child, and the best thing my mum could do with me was have me exorcized. My mum wrote back and said that she didn't have that kind of money.

'She's an old hag,' said Mum.

'Oh, I don't know,' I said, 'I think I could do with a bit of exorcism!'

Mum and I get on a lot better these days. We'll never be close, if you know what I mean, but we've got something worked out. Mum has been a lot more cheerful since Quigley was declared bankrupt, insane and guilty of fraud. She's got bigger. Her eyes, which used to be dull and filmy, have got some of their sparkle back. She and Hannah Dooley left the First Spiritualists and founded a Household Church. They've called it the Fellowship of Christian Spiritualists of 24 Stranraer Gardens, and they have a lot of fun, singing and dancing and playing the tambourine in the back room downstairs. Once or twice my mum has even gone into a light trance, and, though she hasn't yet contacted anyone interesting, we have great hopes of her.

They reckon it was all Quigley's fault. That Old Mother Walsh had it right, and that Ella Walsh should never have led the church into the ways of men. They are quite down on men, but they seem to like me.

Mrs Quigley and Emily still live with us. They had to sell the house – what remained of it after Brunt had finished with it. Mrs Quigley doesn't say a lot, and what she says, she says quietly. Sometimes, if she's good, my mum lets her chop the vegetables. Emily turns out to be really quite decent. She has had a crisis of faith since her old man was put in the bin, and, a month or so ago, she took all her C. S. Lewis books out into the garden and burnt them. For some reason, shortly after the First Church of Christ the Spiritualist took its number out of the phone book, she started to forget to lisp. Who knows, one day I may marry her. On the other hand, I may not.

I used to think sex was all about condoms and fellatio and getting girls to show you their underwear. These days it seems something more mysterious, but also somehow more real. As if it's just over the horizon, waiting to happen to me, as weird and wonderful as all the things that happened last autumn.

I think about the aliens quite a lot. I still think they're out there. I think they're still spacenapping people, if you want to know. Not in the obvious way. I don't think they cruise into our atmosphere in *saucers,* exactly. But, whatever name you choose to give it, *something* gets into humans one way or another and makes them do things that are very hard to understand.

I'm staying as far out of it all as I can. I'm based on the moons of Jupiter from now on, and the only time I'll come back to earth will be strictly on a day-trip basis. I'm behind that glass that separated us from Pike that night on the Common. I never wrote to that box number. I never will. I keep the piece of paper in a tin next to my dad's glasses – the ones he'll never come back for – but I know I'll never use it.

You see, I was a little kid a year ago and I made the mistake kids make. I let things get to me. I let them all get to me – Quigley and Pike and my mum and Mr Marr. Most of all I let my father get to me. I let him get under my guard. But I'll never let anyone do that again. From now on I'll never let anyone under my guard. No one gets close to me. Not ever.

AUTHOR'S NOTE

The Wimbledon Dharjees are, of course, an entirely fictitious Islamic sect, but the group from which they are alleged to come, the Nizari Ismailis, are a real and well-documented group of Shiite Muslims. A full account of the true, and incredible, story of Hasan the Second, the Twenty-third Imam of the Nizari Ismailis, is to be found in Bernard Lewis's *The Assassins* (Weidenfeld & Nicolson, 1967). Robert's one guide to his assumed religion, *Morals and Manners in Islam, a Guide to Islamic Adab*, by Marwan Ibrahim Al-Kaysi, was published by the Islamic Foundation in 1986.

Unfaithfully Yours

Nigel Williams

ISBN: 978-1-47210-674-2 (HB) £18.99
ISBN: 978-1-47210-683-4 (Ebook) £12.99

When Elizabeth Price engages a private detective to investigate her husband's suspected infidelity, she unwittingly sets off a chain of correspondence that will reunite four formerly close-knit couples. They all live just a few streets away from each other; they are all still married; so how – and why – did they become so estranged? In a series of painfully and often hilariously revealing letters, from love notes to condolence messages, all becomes clear.

Unfaithfully Yours is an uproarious and poignant portrait of four marriages; a tale of late-flowering love and suburban intrigue. It heralds the return of one of our finest comic writers, in peak condition: all hail Nigel Williams, chronicler of England's sleepy suburbs, where all is not quite as cricket as it seems . . .

'A brilliantly witty writer.' *Sunday Times*